ICE
CAP

Also by Chris Knopf

Bad Bird

Short Squeeze

Black Swan

Hard Stop

Head Wounds

Two Time

The Last Refuge

ICE CAP

Chris Knopf

MINOTAUR BOOKS

A THOMAS DUNNE BOOK

New York

A THOMAS DUNNE BOOK FOR MINOTAUR BOOKS.
An imprint of St. Martin's Publishing Group.

ICE CAP. Copyright © 2012 by Chris Knopf. All rights reserved. Printed in the United States of America. For information, address St. Martin's Press, 175 Fifth Avenue, New York, N.Y. 10010.

www.thomasdunnebooks.com
www.minotaurbooks.com

Library of Congress Cataloging-in-Publication Data

Knopf, Chris.
    Ice cap : a mystery / Chris Knopf. — 1st ed.
        p. cm.
    "A Thomas Dunne book."
    ISBN 978-1-250-00517-5 (hardcover)
    ISBN 978-1-250-01425-2 (e-book)
    1. Women lawyers—Fiction. 2. Hamptons (N. Y.)—Fiction. I. Title.
    PS3611.N66I28   2012
    813'.6—dc23
                                                            2012005481

First Edition: June 2012

10 9 8 7 6 5 4 3 2 1

To the Polish.

An accomplished and underappreciated people.

Acknowledgments

My greatest debt in the making of this book is to the Polish people who supplied so much useful information on Polish food, festivities, family dynamics, names, places, and cultural nuance, both here in Southampton and New Britain, Connecticut, and in the old country. Notably, Pawel Bula and Adrian Kecki. Matters of the law were managed by my crack legal team: Norman Bloch, Cindy Courtney and Rich Orr, and their law student son, Andy Orr. Paige Goettel handled French duties, with some excellent assistance from Mark Bonnet, who also advised on technology issues. Dr. Peter King told me how to kill someone by inducing a heart attack, and get away with it. Don't mess with either of us. Nancy Dugan gave me a native's guide to Carnegie Hill and the Upper East Side of New York City. If you notice inaccuracies in any of these renderings, the fault is all mine, not my advisers'. My staff of pre-submission readers, Randy Costello, Bob Willemin, Mary Jack Wald, and Sean Cronin, performed their usual editorial magic, this time under a very tight deadline. Anne-Marie Regish threw in her usually stellar logistical support, and Mary Farrell continues to endure the relentless imposition of her husband's literary compulsions.

ICE
CAP

1

It would have been the blizzard of the century if a bigger one hadn't hit a few weeks later. But for the people of the Hamptons marooned in the off-off season of mid-January, it was like we'd been plucked from the end of Long Island and dropped into the Arctic Circle.

For me, it was another opportunity to praise my Volvo station wagon, both steadfast and true, no matter how little maintenance or care I remembered to bestow upon it. That evening the biggest challenge was identifying the car among the other giant heaps of rapidly building snow in the parking lot behind my apartment. I was only out there because I got a call from one of my clients, Franklin Delano Raffini, aka Franco—an ex–investment banker who'd served time for killing his girlfriend's husband with a rotisserie skewer before the husband could kill him with a steak knife.

"You gotta get over here, Jackie," he said via cell phone, the words barely audible over the wind noise.

"Not the best time," I said.

"Don't tell anybody anything till you get here. I'm serious. You'll see why."

Another complicating factor was my complete lack of personal preparedness. Snow was hardly unheard of in the Hamptons, but it was usually nothing like this. The best I could do was cowboy boots, black leather gloves that went nearly to the elbow (bought for more heated circumstances), a leotard, jeans, and lots of layers under my orange barn jacket.

I thought I'd overdone it until I hit the outside air and felt like the skin on my face was being cryogenically removed. I found the car and dug my way to the driver's-side door with an old aluminum fry pan. Inside the car somewhere was an ice scraper. From the driver's seat, I climbed into the back and dug the scraper out from under a stack of file folders, a pair of jumper cables, a box of Kleenex, a birdcage, a beach umbrella last used five months before, golf clubs never used, and other unrelated items whose origins had been lost in the mists of time.

When I finally finished clearing about two feet of snow off the car with the fry pan and scraper, another inch or two had already started to form. The engine had been running, however, so the defrosters and wipers kept the glass clear. The greater issue was the most fundamental—could I really drive in this stuff?

Even if snowplows had been as prevalent on Long Island as they were in Buffalo, there was no way to keep up with the snowfall. So the only choice wasn't driving over, it was driving through.

At least I'd been taught by my father how to handle a car in the snow. He had his faults, but denying his daughter instruction in the many things he thought her too stupid to master on her own was not one of them. So whenever a snowstorm hit the area, however meager the accumulation, we'd venture forth in one of his ungainly American land yachts for a lesson, which was usually delivered in harsh and condescending tones, just to ensure that even an effort to preserve my safety would be remembered with a tinge of hollow disappointment.

The first trick was to go easy on the gas pedal, refraining at all times from spinning the wheels—a circumstance from which, my father impressed upon me, it was virtually impossible to recover. That day, I thought the whole thing was impossible, so I was more surprised than triumphant when I felt the car move forward out of the parking spot, across the lot, and out into the street.

From there it was a short hop to Montauk Highway, the main east-west thoroughfare that connected the string of villages that comprised the Hamptons, and thus the only road the authorities were committed to keeping as clear as possible. This meant that successive plow passes during the day had formed a small mountain ridge at the end of my side street. As my father had taught me, this circumstance called for an opposing strategy: drop to a lower gear and hit the gas.

I felt it was every bit as unlikely that I'd be able to smash my way through a wall of snow as it was getting under way in the first place, which is probably why I didn't consider the consequences of success until I found myself in the middle of Montauk Highway, perpendicular to the flow of traffic and directly in the path of a very large pickup. I cranked the steering wheel hard to the right and kept power to the wheels, allowing me to spin the rear of the car into the opposite snow-bank, just barely avoiding an ugly collision. For its part, the truck swerved a few times, the edge of the yellow plow whispering past the side of the Volvo and then swinging back into the mass of snow that entombed a row of cars along the curbside.

"Idiot," I said to myself for a variety of reasons, including the fact that I was now irrevocably lodged inside the packed snow.

I looked in my mirror and saw a woman in heavy coveralls, about the same color of my barn jacket, jump out of the truck and slip-slide toward me through the swirling haze. I rolled down the passenger-side window and prepared myself for a well-deserved rebuke.

"Are you all right?" she asked, looking anxiously through the open window. Her long brown hair, streaked with gray, was salted with snow-flakes, and her angular, dark face was lit up with concern.

"I should be asking you," I said. "I did a really dumb thing."

"Everybody's dumb in a snowstorm. You stuck?"

"Oh, yeah. How would you feel about pulling me out?"

"I'd feel fine about it," she said. "Don't go anywhere till I get back."

She jogged back to her truck, jumped in, did a three-point turn, and drove a short way past me. Then she got a chain out of the truck bed and hooked us up. She gestured for me to roll down my window again.

"Just help me along with some gentle acceleration. No stunt driving necessary."

"What's your name?" I asked.

"Dayna Red. I tell people it's a house paint. Nobody believes me."

I told her my name and profession: counsel to the region's impoverished miscreants or merely misled, one of whom had sent me an urgent call that I felt irresistibly compelled to answer.

"Not in this weather you aren't," she said.

"What if I hired you?" I asked her.

"Plow job?"

"Escort. I need to get over to Seven Ponds in Southampton."

She leaned into the car, bringing some more of the storm with her. A white dust started to form on the accretion of papers, soda cans, and empty cigarette packs that filled the passenger seat.

"I just came from over there. They haven't plowed yet."

I wrote the address on a handy piece of paper.

"You know where that is?" I asked her.

She studied the paper.

"Sure. Tad Buczek's place. Metal Madness."

Metal wasn't the only thing mad about Tad, but it figured largely. Like my late husband's family—the honorable Swaitkowskis—Tad's family had made the calculation that tens of millions of dollars in hand from real-estate developers was better than bushels of potatoes you had to go to the trouble of growing, harvesting, and selling into a saturated market. Tad's share of the bounty was substantial—enough for him to retain fifteen acres of mixed fields and woodlands for himself, on which he established one of the more irregular local homesteads, even by the rigorous standards of the Hamptons.

Always a connoisseur of large agricultural machinery, Tad harnessed his new wealth to embark on a major acquisition program, focusing on earth-moving equipment, until his property was littered with backhoes and bulldozers, excavators, dump trucks, and articulated haulers. Zoning disputes quickly erupted, led by some of Tad's new neighbors, the wealthy owners of colonial-style and postmodern minimansions that rose up from his family's former potato farm.

Tad eventually reached a settlement, which in my former life as a real-estate lawyer I helped draft, and which required him to store his earth-mover collection within a pair of huge pre-fabbed steel buildings designed to enclose things like assembly lines and commercial aircraft. The deal was sealed when he sited the buildings within a grove of pine trees deep inside the property, thus rendering the entire operation essentially invisible.

What his opponents hadn't figured on was Tad's purpose in acquiring the earth-moving equipment in the first place, which wasn't simply to warehouse a fleet of lumbering machines but rather to apply them to the purpose for which they'd been originally engineered.

Moving earth.

The land, cleared of the offending eyesores, was soon in the midst of a massive transformation. Out of acres of flat, unobstructed potato fields grew huge hills, plateaus, pyramids, and berms that circled into themselves like ancient fortifications. Much of this required massive infusions of fill, which meant a steady procession of dump trucks importing sand, gravel, and rough soil from as far away as North Jersey.

Another flood of lawsuits resulted, but there was little the neighbors could do about this one. There was no law or statute prohibiting the physical alteration of a person's private land, provided it had no negative impact on the adjacent environment, water supply, or septic systems. Offenses Tad studiously avoided.

Better yet, the work was done in fairly short order—barely six months—after which Tad set to growing grass and planting trees and bushes on his freshly terraformed estate, softening the edges of the artificial earthen shapes until they took on the character of a naturally molded landscape, one of such verdant beauty that any complaint seemed fatuous at best.

The subsequent goodwill helped Tad weather the next explosion of outrage.

"I'll have to put the plow down when we turn on David Whites Lane," said Dayna after pulling me out of the snowbank and walking back to my car. She asked for my cell phone number. "I'll call you, and we'll keep the connection open. Keep it on speaker. Better than a walkie-talkie."

The snowfall might have abated some as the sky above darkened to a deep, sooty gray. But snow still filled the air, blown into a chaotic frenzy by the increasing wind. That was one of the costs of living close to the ocean. Whatever lousy weather you could have out here, the wind always made it that much lousier.

Almost a half hour later we reached the intersection of Montauk Highway and David Whites Lane. I asked Dayna to give me a few minutes to clean the ice pack off my wipers and the congealed snow and road grit out of the grille. It took longer than I hoped, hampered as I was by icy needles being driven into my face. I knew there were buildings on three corners of the intersection, but with night completely settled in, they only looked like ghostly shapes within the blustery haze. I made it back into the car thinking it may not ever be safe to emerge again.

"They're saying it's the blizzard of the century," said Dayna over my exotic new smartphone, a type that provides everything short of teleportation. "Could get three feet, not including drifts. The governor's shut down the whole island. Nonessential travel's forbidden."

"Sorry if this gets you in trouble."

"I'm essential, honey. Which means you're also protected. It's like diplomatic immunity."

"I know the cops around here pretty well," I said. "Good luck with that one."

Even with her heavy four-wheel-drive truck, knobby tires, and snowplow it was slow going. Every so often the load in front of the plow grew so large she had to increase the angle of the blade and shove it off to the side. Then we'd back up a little and take off again—her easing along what she hoped was the road surface, now completely obliterated by a blanket of deep snow, and me transfixed by the two red lights on her tailgate and the pale light over the truck's license plate that read WOODCHIK.

I never would have made it without her. No way, no how.

"Wood Chick, you're the aces," I told her over the phone, deciphering the vanity license plate.

"Now I'm embarrassed."

"Don't be," I said. "I'm just trying to be nice."

"My own fault for plastering that name right on my ass. With encouragement from people I'd be better off ignoring."

"I know people like that."

"Tad's place is getting closer," she said. "During the day we'd have a visual by now."

She meant we could have seen one of the towering metal sculptures that comprised the loony installation Tad had created and named Metal

Madness. The sculptures, mounted atop Tad's ersatz mountains, were built from twisted sheets of steel welded into abstract shapes that thrust high into the sky. And consequently, they are the latest cause for neighborhood angst and costly legal maneuvering, which I was grateful to leave behind, safe within my current career as a full-time criminal attorney.

Seven Ponds wasn't even a place name; it was just a few roads of the same or similar names that crisscrossed a semirural swath north of Southampton Village. And by my reckoning, there was only one pond named Seven Ponds, which must have been either an act of clever misdirection or the product of some ancient real-estate broker's imagination.

These days I'd call the area mixed use, with farms like Tad's mostly developed, and the remaining open land, preserved in land trusts, slowly succumbing to natural reforestation. The few auto-repair shops, roadside markets, and tractor dealers from back in the day were also taking on a disintegrating, superannuated hue.

Tad's place was at the northernmost limit of that area, describable as the foothills of a little forested ridge that runs down the spine of the South Fork. This meant that Dayna and I had a hard fight up a relatively modest grade, with lots of starting and stopping, punctuated by fruitless spinning of wheels, just as my surly father warned me about.

"A little less torque might help," I said to Dayna over the phone. She grunted and proceeded slowly but relentlessly, with or without my advice. I followed in the same spirit.

After what felt like hours, because it almost was, we finally reached the head of the driveway that led into Tad Buczek's place and were heralded by the words METAL MADNESS punched out of a slab of aluminum that hung above the entrance.

"At least it's downhill from here on," said Dayna after making a tentative run at the top of the driveway. "You ready?"

"I've waited all my life."

"I could chain us together again, which might keep you from getting stuck, or just pick my way along in the hope you can keep a safe distance and stay under way."

"That's what I've been doing," I said.

"This is different. There're no road markers. I'll be driving blind."

"Unchained sounds more like me," I told her.

"Okay. Here we go."

Dayna dropped the plow and turned into the driveway. It was the deepest snow we'd yet encountered, undisturbed by traffic of any kind. I could see all four wheels of the pickup throwing up tiny wakes, half spinning, half digging in. It wasn't a slow passage—Dayna needed the velocity to attack the heavy snow, some in drifts that crested over the top of the plow.

"Are we headed to the house?" she asked over the cell phone. "If so, we'll have to make a hard left very soon."

"Let me make another call and I'll tell you."

I hung up and tapped Franco's number from the list of recent calls. It rang a few times before he picked up.

"I see two sets of lights," he said. "Is that you?"

"It's me and a plow. Where are you?"

"In front of the big pergola. Tell the plow not to run me over."

I hung up and did just that. I told Dayna the pergola was halfway between the upcoming left and the main house. She said, "Roger that," and slowed down to take the left. I crept up behind, praying I had the momentum to stay stuck to the slippery road surface and still make the turn.

We both made it around, and I saw the lights mounted above the truck's plow kick up to high beams. I tucked up closer to her rear bumper, feeling more secure at the slower pace she'd chosen. It was still fast enough to cause the snow to explode out from the front of the truck and wash into me from either side and above. My windshield wipers, already compromised, soon surrendered, and I picked up the phone to tell Dayna I had to stop when I heard her voice over the speaker.

"There's a guy waving at me," she said.

"Stop there."

She actually drove a little past him so he was at my passenger-side door when I stopped. I rolled down the window.

"So Franco, what up?"

I assumed it was Franco based on the prominent nose and thin black mustache and goatee, which were the only identifying features. The rest was a snow-covered wool coat and baseball cap. When he greeted me, in his Italian-inflected English, more a lilt than an accent, I was sure it was him.

I got out of the car and stumbled around to the other side. Dayna approached and asked if I was all right. I introduced the two of them and they peeled off their gloves to shake hands. Franco gave a neat little bow.

"Jackie, I need to show you something. Ms. Red, you better wait here, if you don't mind."

"I'd rather come," she said.

"She can come," I told him, not knowing exactly why. I had nothing to fear from Franco, but you quickly grow connected to people, even strangers, who deliver you through dire circumstances. I wanted her nearby.

"Suit yourself," he said, turning and then tromping under Tad's giant pergola through the deep snow, guided by a bright flashlight made less so by the tiny snowflakes that streamed down through the woody vines and open beams of the structure above. I cursed the lack of a hat.

It wasn't a long walk, blessedly, as I quickly grew weary of the trudge, a misery compounded by the slippery soles of my cowboy boots. We were at the far end of the pergola, in an area that was partially covered by a hard roof, under which Tad had a wooden table for al fresco dining. On top of the table was a long white mound, at the fringes of which I could see the edge of a blue tarp. Franco waited for us to come up to him, then took a piece of the tarp in his gloved hand.

"Uh-oh," Dayna said under her breath.

"You wanted to come," Franco said to her, then flipped the tarp over the mound, sending the covering snow flying into the air, where some of it was blown back and hit me in the face. I wiped my eyes and followed Franco's flashlight as it outlined the prone figure of a large man, finally stopping at the red-and-gray mash that used to be the defiant and hard-headed skull of Tadzio Buczek.

.

2

"I know, I know," said Franco. "I shouldn't have moved the body."

"You moved the body?"

"I know I shouldn't've. He was out there in the middle of the field. I had to get him somewhere out of the snow, it was coming down so fast. I dragged him on the tarp."

"Whoa, back up," I said.

Franco's body quaked from the cold. He lifted one foot, then the other, swaying side to side.

"I'm about to die here myself," he said. "Been out in this crap for hours."

"I have blankets in the truck," said Dayna.

"Get 'em, if you don't mind," I told her. She turned and left.

When she was out of earshot, I said, "Give it to me. All of it, and straight down the middle. This is no time to bob and weave."

I'd inherited Franco, born in Milan and educated at Duke University, as a client when I took over the East End branch of Burton Lewis's pro bono law firm, which specialized in defending the poor, disenfranchised, and occasionally innocent. I'd been on the job about a year, after Burton saved me from my old real-estate practice, which was already succumbing to an unplanned and financially disastrous slide into criminal law. Now that Burton, one of the Hamptons' certified billionaires, was paying me, I could afford to give in and complete the transition, for better or worse.

Franco had been convicted of manslaughter and was doing time up at Sanger Penitentiary. After reviewing the case, I was able to knock off almost half the original sentence, which led to an early release. This made Franco a very grateful man, and even more so when I got him a job with Tad as a general handyman, the felony conviction having put a slight dent in his banking résumé.

This probably encouraged him to think I'd be willing to do anything for him, including driving my blessed Volvo through blinding snow, subzero temperatures, and gale-force winds.

Franco shoved his hands even deeper into his pockets and looked up at the pergola, gathering his thoughts.

"Zina called me from the house, telling me Tad had gone out to check on the main woodshed," he said. "It's got a pretty flat roof, something we built last fall, not expecting this kind of ridiculous snow. Roofs are collapsing all over the place, so this was a logical thing to do. Only, a ten-minute checkup turned into an hour and a half, which was a little out of the ordinary, even for Tad."

"And you said you'd go look?"

"Sure, absolutely. Our shack is closer to the woodshed than the main house, so no prob. And you don't say no to Zina."

Zina was Katarzina, Tad's wife. Or, like most people thought of her, his mail-order bride, having arrived from Poland only two years before. With high cheekbones, slanted eyes, and a coarse shock of nearly blond hair, Zina was a legitimate beauty, thirty years younger and a hundred pounds lighter than her homely American husband.

"So you found him," I said, throwing the tarp back over.

"On the way to the shed. At the base of Hamburger Hill. I stepped on him and fell right on my face. I thought it was a hay bale or something. Lucky I took the trouble to look back. It just about stopped my heart, seeing him there. Probably why I lost my mind and dragged him over here. Fuck, it's cold."

"Dayna's bringing blankets. So what did you do after you brought him here?" I asked.

He looked disappointed in me.

"Called you, what do you think? As soon as I realized my massive stupidity. They're gonna hang me for this, aren't they? Convicted felon. Killer of men. Stupid Dago puts the gun in the hands of people who'd be just as happy to shoot him."

He hung his head in abject remorse, although a little more theatrically than served his purpose.

"Hey, stop talking like that," I said. "Nobody's persecuting Italians."

He nodded, again a bit too contritely.

"You're right. I'm sorry. And way too paranoid."

"Stupid Dago . . . with a degree in economics. Jeez."

I studied him, with meager result. The weather was too stormy, it was too dark, and he was too buried inside his clothing to get a reliable read off his face. I liked Franco, mostly, and trusted him, somewhat, so I'd have to go with that for the time being.

"Did you touch anything with your bare hands?" I asked him.

He put both gloved hands in front of his face and shook his head. "No. Never. Had gloves on the whole time. Too cold not to."

I dug my phone out of its holster and held it up to him.

"I'm calling Southampton Town Police. Anything else you want to say before I do?" I asked.

I looked at him without speaking for a few moments, in case there was something else in there yearning to come out, but it didn't happen.

"'Or forever hold your peace'?" said Franco. "I've heard you say that before."

"I still mean it."

"No. That's all there is."

I didn't completely believe him, but I called anyway, knowing that clients come and go, and although I was both morally and legally bound to put their interests first, I had another constituency to care for: the local police, without whose trust and goodwill I'd be out of business faster than a snowflake dissolves on the tip of your tongue.

Not surprisingly, I had Detective Joe Sullivan's cell phone on speed dial.

"This can't be good," said Sullivan, answering the phone.

"That's nice. Just assume the worst. Okay, it's not good." Dayna showed up with a flashlight of her own and a stack of blankets, one for each of us. From what I could see of Franco's face, he looked grateful. "I have a DB laid out on a picnic table. Tad Buczek. Big-time trauma to the head."

I told him where to find me and the body. I didn't mention the others. That could come later.

"Crazy Polack."

"Watch it."

"Sorry. I meant that respectfully. Most of my friends are crazy Polacks. We've only got the four-wheel units out. Stay on the line while I get one over there, then I'll come back and you can tell me what happened."

Like I knew what really happened. I held the phone away from my mouth.

"You sure no one saw you discover the body or move it here," I asked Franco one more time. "No other witnesses?"

"I'm telling you, no."

"And Zina doesn't know."

"No. I only called you," said Franco with a shiver that was probably not entirely from the cold.

"Maybe we should wait in the truck," said Dayna.

I shook my head. "Cops like simple stories. 'We met up with Franco, we came here, we waited.' But there's no reason for you to suffer. You've done a lot already."

She shook her head this time. "This is more interesting than sitting around watching the snow fall."

Sullivan came back on the line and I briefed him as thoroughly as I could, with all the information I had at hand. Given where we were at that point, there was nothing to hide, no client confidences to defend. I knew Franco's decision to call me before calling the cops wasn't going to sit well, however.

When Sullivan was done grilling me, I asked him what I should do next.

"Stay put, exactly where you are."

And so we stood, silently, each doing his or her little improvised dance, trying in vain to generate a little body heat. Dayna cupped her gloved hands in front of her mouth, her steamy breath slipping through her fingers only to be whisked away by the wind. The only person there who was indifferent to the weather was Tad Buczek, now just a long, inert mass whose presence I nevertheless felt. I remembered my late husband, Pete Swaitkowski, introducing me to his uncle Tad, who was a big man all over, with enormous workman's hands. He didn't have much of a chin, and his eyelids hung nearly at half mast, conveying the cartoonish cliché of a classic doofus. Except Tad was anything but. In fact, the ongoing battle with his rich and presumably sophisticated neighbors had earned him a reputation as a crafty and unpredictable adversary, and thus a near folk hero within the Polish community. Only a near hero, because he also had a reputation as a ball breaker with a hair-trigger temper. Rumors of crazed and brutal brawls had for years been part of family legend, events Pete could never quite confirm or deny.

None of which lessened the sad shock I felt closing in around my heart as I stood in the dubious shelter of the pergola and contemplated the ruins under the white-flecked sheet of blue plastic.

Danny Izard was Sullivan's patrol officer of choice whenever the call came from Jackie Swaitkowski. This was fine with me, because I liked Danny Izard and he liked me—a bond reinforced by a few occasions where he'd likely saved my life. Accomplishments he refused to take credit for or regard as anything particularly special.

We saw blinking blue and white lights out on the driveway. Then the jittery approach of a pair of flashlights carried by two people dressed in heavy black clothes and hats with earflaps pulled down and snapped beneath the chin.

"Hey, Jackie, what're you doin' out here?" said Danny. "You must really like the snow."

"What snow?"

"What do we got?"

I pulled back the tarp and Danny and the other cop, a stubby hedge-hog of a woman named Judy Rensler, scanned the body with their flashlights, just as we had done not that long before. Nothing had changed.

Judy immediately started taking photos with a battered digital Nikon. The stinging brilliance of the flash caused me to turn my eyes away from the body.

"It's Tad Buczek," I said to Danny. "Franco Raffini here found him at the base of one of Tad's homemade hills and dragged him here," I said, getting the worst of it out in the open right away.

"Why'd you do that?" asked Danny, an edge in his voice. He stuck the flashlight in Franco's face.

"I don't know. The storm, I guess. It's not that far from here, where I found him. Want to go take a look?"

He turned and started to walk up the grade behind us, but I stopped him.

"What about the CSIs?" I asked Danny.

"On their way. As best they can."

"I can plow the drive again," said Dayna.

Danny looked over at her. "Excuse me, ma'am, you are?"

"Dayna Red," I said. "She and her pickup got me over here."

"Okay, sure," said Danny. "Thank you very much."

After Dayna left, the rest of us walked along a path of footsteps in the snow, now nearly refilled and barely defined enough to follow to a spot at the base of a huge circular mound with gently curved sides that Tad called Hamburger Hill. On top of the hill Tad had built a huge metallic mobile. In the summer, it was driven by water pumped up and out from the sculpture's extremities, so it looked like a giant sprinkler hallucinated by Salvador Dalí. Now it stood motionless, covered in a thin layer of snow.

Franco brought us up to where he claimed to have stumbled over the body. You could see where a lot of snow had been disturbed, even though the edges were softened by the added accumulation. There were faint depressions in the pattern of footprints leading up to the spot from the opposite direction, which supported Franco's story pretty thoroughly.

After Judy took some more pictures, she let Franco walk around the crime scene and act out how events unfolded. Danny and I both took notes in little notebooks using regular pens, stopping every few minutes to brush the snow off the pages, which in my case smeared the blue ink.

"So you went back to your living quarters to get a tarp," said Danny, counting the footprints with the beam of his flashlight.

Franco nodded. "All our equipment's in a barn next to the shack where Freddy and I live. Freddy's the other hand. I knew the tarp was the only way I could drag a guy as big as Tad. I almost asked Freddy to help me, but I'm glad I didn't. It's a little downhill from here to the pergola, so I made it on my own. Barely. Tad's a lot of dead weight. Sorry, didn't mean it like that."

Danny gently brushed away the lightest snow from the spot Franco had designated. Underneath were chunks of red ice and snow. Danny pointed to where he wanted Judy to take some more pictures. Then he fished a roll of yellow tape out of his pocket and tore off a piece. He stuck it to the ground with a pen, using the butt end of his semiautomatic as a hammer.

"The CSIs will be screaming over this one," Danny said.

"Can't blame the weather on you," I said.

"They blame everything on everybody."

After that, we walked back down to the pergola and out to the driveway in time to meet a pair of white vans—one from the chief medical examiner's office, the other from the county forensics unit who shared quarters with the ME up in Riverhead. Dayna Red had cleared the way for them and was facing the unmolested snow that covered the way to the main house. Without discussing it, we all knew it was time to go see Katarzina and break the news.

When Tad was still a potato farmer, he tore down the original family farmhouse and built what I think was intended to be a Californian hacienda. It was only one story, but it stretched across a considerable chunk of real estate. The wide, gently sloping hip roofs added to the low-slung effect. Underneath were both enclosed rooms and open spaces, divided by large panes of fixed glass. By that description, it should have been an architectural delight, but Tad had managed to imbue the place with a kind of shabby gloom. Having lived as a bachelor for most of his life, it was an atmosphere entirely of his own making that two years of Zina's influence had only begun to dispel.

I followed Danny and Judy across a broad covered patio that led to the front door. Franco and I followed a few steps back. Dayna was happy this time to wait in the truck. When Danny rang the doorbell, a light flashed on above our heads, then another in the living room visible through narrow side windows.

There was a click at the door, which then abruptly swung wide open. It startled me, as I was expecting something a little more tentative. Zina Buczek stood in the doorframe, her sharp features exaggerated by the light above and the effect of a pair of barrettes that pulled her hair back and stretched her forehead. She stood silently, staring at the cops and waiting, braced for what was to come.

Danny had done this before and, being a person of essential decency, spoke the words with just the right tone and pitch. Zina stood motionless, but her cat eyes began to widen and flicker back and forth from cop to cop.

"What is this you're saying?" she asked, her accent thick with Polish inflection. Danny was forced to repeat the whole thing.

"No, it is not true," she said, her shoulders now sagging as she reached back to the door handle for support. Judy stepped forward and took Zina's arm.

"Sorry, ma'am," she said. "Let me help you back inside."

Danny followed after telling us to wait on the patio. I knew it was the right call, but the brief blast of warm air from the house had left me even more disappointed by the relentless cold.

A few minutes later, Danny stuck his head out.

"She wants to talk to Franco," he said.

"Not without me," I said.

The door closed again. Franco stared at the ground, keeping his comments restricted to wordless mumbling. A minute later, Danny let us in.

The twin sensations brought on by the heat and incandescent light nearly gave me vertigo. The air on my face was drier but somehow heavier than the chilly stuff outside. It soothed my burning cheeks. Franco snatched off his hat and scratched at his curly hair as if relieving a long-denied itch. We stood on dark gray tile that extended into the living room, the snow melting off our boots and blending into puddles already formed on the floor. Directly in front of us was a pair of sofas facing each other, separated by a dingy area rug. Zina and Judy sat on one of the sofas and Danny stood a respectful distance to one side. He wrote in his book. Judy held both Zina's hands in hers. Zina looked up at us as we came forward. Her fine-skinned face was paler than usual, but her eyes were clear and dry. I realized in the better light that she was wearing pajamas made of a heavy gray flannel that I'd mistaken for a sweatsuit.

Franco started to say he was terribly sorry, but she cut him off. "He was dead when you found him, you are sure," she said.

Franco held his hat in front of him with both hands and looked up at the ceiling. Danny watched him carefully.

"Yes, Mrs. Buczek. There was no doubt. I'm terribly sorry."

"You don't tell me right away, but you call Jackie. What does that mean?"

"It means I didn't know what to do. I'm sorry for that, too."

"You think Franco do this?" she asked Judy.

"No one's been charged, Mrs. Buczek," she said. "We're not assuming foul play."

"Foul play?"

"That anyone caused your husband's death. Or if it was an accident. It's too early for that."

Zina stared off into the middle distance and slowly nodded, as if trying to absorb the information, if not the entire situation. Meanwhile, Judy went through the usual brief: Did Zina have anyone who could stay with her? Anyone she could call? Could they drive her somewhere? Still looking into nothing, Zina shook her head.

"There's nowhere for me now. Nowhere to hide."

Franco still stood silently, head bowed, hat in hand. The wind blew a spray of snow into a picture window across the room. I looked over and saw the blue lights from the white vans flickering through naked tree limbs and heard the sound of Dayna's plow rumbling up to the house, the truck's high beams briefly striking one of Tad's metal art pieces, this one a type of stork or crane, its long beak pointing back toward the pergola as if aware of, but indifferent to, what lay there.

3

Burton Lewis was born with more money than even the most enterprising spender could ever spend. His entire family had died off soon after he graduated from law school, so he'd have a right to question the value of the cosmic trade-off. Though he never did, at least not to me.

Part of his inheritance was a colossal law firm on Wall Street that specialized in what you'd roughly categorize as tax law, but that barely described the actual pursuit: mediating between the wealthiest people on earth and the U.S. government over the price of doing business at the center of the world's biggest economy.

Burton liked the work, despite having started his career in a storefront legal defense practice in the South Bronx, an antecedent to the extensive pro bono enterprise he'd built up across the region and for whom I ran the Eastern Suffolk County franchise.

I liked him, a feeling I concentrated on while avoiding the more intense emotions he could touch in me, which would have been for naught given Burton's orientation. Nevertheless, he liked me, too, which I had a hard time understanding but was devoutly grateful for.

"So, no charges levied against Mr. Raffini," he said to me over the phone when I called him the morning after the to-do at Tad Buczek's.

"Not yet," I said, "since there's no direct evidence Franco had any role in the death."

"It was good of you to drive over there, given the conditions. Though impulse control has never been your strong suit."

I didn't try to argue that point. Instead, I shared what Zina had said: "There's nowhere for me now. Nowhere to hide."

"Interesting," he said.

"You bet. We pressed her to say more, but she clammed up after that. Though it's not enough to slow Sullivan from bringing Franco in for questioning. This afternoon, assuming the roads are clear enough for the governor to lift the travel ban."

Burton huffed with scorn.

"What seems to be the state's difficulty? I've been on the snow-blower since daybreak. The drive and pathways are now perfectly clear."

That the driveway leading to Burton's mansion in Southampton was about half the length of the Long Island Expressway gave his case some credence. Burton liked to do this sort of work himself, despite an extensive and eager domestic staff, which was another reason why the guy held such a persistent grip on my affections.

"I'll tell you what I know when I know it," I said to him, then hung up and went back to my focus of the moment—staring in the bathroom mirror at an odd little red splotch on my cheek, arbitrating between what could have been one of my ridiculous freckles, late-life acne, or some sort of fatal carcinoma.

According to the calendar, I was about to bump up against a birthday that would put me within spitting distance of forty, a milestone I was ashamed to admit felt a bit daunting. This had led to heightened vigilance over signs of impending decrepitude. Both my parents had died relatively young, within a few months of each other, so that might have been one factor. Or the only factor. Or maybe I was just a coward.

I was in my apartment in Water Mill, a subsection of Southampton you crossed through on the way to Bridgehampton and other eastern reaches of the South Fork. I used to live in a house my late husband had built not far from there, but after being attacked and nearly raped and killed there one night, living alone in the woods had lost its allure.

Across the hall from the apartment was my office, giving me one of the shorter commutes in the Hamptons, a distance often traversed in bathrobe and slippers, as it was that day. My apartment and office encompassed the entire second floor of a building that housed a Japanese restaurant and shabby little art gallery on the first. It was my empire, my province, my paradise on earth.

I made a cup of coffee and barely had time to boot up my computer when the cell phone played the first instrumental stanzas of "Should I Stay or Should I Go." I picked it up.

"So you're obviously alive," said Harry Goodlander. "I'm glad."

Harry was my boyfriend, a word I never felt comfortable hearing inside my head, much less passing my lips. Not because I didn't care for Harry, but I could never think of him as a boy, or a friend, in the traditional sense of the term. Of course we were friends, but of the abiding, confusing, gut-wrenching type that transcends the banality of the standard definition.

And if you saw Harry, you'd agree no standard definition could ever quite apply.

"I'm glad, too," I said. "Were there doubts?"

"I called a few times last night. When you didn't answer, I figured you were either stoned silly or frozen under a snowdrift."

"That's so sweet. So you called the authorities?"

"Actually, I went back to the Knicks game," he said. "They won—a bigger miracle than your apparent survival."

"As it turns out, I was already with the authorities. The cops, to be specific. Want to hear about it?"

He did, and I spared no detail in the telling of the tale. Patience with my excesses, in all their forms, including a tendency to go on and on about something well beyond the necessary, was Harry's most appreciated quality. Okay, second most appreciated.

"Sorry about your uncle," he said. "Pete's uncle. Terrible thing."

"Thanks. Though I can't say I liked him that much, which I hope doesn't bring all kinds of bad karma down on my head."

"I don't think that's how karma works. Not that I'm an expert. Can I bring you breakfast? The government is letting us out of our houses. Just in time to avoid a constitutional crisis."

"I'm in the mood for things hot, sweet, and slippery. Cardiologically impure. I'll work it off in the spring," I told him.

"On it."

I went back to my computer, or rather my worst addiction. Plagued as I've been my whole life by an uncontrollable curiosity about all things large, small, and in between, the allure of that silvery machine has proven nearly, maybe totally, irresistible. To me, modern computers are, in fact, intravenous tubes you jack directly into the arterial throb of global information. The World Wide Web is not so much a vast repository of fact and opinion but a living organism, a seething, voracious creature ever expanding toward the infinite.

And for me, pure joy.

Thus lost as I usually was in the digital chase of the moment, I didn't immediately notice the chime that warned someone was at the outside door. I probably assumed it was Harry, so by the time I looked at the monitor connected to a security camera mounted above the door, the person had just begun to turn away. I tried to follow him with the camera, moveable by a little joystick, but all I saw was another man, shorter and rounder than the first one, though equally bundled against the cold weather. They hadn't rung the bell but had merely walked inside the field of a motion detector, which triggered the chime. And now they were moving away, back toward the parking lot and out of my electronic field of vision.

I once shared the top floor with a bunch of grumpy surveyors, so when I took full possession of the space, this kind of thing happened a lot. But not in recent months. I was tempted to run downstairs in my robe to see if I could catch a better look, but something held me in my seat. Maybe Burton's remark about impulse control.

Almost by reflex, I switched on the digital recorder that captured feeds from the security cameras—one outside, and two in the hallway facing the apartment and inner office doors. The recorder was good for a week before I had to clean out the hard drive.

I crossed the room to a keypad that controlled the alarm system and punched in the activation code. Then I threw the massive deadbolt on my office door.

Safe, but now afflicted with a type of vague apprehension that always made me feel slightly ill. A warning light had flicked on inside my head, so, real or imagined, the rest of my physiology quickly followed.

"Dammit."

Harry set off the next chime. I knew immediately it was him by the sight of his charmingly bald skull filling the security monitor. At about six foot eight and then some, he nearly reached the height of the hidden camera. He also had a key, which he was using to get through the door. I shut off the alarm, threw back the deadbolt, and waited for him to reach the top of the stairs.

"Wow. An official greeting," he said. "Complete with formal wear."

"This is all we wear in these parts, mister."

When we were inside the office, I switched the alarm back on and turned the deadbolt, causing Harry to arch an eyebrow.

"Paranoid, are we?"

I told him about my two near visitors.

"Probably nothing," I said, "but you'd be the first to tell me to take normal precautions."

"Where's the Glock?" he asked, referring to my trusty semiautomatic.

"Where it usually is," I said, flicking my eyes toward the spot and winking, as if there were others in the room we needed to trick. "So, what's in the bag? Some form of enticement?"

"I hope so. Ham-and-cheese omelets, bacon strips, and two gooey cinnamon buns. Artery clogging, as specified."

"Good. Let's eat."

Harry was a freelance logistics expert, specializing in the sourcing, procuring, and transporting of the daunting and improbable. If you had something odd to ship—say, an orangutan from Sumatra to Tallahassee, or very big, like a full-scale reproduction of the Trojan Horse, Harry was your man. So if I'd ordered a breakfast of torofugu and gingersnap cookies, he'd definitely deliver.

Harry and I had been an on-and-off-again thing some years before, and now we seemed to be fairly securely on, for which I credit him, both for his persistence and the willingness to adapt to me without asking for a whole lot of adaptation in return. Unless you count my willingness to have him be whatever he wanted to be. Not just willing, but eager, since his Harry-ness was what appealed to me from the beginning. Why mess with that?

My Jackie-ness had been the issue, now tentatively resolved. Although, like most neurotic, ambivalence-ridden females of my time, my emotional fingers were never completely uncrossed.

After breakfast, spent in luxurious avoidance of all things responsible, personal, or professional, Harry generously helped me take a shower, which was fun for both of us, then left me to go about the rest of the day, the morning now exhausted but well spent.

The snow had not only stopped, the sun was ablaze and the sky without a cloud. The cold, however, bit even deeper, stuck as it was in single digits, unusual for our part of the world. I feared for the tulips and daffodils, buddleia and miscanthus that grew along the back of my building, though I'd been told by a native Vermonter not to worry if there was plenty of snow cover, which remarkably enough served as insulation. Who knew?

I'd arranged to meet up with Franco Raffini at a diner on Montauk Highway a few miles south of Southampton Town Police headquarters. This was a tradition of mine when escorting my clients to visits with the cops, events I mostly strove to avoid, though with a case like Franco's, not so easy to do. By every definition, he was a material witness if they chose to anoint him one, and could thus become quickly embraced by their tender mercies whether I liked it or not.

The diner was the perfect place to hash out the ground rules—the most important of which was to keep your damn mouth shut unless I gave you permission to speak. You'd be surprised how many people found this impossible to do.

"What am I going to say?" I asked Franco over two cups of coffee, a turkey sandwich for him, and a yogurt for me, fooling him into thinking I ate like a bird.

"To keep my damn mouth shut unless you give me permission to speak. Even though I'm Italian, a race of bigmouths."

"Italians aren't a race, and I never said that. You gotta lose this ethnic persecution thing. The governor's Italian, for God's sake. Like his father, also governor. Sometimes I think all of Nassau County is

Italian, per capita the richest county in the country. For an oppressed people, you're doing pretty well."

"You're right. Sorry. It's transference. My father oppressed me, so I blame it on you Anglos."

"Don't call me an Anglo unless you're spoilin' for a fight," I said. "I'm Irish. We know a thing or two about oppression."

Now that he was out from under his snow gear, I could see his face, which was still long, poorly shaven, and somewhat morose. Undoubtedly, he'd had a far more bright-eyed and chipper demeanor back in his investment banker days, when he had a prestigious job on Wall Street, a summer house in Hampton Bays, a stunning wife, and two kids. Losing all that—including most of his liquid assets in the subsequent divorce—and doing three years in prison had brought on predictably corrosive effects. Still, I imagined I could see glimpses of a prior Franco occasionally peek through, an intimation of the crafty intelligence and drive that had earned him the opportunity to execute such a precipitous fall from grace.

"This would also be an excellent time to tell me the truth about last night," I said. "All of it."

This was the other reason I liked prepping my clients at the diner. There was something about delivering harsh words in a public place that undermined their natural defenses.

I saw Franco's eyes shift toward the door, as if contemplating escape.

"I told you already," he said.

"You haven't met Joe Sullivan," I said. "He knows people are bullshitting before they do. Anyway, it's insulting to think you can't open up to me. I trusted you enough to get you sprung out of Sanger. You're supposed to trust me back."

He'd been about to take a bite of his sandwich when I said that. He pulled it away from his mouth. His sad eyes grew sadder. "I trust you, Jackie. If it was just about me, it'd be different."

He tried again to make a little progress with his sandwich, but this time I took it away from him and dropped it back on the plate.

"I knew it. Dammit, Franco, you're not supposed to hold out on me. I'm your lawyer. I'll protect your confidences."

He looked unconvinced. "No. You won't give them up. You'll browbeat me into giving them up myself. I don't look forward to that. Some people don't know how to let up."

When he said that, I noticed I was halfway out of my seat and nearly stretched across the table. I sat back and straightened my clothes, brushing lint off the shoulders of my jacket in a caricature of regained composure.

"Okay," I said. "I promise I won't do that."

"What?"

"That thing I do. That not-letting-up thing." He wasn't the first to point out this tendency, so maybe I was a little sensitive about it. "I'll respect your boundaries. And there's always attorney-client privilege. If I reveal stuff without your okay, you can get me disbarred. Not that I would."

One of the least appealing features of Franco's bedraggled face was that crummy little mustache and goatee, composed of wiry, black, thinly distributed hair that, combined with a pair of bulging, closely set eyes, gave the general aspect of a small nocturnal mammal. A sick one at that.

"You're gonna be unhappy with me," he said dolefully.

"I'll only be unhappy if you keep trying to squirm out from under this."

He snatched his sandwich off the plate and sat as far back in the booth as he could, clear of my reach. He took a bite that was too big to talk through, so I had to wait.

"So, you have to keep this to yourself if I ask you to, as, like, my lawyer," he said.

"Absolutely," I said, even though that wasn't quite true.

He rubbed his scraggly facial hair and shut his eyes tight, the outward expression of an agonizing internal debate.

"Tad went out there to check on the woodshed, but that's not the only reason," he said, the words nearly wrenched from his throat.

"Okay," I said. "Then why?"

He squeezed his eyes even tighter and rolled his head like a blind piano player.

"He was looking for Zina," he said with a burst of exhaled breath, as if he'd saved it up to help force the admission.

I allowed a few moments for him to recover.

"How do you know that?" I finally said.

"He called me on my cell. Asking if I'd seen her, then saying he was heading out to look. By then it was snowing like a bastard, and her car was still in the garage, so he figured she had to be out there on the grounds. I said I'd help him search. He told me to stay put, but to keep my cell on. He'd call me after securing the woodshed, and if she hadn't turned up by then, we'd plan a search. That was the last I heard from him."

He looked out the dirty window at a small mountain of winter grime piled there by the successive labors of snowblowers, shovels, and plows. He shook his head haphazardly, like people do when they're listening to an unwanted internal monologue.

Then he looked right at me, the odor of ill-concealed deception hanging over him.

"You knew where she was," I said, suddenly seeing the truth, at least the part of the truth advertised by his tormented eyes.

He lurched back as if I'd taken a swing at him. "How can you say that?" he asked.

"Come on, Franco. If I can see it, Joe Sullivan can see it. You know what that means."

Detectives and other skilled interrogators will tell you it takes a nearly superhuman grip on self-control to keep a secret. It isn't that people are so driven to tell the truth. In fact, lying is so much a natural part of day-to-day existence, it's a wonder there's any truth spoken in the world at all. But an interrogation isn't a day-to-day thing. It's a mental pressure chamber, so concentrated and relentless that the secret eventually strains to reveal *itself*, begs to be free just to escape the agonizing scrutiny.

Franco had been there before. He didn't want to go back.

"Dammit, Franco, you knew where to find her, didn't you."

His buggy eyes opened even further, until the whites surrounded his dark irises.

"I did. All I had to do was look over at her lying in my bed. Sheet pulled up to her throat, finger at her lips, warning me not to say anything that might give us away. And that I didn't do. I swear it."

4

Even when operating on different sides of a perennial contest, you get to know and befriend people, especially if you're contending a lot over a long period of time. I felt that way about Detective Joe Sullivan, a buzz-cut blond with a body like a slab of marbled beef and a social conscience as finely tuned as it was thoroughly disguised.

I first met Joe when he was a beat cop patrolling North Sea—the scrub-oak-littered and formerly semi-squalid outer suburb of Southampton Village—and I was still a sloppy, overly compensated real-estate attorney. As things evolved, we got more and more enmeshed in the same cases, the same shared experiences, until it became a matter of routine, and along with that, a settled sense of mutual respect, if not out-and-out affection.

Sullivan's boss, on the other hand, was a whole different kettle of fish. Mutant fish, to stretch the analogy. When you first met Ross Semple, the chief of police, you immediately thought the guy was in the wrong job. What the right job would be was hard to tell. Maybe college professor or actuary or master of black ops for the CIA.

Learning that he was widely considered one of the best in his ill-suited profession never quite shook that initial impression.

So I had the usual mixed feelings when Sullivan said Ross wanted to meet with me after we chatted with Franco.

"You and I will chat," I said. "Franco will listen."

"Sure thing, Jackie," he said, leading us along a familiar path through the squad room to a drab little conference room in the back. Sullivan chose it to stress the informality of the occasion, bypassing the official interrogation room with its one-way mirror and hard metal furniture. "What can I get you—water, coffee?"

"We're all set," I said. "This won't take long."

Joe went through the pretense of making us comfortable by holding our chairs and bringing in an unasked-for tray with glasses and a pitcher of water. If there'd been a stereo, we'd be listening to a little light jazz.

"Heck of a winter we're having," he said to Franco as he sat at the table. "Must keep you busy over at Tad's."

Franco gave a tight little smile, his lips literally sealed.

"For the record, Mr. Raffini is here voluntarily to assist in the police investigation of Mr. Buczek's death," I said.

"And we appreciate that, Mr. Raffini. We do."

From there, I gave a description of the night based on all the facts and events I understood the police to already know, in chronological order. Sullivan took notes, nodding along with the story. He asked Franco a few questions, most of which I answered for him, such as did he hear or see anything out of the ordinary before coming across the body in the snow.

Franco shook his head and looked over at me.

"Go ahead," I said.

"Nothing," he told Sullivan. "There was just a lot of snow and wind, could hardly see or hear anything else."

"Did you call out his name when you were searching for him?"

I gave him another go-ahead nod.

"I wasn't searching. I was heading over to the woodshed where Zina said Tad had gone to check things out. I figured I'd find him there shoveling the roof or propping up the walls. It wasn't like Tad to walk away from a job until he was satisfied it was done. Even in a big storm."

Sullivan continued to write down notes, a lot of notes. I wondered if they said "All work and no play makes Tad a dull boy."

"How was your relationship with Tad?" he finally asked. "You guys get along?"

"They got along fine," I said. "That's not what we're here to discuss."

"Understood. How about Mrs. Buczek?" he said. "How'd you get along with her?"

Franco sat as still as a statue.

I stood up. "Okay, Detective. It's been fun. Gotta run."

"Sit down, Jackie. You and I need to talk a little. Franco can wait for you in the lobby. Unless you don't want to hear what I have to say."

Not much chance of that, I thought. So I sent a slightly rattled Franco out of the room and tried to look indifferent.

"What?" I said.

"You know he's been boinking the Polish missus," said Sullivan, not even looking up from his notepad.

"Who told you that?"

He looked at me indulgently. "Your boy's been down this road before. Diddling some guy's wife. Then the guy ends up dead."

"Totally inadmissible," I said.

"Not if the ADA can help it."

"Never happen."

"Why'd he move the body?" he asked.

"He panicked."

"Over what?" he asked.

"Like you said. He's been down this road before. He thought he'd be implicated."

"He's implicated anyway. So why move the body? Nobody does that for no reason."

"Does this mean he's being charged?" I asked.

"I'm waiting on forensics. The ADA wants more tangibles, but we're dealing with the world's lousiest crime scene. It'll take too long."

By the ADA, he meant the assistant district attorney, the underling who actually did all the work in the District Attorney's Office. I didn't know what the DA actually did herself. I just knew she terrified me.

"Franco's not a flight risk," I said.

"The hell he isn't. What does he have to lose?"

"He doesn't want to go back to prison."

"It's looking bad, Jackie. As bad as these things get. Second-degree premeditated is the best you're gonna get unless we started talking plea. And we can start talking anytime you want. Every hour that goes by, the deal gets worse for you."

Sullivan was not an easy read, an important professional advantage. But it didn't take an intuitive genius to figure out where this was going.

"You're not waiting on forensics. You knew all along you were charging him."

It was a crappy thing to do and he knew it.

"The murder of a prominent local guy, even a nutbag like Tad, is serious business," he said. "Ross does not want to lose control of this one."

"The ends justify the means."

"Unless you can tell me something I don't know that would change my mind, Franco's about to get his rights read. I didn't have to give you this chance," he added, maybe a bit defensively.

I frantically ran through the facts and suppositions of the case, hoping the added pressure would squeeze out an important insight, but all it did was confirm what Sullivan was saying. Things were as bad as they could get.

"I want copies of all the crime-scene photos and forensics reports," I said.

"Done."

"Let me talk to him," I said. "One more time."

Sullivan left the room for a few moments, then came back with Franco, who was escorted by a uniformed officer. They closed the door and left us alone.

"What's going on, Jackie? They're all looking at me out there."

"They're gonna arrest you, Franco. For killing Tad Buczek."

His face fell so far I thought it would slide off his head and onto the floor.

"Oh God, no."

"There's so much circumstantial evidence, they don't think they need forensics. They're more afraid of you taking off than rushing into a botched case."

"You knew about this?" he asked, his dejection suddenly replaced by a flash of brilliant anger.

I fought to keep my voice calmer than I felt. "I didn't. I would never do such a thing. It would be stupid, immoral, and completely unethical. They fooled me, too. I'm sorry."

I don't know if he believed me, but he looked like he wanted to. At that point, I was all he had. The loss would be too great.

"I can't make bail," he said.

"I'll work on that. Right now, you really, really need to tell me everything you know. Or saw, or did. Anything that could influence how they write up the charge. And make it quick. We don't have much time."

"I know I didn't do it—does that count for anything?"

I didn't answer that. I just waited for him to run through whatever calculations were going on inside his head. It didn't take long.

"Tell them I'll go willingly," he said. "The world hates me anyway.

Just throw me in a hole and leave me there till I die. You'll all be better for it."

I sat with him while they read him his rights. He only looked at me during the part of Miranda where it says you have the right to an attorney. The look said, *Fat load of good that did me.* I kept my composure, for his sake, and to deny the regular cops the sight of me blowing my top. It wasn't until they led him away in handcuffs that Ross Semple showed up, wearing his customary striped polyester shirt, conflicting tie, and bottle-bottom glasses. I waited until the door shut behind him.

"Fuck you, Ross. You suck."

"Detective Sullivan had no choice. It was a direct order from me. He almost quit over it. He's a good cop."

"Unlike you."

He held a manila folder under his arm and a lit Winston in his right hand. As far as anyone knew, Ross was the only public official on Long Island who still felt free to smoke in the office. It wasn't that he hadn't read the memo. No one had the guts to send it to him in the first place.

"Raffini's the guiltiest man in the world, and you know it."

"No, I don't. And neither do you. All you have is circumstantial. With that blizzard, that's bloody all you'll get."

This seemed to amuse Ross, a response that nearly moved me from merely irate to irredeemably enraged.

"Interesting choice of words. You did notice all the blood at the scene."

"Of course."

"But you didn't notice all of it."

He offered me one of his cigarettes. I refused dismissively, despite the sudden surge of yearning.

"It was dark and a little stormy," I said. "Though you could see some blood under the top layer of snow."

"And ice."

"Ice? I guess so," I said. "All I saw was bloody snow."

"As you say, the conditions were lamentable. You would have had to dig deeper into the drift to discover the bloody ice. The bigger chunks."

"I didn't see any chunks. Where are we going with this?" I asked.

Even my angry mind knew to pay attention when Ross was taking you on a little mental journey. The destination could be perilous.

"We haven't found the murder weapon, but we have something you might call the pre-murder weapon," he said.

"I don't follow," I said. "Maybe you could just tell me without the twenty-questions game."

"What fun is that? With all the blood, you wouldn't know that the blow to the top of the head wasn't what killed him. And it didn't take an ME to see the lethal wound once it was washed off."

"I'm listening."

"It was a big damn hole, right beneath the occipital bone, where the spine and brain stem converge. There are marks on the back of the neck that could be from a boot, but too vague to confirm. But the hole itself took some precision."

"With what?"

"We don't know. We're more encouraged by what struck the original blow to the head. It was tossed about twenty feet from the scene. An eagle-eyed CSI saw a suspicious-looking depression, like a filled-in footprint, though off by itself. " He took a last draw off his cigarette and dropped the butt in one of the water glasses. "Did you know you can get fingerprints off an ice cube?"

"No."

"Conditions have to be perfect. It has to be very cold. The ice can only be held for the briefest of moments. Just long enough for the oils in the fingers to leave an impression but not so long that the person's body heat melts the little ridges beyond recognition. The next trick is to keep the ice frozen hard enough to dust and pull the prints. Who would have thought to bring frozen nitrogen in a big cooler into a snow-storm? Why, the wizards at the Suffolk County forensics lab. People here call them the creep geeks. Little do they know."

Ross would know, I thought. Terms like "creep" and "geek" would be very familiar to him.

"I bet you're eager to get to the point," I said. "Lord knows I am."

He lit another cigarette, which he held by the tip and tried to make little smoke circles with. I'd seen him try this before. It hadn't worked then, either.

"It was a piece of ice, the biggest and heaviest at the scene," he said. "One half covered in blood. The other, remarkably, showing three good-sized partials. Enough to make a conclusive identification."

"Hence the arrest," I said, not wanting him to drag it out any more than he already had.

"That's right. Your amorous Latin. Franklin Delano Raffini."

5

I know I had a reason for marrying Pete Swaitkowski, I just can't remember what it was. Probably because I'm attributing a far more sophisticated motivation than existed at the time, an invention retroactively imposed in the years following his death.

There's a simpler explanation. He was a very handsome, kindly, and cheerful guy with a lot of money earned the same way Tad Buczek earned his: the conversion of potato plants into postmodern vacation homes. And he was the first to identify certain buttons of mine, which he pushed with effortless ease.

His windfall came the year he graduated from college. The day after receiving his share of the family farm, the largest on the East End, he sold it. From then on he devoted his short, happy life to unencumbered bliss. Not in the chemical sense—he barely sniffed a drink, much less a spoon of cocaine, and his only sexual excess I'm pretty sure was with me (if he had any energy left after that, more power to him). His abiding state of delight was the natural kind, born of his good nature and, frankly, a mind unfettered by the demands of serious introspection.

The only outsized indulgence he had, made possible by unearned wealth, was a top-of-the-line Porsche Carrera Roadster, which of course killed him when he drove it into a giant oak tree at 120 miles an hour.

Though I'd always felt welcomed and accepted by his family, made up of his two parents, half a dozen siblings, and nearly countless aunts, uncles, and cousins, we hadn't been married long enough for me to have been completely absorbed into the tribe. Soon after the funeral, I drifted away, and those relationships became confined to saying hi on the street or catching up for five minutes in the aisle of the grocery store.

So I had some trepidation when I looked up his mother's address, his father having passed away a few years before. She was the best choice anyway, being the former Paulina Buczek, Tad's sister. The last I knew, she was living in a town house condominium in Southampton Village.

She was still there. I had her phone number as well, but thought it better to just ring the doorbell. I'd learned long ago it's far more difficult to put a person off when they're standing on your doorstep than when you're merely a voice at the end of the telephone line.

That theory was sorely tested by Paulina.

"Well, Jackie O'Dwyer," she said to me, peering into my face through thick, square-framed glasses, her mouth set in an uncommitted straight line. "Fancy that."

"I'm awful sorry about Tad. I was there the night they found him."

She looked more or less as I'd last seen her. Her hair was a different color, nothing found in nature—a sort of mahogany red leaning toward magenta. It was stacked on the top of her head, held in place by invisible, unnatural means of support. Her jaw still had its hard angles, though the rest of her had bulked up considerably. Her hands, thicker than most men's, still proudly testified to the brutal labors of her early potato farmer's life.

"So they tell me," she said. "You were there with the fellow that killed him," she added with something less than condemnation, but not much.

"I'm his lawyer," I said. "That's why he called me over. I wouldn't blame you if you didn't want to talk to me, but somebody has to defend Mr. Raffini. At least you know me. You know I'm a fair person."

"Don't know that anymore, Jackie. Not a big fan of lawyers. Papa called 'em bloodsuckers."

Great, I thought. Nice to hear.

"Maybe not every single solitary lawyer is sucking blood, Paulina. Some suck wind."

Her iron face eased a bit. Without even thinking about it, I'd tapped into the basic source of my goodwill with the Swaitkowskis and their kin: my sense of humor—not necessarily the same as theirs, but on a similar frequency.

"Well, I don't know what I can tell you, Jackie. I haven't kept very close tabs on Tad, except what I'd read in the papers."

"You knew I was there the other night. And that I was representing Franco Raffini. That's pretty intimate knowledge," I said lightly, to make it sound more like a compliment than an accusation. Which is how she took it.

"I have my ways," she said.

"Can't we talk a little bit? What can it hurt?"

She stepped away from the door, still reluctant, but letting me in.

I looked around her living room and was glad to see Paulina's approach to interior decor had held firm. For those who think taste and style are entirely subjective, arbitrary judgments, with no absolute right or wrong, I offer Paulina Swaitkowski.

You don't see a lot of shag rugs anymore, so you probably won't remember they often came in a blended array of colors no one wants to ever see again—avocado green, fluorescent orange, mustard gold. Paulina had the entire apartment thus carpeted, which probably served one good purpose—distracting you from the hideous furniture. Could I call it Southern Italian American/Bollywood/'60s Disco a- Go-Go/ fifteenth-century baroque chic? That would be the most descriptive, but no one would believe me.

"Place looks great, Paulina. You always did have a flair."

"It's an instinct, Jackie. You can't teach it."

She sat in an overstuffed, wood-framed monstrosity of indistinct origin, leaving me to the long, padded bench beneath the Clock. The Clock was mostly brass, and the face itself was only about a foot in diameter, though it represented, I think, the sun, from which radiated long, brass spikes that more than tripled the total circumference. I'd never sat on the bench for fear it would somehow fall off the wall and I'd be impaled by one of the spikes. And now, there I was.

"Still struggling with the hair, I see," said Paulina.

This is the sort of thing Paulina always felt entitled to say, even with subjects more or less off-limits to my own family. Personally, I'd grown comfortable with (resigned to) that giant reddish-blond ball of fuzz that God had blessed me with in lieu of normal hair. I wanted to tell her that at least the color was the one I was born with, unlike some others in the room.

"Had you been seeing much of Uncle Tad in the last few years?" I asked.

"No," she said, without hesitation. "Truth be told, I haven't spoken to him since Papa died and he couldn't even trouble himself to come to the funeral. I heard he said, 'What's the point of missin' the game just to fuss over some dumb bastard who's dead anyway?' Isn't that terrible?"

I had to agree it was. Though it sounded like Tad.

"What about before that? I'm just trying to get an idea of what his life was like."

"You know as well as I. His life was"—she paused for emphasis—"crazy." She scowled, at her brother for being the way he was and at me for asking the question. "What he did to the family," she added, "it's inexcusable."

"I know he did a lot, but what do you mean exactly?"

"Well," she said, rolling her eyes around the room as if his manifold offenses were among the banal homilies etched on the plates and painted pieces of wood she'd hung on the walls, "destroying that property with his bulldozers and shovel things, and piling it up with junk. And then actually fighting with the neighbors when they rightfully complained. He made sure that everybody knew what they all thought about us anyway: stupid, primitive Polacks." Then she added another pejorative referring to a specific minority who might have come into unexpected money, which was too ugly to repeat.

"And then he goes over to Poland and buys himself his own private whore," she said, leaving the end of the sentence suspended so I could fill in the blanks with the worst possible conclusion.

It was a side of Paulina I knew existed but rarely saw. Though not for nothing, she *was* Tad Buczek's sister.

"So he had a few enemies," I said.

"A few? I think you could divide up the town in two groups: the people who hated him and the rest who thought he was just a jerk."

"What about the people who worked for him?"

She sat back in her chair, suddenly reticent. "I wouldn't know about that."

"I know Franco's pretty new, but what about Freddy and his wife—what's her name again?"

She looked defiant. "You know perfectly well who she is."

"I do?"

Now she looked both defiant and annoyed. "Don't try your lawyerly tricks on me, young lady. In the eyes of God, I'm still your mother-in-law."

I was honestly baffled. I hoped it showed.

"I'm sorry, Paulina. I'm not trying to be dense here. I don't think I ever met her. I just knew Freddy's wife looked after the house while Freddy worked on the property. That they went back to the potato days."

Her face softened down to the merely hard-edged. "I guess you wouldn't have seen her at family gatherings. She never came. Felt ashamed, is what I think."

"Why ashamed? Not around our family."

"Her family, too," said Paulina. "You really don't know. She's your Peter's aunt. Papa's sister. Aunt Saline."

I spent the rest of the day attending to my other, nearly neglected, clients. Making enough progress to be technically beyond reproach from everything but my conscience. The next morning the Hamptons were back in the freeze locker. It was five below when I woke up and so cold in the apartment I thought my furnace had failed on me. When I jumped online to find a furnace-repair person, I checked the weather report. Then I turned up the thermostat and hot air flowed through the registers. It was almost disappointing to learn that the furnace was fine and it was the world that was malfunctioning.

I got back in bed after going through these shenanigans, now wearing a down vest over my flannel pajamas and, lying flat on my back, I tried to figure out what I was going to do next. The allure of coffee loomed large, but I forced myself to contemplate more ambitious stuff.

One of the games I play with myself is, What would you least like to do right now? I play this because it's often the one thing I ought to do. It was no different this time. The next thing I had to do was pay a call on Zina Buczek, even though I didn't feel like it.

I tried to interpret this reluctance, and couldn't, so quickly stopped trying. It didn't matter, because while lying there in bed, I'd already made up my mind that this was the only reasonable course of action.

At least the sun was out. With a vengeance. How could it be so cold when the world was so bright? I wore a new set of insulated hunting boots that arrived in the mail the day before from L.L.Bean, along with a pair of flannel-lined blue jeans. The steamy clouds generated by my breath looked for all the world like cigarette smoke, a habit I'd almost credibly begun to overcome. So now I could just pretend!

The Volvo turned over unenthusiastically, the engine running as though not all the cylinders were completely in the game. So I let it sit and warm up for a while as I sat huddled in multiple layers of fleece, down, and canvas, feeling fairly miserable.

Traffic on Montauk Highway moved sluggishly, as if everyone felt a little fragile, as if we might shatter if struck by hard objects. The blasting sun was mostly behind me as I headed west, which was a blessing. The announcer on the radio said not to expect much change in the temperature over the next few days, when it would warm up, but likely snow again. If we got more than three inches, we'd break the all-time Long Island record. Good for us.

The plow crews had been honing their skills since the last big storm, and Montauk Highway was now reasonably opened up. The rain had done its part as well in shrinking the mounds and now, with the deep freeze, had encased the world in a glittering crystal glaze.

Once I turned up toward the Seven Ponds area, the effectiveness of the road crews faltered. There were really only one and a half lanes, so each oncoming vehicle presented an opportunity for negotiation. The general ground rules called for the one closest to a driveway or some other indent to pull over and wait. Unless it was a big truck, in which case, size dominated. On a different day, this would have been cause for confrontation, but I was in a malleable mood, subdued by the unforgiving elements.

I eventually reached the Buczek place, guided by the tops of Tad's larger metal sculptures, which were easily seen from some distance shooting above the treetops. The long driveway was only roughly cleared, the most serious effort handled by Dayna Red several days before. I had to stay inside a pair of tracks that barely accommodated the Volvo's wheelbase, sliding a little at the hairpin turn but making it all the way to the house with no further incident.

I found a convenient slot to park the car, and after shutting off the engine, rummaged around in the pile on the passenger seat for a pen and my little spiral-bound notebook. When I found it and went to open the door, there was a guy standing there looking in my driver's-side window. I yelped, then rolled down the window.

"Sorry for yelping," I said. "You startled me."

He had a round face with cheekbones so plump they seemed to squeeze his eyes into narrow slits. Tufts of gray hair squirted out from a baseball hat. Mets. Not a good sign.

"What can I do for you?" he asked in a hoarse, high-pitched voice.

"Is Mrs. Buczek home? I need to talk to her."

"What's it about?"

"I'd rather discuss it with Mrs. Buczek. Is she here?"

I started to open the door and smiled politely until he stepped out of the way.

"Are you Freddy?" I asked, guessing it was Saline's husband, though I barely remembered him.

His slitty eyes narrowed, but he put out his hand. "Fred Lumsden."

I felt like I was shaking an inflated version of the human hand.

"Jackie Swaitkowski. I'm Franco's attorney."

"So I heard. You was Tad's niece?"

"By marriage. To the late Pete."

"Oh, yeah. Sorry about that. Pete was a fun'un."

"He was indeed. So about Zina, I'm assuming she's in the house."

"Couldn't tell you. Hardly ever talks to me. Saline oughtta know. Don't know where she is, either."

And what, in fact, do you know? I thought uncharitably.

"Okay, thanks," I said, and crunched over the icy snow to the front door of the house and rang the doorbell.

I waited awhile, but finally the door opened, although just a crack. "Yes?"

I knew it was Zina by the accent, though I couldn't see her.

"This is Jackie Swaitkowski, Tad's niece." I thought I'd open with that. "And Franco's defense attorney. Could I talk to you for a few minutes?"

"Talk about what?"

"You were Tad's wife. Anything you have to say is important."

"That's what you think. You weren't married to Tad."

"Can I come in?" I asked. "It's very important." There was a long pause and the door started to creep closed. "I'm a fair person, Zina. I only want to get at the truth. For everyone's sake."

Not an entirely true statement, but it could still turn out that way. The door started to open again, though still no sight of Zina.

"I need to change into something more decent," she said. "Wait there."

Then she closed the door and I got to stand there for ten minutes thinking I'd just been given the bum's rush. I was about to ring the doorbell again when the door swung open.

It was Zina in a burgundy fleece outfit—nominally workout gear, though more the decorative variety. There were elastic bands at the wrists, waist, and ankles, and the zipperless top fit with little capacity to spare. The most striking feature was the neckline, which took a steep plunge, leaving much of Zina's boobs on display. Though they were seemingly unsupported, I strongly suspected some superstructure was cleverly concealed under the fleece. I hoped so, for my own self-esteem.

On her feet were black slipper socks made of knit wool with black canvas on the soles, which made a scraping sound as she led me from the foyer into the living-room area.

I wondered what the hell she'd changed out of. A corset, heels, and thigh-highs?

She slid into the corner of a sofa with her feet up, supported by the sofa arm. I'd seen similar poses in high-end fashion magazines. I plopped straight down on the opposite couch, leaning slightly forward with both feet on the ground.

"Should I be calling my lawyer?" she asked. "I've already spoken to the police. Twice. I don't know what is expected of me in this country."

"You can if you want," I said. "Nothing you tell me is legally binding. It's just a conversation."

She found that amusing. "Nothing's just a conversation, Jackie. In America or anywhere else."

"We have a thing over here called a deposition, where they come to your house and you have to swear an oath that you're telling the truth, just like you would in court. That's not what I'm here for. I just feel like I should get your take on things. You know Franco, and Tad was your husband. What do you think happened?"

She looked down at her hands, not her fingernails exactly, since it wasn't preening. It was stalling for time.

She looked up and locked onto my eyes. "I don't know what happened, and that's the truth. I'll swear an oath to it."

I broke free of the stare and looked down at my empty notebook page.

"So tell me what you do know about the night he died," I said.

"There's nothing to tell. Franco called to say he was worried about the roof on the woodshed. I tell Tad, who don't want to deal with this and would rather watch basketball game. But then he curses and tells me he better go shovel snow off the roof. He takes the phone and tells Franco to meet him at the shed. Then he leave. An hour later, I'm wondering what's happening, so I call Tad's mobile, but he doesn't answer. Neither does Franco. Next thing I know, you people are telling me Tad is dead."

"Can you think of anyone who might have been angry at Tad, who might have wished him harm?"

This was also amusing.

"You're kidding, right? Everybody wish Tad harm. Even some of his own family." She looked at me pointedly.

"But no one person or persons who stand out, who might actually be mad enough to commit this crime."

She shook her head slowly, contemplatively.

"I don't know that many people here. Tad hardly ever take me anywhere. Do you think he would go around and introduce me to his enemies?"

Good point, I thought.

"So how'd you guys meet?" I asked, trying to sound like we were just hanging together at a cocktail party.

She cast her eyes back toward her hands.

"The Internet," she said, turning the *r* into a trill. "Polish-American chat room. Probably disgust you."

She smoothed the tops of her fleece pants as if they needed smoothing.

"Not at all. Why should it? Everyone likes to chat with people from the same background."

She relaxed into the sofa as if her body had given off a sigh. I'd said the right thing.

"It's lonely when there's so many people all around and none of them you like talking to. Tad was easy to talk to. On the Internet. His Polish not so good, but my English better. I like the artistic conversation. I wanted to be an artist. Not so good as Tad, but I'm young yet. I could learn."

Even with a more confining definition of art than what prevails today, Tad's crazy sculpture clearly fit the criteria. Just because they were objects of controversy didn't mean they weren't legitimate artistic expressions. It was Tad's brutish, hulking ways that probably caused people, including me, to assume it was all just belligerent lunacy.

"It must have been tough to live with an artist," I said. "I've read biographies of people like Picasso and Gauguin. Bastards all."

She telegraphed a blend of ruefulness and resentment, although I might have overinterpreted her meager body language.

"It was harder after the marriage. Tad was not so much around anymore. Business, he said. I understand business. My father was a businessman in Kraków. Not see him too much either. But when he come home, it was Christmas and birthday all in one. With Tad, it was sports on television and dirty clothes. That's okay. People are different. You want something to eat? To drink? I can call for it."

I hate to let people put themselves out for me in these situations, yet I always do, the lurking need always overpowering the social inhibition.

"Coffee?" I asked.

Zina got up from the couch and walked out of the room through a dark passageway. Abruptly alone, I took the time to look around, noting the heavy furniture, earthy colors, and dismal art on the walls. The windows were large, however, giving a nice view of the ice-lacquered snow gripping the landscape beyond.

Zina came back in short order, walking into the room with a languid saunter more appropriate to the catwalk or casting studio.

"It's coming soon, with some snacks," she said. "You'd think I'd ordered up the moon."

"I appreciate it."

"It's nothing for me. I just have to ask Saline. I don't have to lift a finger. Like I'm not able to? It's what Tad wanted. He had Saline here long before me. Didn't matter if I didn't want another person doing my work for me. But it's not too bad. You get used to it. Stupid thing to complain about, yes?"

I disagreed. "That some may find this a nice setup doesn't devalue the quality of the complaint."

She brightened at that. "That sounded so nice. I want to learn to speak like you. Do they teach you that in legal school?"

"I was an English major in college. And it helps to be born here. But there's no reason why you couldn't improve your language skills. With your resources you could hire a private tutor. Or just go back to school."

"I have a college degree. In economics. That surprises you?"

It did, but I wasn't going to let it show.

"Not at all. Explains why Franco said you were so bored. And lonely."

Technically, I'd just violated my client's confidence, but she'd served up too good an opening to pass up. Franco wouldn't be the only one who could make the same observation. It was only a teeny little violation to ascribe it to him.

"He tell you that?" she asked, I thought warmly.

"So, did you and Franco talk much?"

Her expression stayed close to neutral, but she didn't answer right away. She did, however, rub the top of her thigh again as if flattening invisible creases in her synthetic pants. I tried not to read too much into it.

"A little. Franco is a very intelligent man with a fine education. Only, you wouldn't know that. He keep a low profile."

"Okay, Zina, I have to ask this if we're going to talk about Franco." As if she was the one who brought him up. "Do you think he could have killed Tad?"

She shook her head very slowly, though without hesitation.

"No reason. He was grateful for the job. And Tad was not a bad boss. You can ask Freddy. He's worked for Tad for twenty years. Tough, but fair. They always knew where they stood."

"Sometimes the reason's not so obvious."

"I thought you were on his side?" she said with a hint of levity. "No, no reason. I think he almost liked Tad. They got drunk together a few times. Freddy can't. He's triple-A."

"Two A's. Alcoholics Anonymous."

This would have been an appropriate time to bring up her affair with Franco, but I was afraid that might shut down the conversation. It would have to come out eventually, since the cops had the same story. I just didn't want her to associate the disclosure with me if I could avoid it. Not when I wanted her to keep talking.

"The night Tad was killed, you said there was no place for you. Nowhere to hide."

She stiffened, not unlike the way she had that night, and looked away from me, toward one of the big living-room windows.

"It was just silly talk," she said. "I was unhappy in Kraków. I never thought I belong there. And now I don't belong here, either. It means nothing."

I still considered myself a newcomer to the legal game, even though I'd been at it for almost fifteen years. But that was long enough to know that when a client or witness says something means nothing, it usually means something.

I was still loath to push her beyond her limits, but not all of me was on the side of restraint. So I just said it.

"If you're sure Franco didn't kill Tad, who did?" I asked.

She didn't like the question, but took little time to answer.

"The whole world knows Tad had many enemies. This is what happens when a man enjoys making other people angry. The more enemies he could get, the happier he was. He told me that himself."

"Would you share that in court?" I asked.

That one slowed her down, but she finally said, "You just tell the truth, right?"

I said that was right, though I spared her the details of cross-examination. That could also come in due time.

I heard the sound of clattering dinnerware coming from the hall Zina had just been down. It was a tea cart, transporting wine bottles and glasses and a tray filled with biszkopty and paluszki, the Polish equivalent of finger food. It was pushed by a tall woman with long, poorly attended, wavy brown hair. She had large hands at the end of long arms, an effect reinforced by her sloping posture. She wore a blue cotton dress—not quite a uniform, but leaning that way. Slim on the whole, she had a little potbelly that seemed to match her slouch.

Obviously Saline, but as with Freddy, I wasn't sure if I remembered her.

Zina ignored her until she'd wheeled the cart up to the coffee table and disgorged some of the load. When she offered me a glass of wine, I demurred but introduced myself.

"I'm Jackie Swaitkowski," I said, holding out my hand. She took it.

"I know. Peter's wife. I'm Saline Lumsden," she said, casting a sidelong glance at Zina. "We talked a long time ago. You don't remember."

I could see echoes of Pete's father drifting around her face. Even a bit of Pete himself, which was a little unnerving.

"His widow, technically," I said with a weak smile.

"Sure. I knew that. I liked Pete."

"Everybody liked Pete."

"Thank you, Saline," said Zina. "Everything looks very good."

It was a tidy balance between acknowledgement and dismissal. Saline kept her attention on me as she took a few more things off the cart. With no coffee in sight, I accepted a cup of black tea that looked, in fact, black.

"I thought Pete made the right choice with you, no matter what anybody said."

There was a statement to make you feel good and bad in equal measure. I chose to lean toward the good.

"Thanks, Saline. We had a few really good years."

She looked over at Zina again, knowing she'd overspent her stay. Zina looked away, and quickly after that Saline dragged the noisy cart back down the hallway. I gave in to the allure of the paluszki, though likely reheated. When Pete was around, I'd totally fallen in love with the buttery, mashed-potato-like stuff.

"Twenty years is a long time to work for anybody," I said. "Was Saline here the whole time?"

"Saline was here first. Freddy come a few years after that. I think of them as built into the house. Like they been here since the farm grew out of the ground. It's not up to me, no matter what I think."

"Though you own it all now," I said. "It's entirely up to you."

She dropped her head back on the couch and slid her right hand across the upper part of her chest, as if bracing against imminent emotional threats.

"I don't know what to do," she said. "It's all so strange."

I drank some of the tea. It was thick and bitter.

"I'm sorry, Zina. I know what it's like to have a dead husband. It's so damn permanent."

She uncurled herself from the couch, stood up, and stretched in fully natural feline fashion, then settled back down, feet on the floor.

"If he's going to leave you, maybe this is the best way," she said. "At least no one else can have him."

She didn't exactly tell me the interview was over, but the climate in the living room took on a seasonal chill. I put down the tea and thanked her for talking to me, which she acknowledged with a lazy wave of her hand, and left.

6

When I got back outside, it was still a brilliant, frigid day. I was glad to get what I could from Zina, though the conversation left me feeling more than a little disquieted. I looked around for Freddy but didn't see him. There were tire tracks in the snow leading away from the house down an extension of the driveway that connected to another, smaller, house, where Franco, Saline, and Freddy all lived, if my recollections from family gatherings were correct. I was tempted to go that way, but after the talk with Zina, I didn't feel up to it.

Instead, I drove back toward the road, stopping at the big pergola. The area off the driveway that Dayna had plowed was only slightly covered in new snow, so I pulled in and put the running Volvo in park. I got out and retraced the lumpy, well-trod path under the pergola and over to the picnic table. The area looked larger and the table smaller in the daylight. The only telltale sign of the night's events was a balled-up wad of yellow police tape. I put it in my pocket and followed the path up the grade to Hamburger Hill.

I tried to read the snowed-over disturbances in the snow, but it was too chaotic. I guessed right on where Franco found the body, brushing aside the top layer to reveal the bloody ice underneath. But I could only imagine where the CSIs found the big chunk of ice. I looked at the tracks that led into the scene from the opposite direction, where Franco had first approached, and then went back again to get the blue tarp. I tried to count the footsteps as I had that night, but realized after all the new rain and snow, it was now nearly impossible.

Hamburger Hill also loomed larger in the harsh sunlight. I looked up and saw two of the lateral members of the sprinkler mobile, one to either side of the scene. The heat of the sun on the burnished metal had apparently melted off any snow that might have collected. So I could see they were basically long, crumpled pipes with boxes at the ends where the water sprayed out.

Not what you'd call a stunning work of art, but I'd seen uglier things in the Guggenheim Museum.

Even under ideal circumstances, crime scenes rarely tell you exactly what happened, as good as the CSIs are these days. But I always felt that science wasn't the only way to communicate with these places. It was probably all spooky imaginings based on what had happened there, yet I usually had the sense that if you just tried to listen, it would tell you something.

So I stood there until the arctic breeze began to burn off my nose, but nothing spoke to me except to say I was acting like an idiot.

It was only when I was getting into my car that a message arrived, not from spectral sources but my own brain.

"Dammit, Franco, what are you not telling me?"

When I got back to my office, there was a message on my answering machine from Dayna Red.

"Somebody named Detective Sullivan wants to talk to me," her message said. "What do I do? I'm supposed to call him back before the end of the day."

She left her cell-phone number, which I immediately called. When I reached her, she told me she had yet to call Sullivan back.

"Not without talking to you," she said. "Not like you're my lawyer or anything, I just don't want to mess this up."

"You did exactly the right thing, Dayna. And I really appreciate it. They've arrested Franco. The arraignment's tomorrow. It's only a preliminary hearing, but they can do some real damage even before the indictment is passed up."

"I don't know what you're talking about, Jackie, but it sounds interesting."

"The point is they'll want to get your statement before tomorrow, hoping it helps the ADA go for some crazy high bail number. My firm can handle almost anything, though I'll need the okay from my boss. Whatever happens, it'll be way above my authorization level."

"So what do I do?"

"Call him back and set a time to meet at your place. I'll be there a half hour ahead and we'll go from there."

"A half hour?"

"That's when he'll actually show up. I know the guy. Don't worry, he's okay despite what it might look like. Just tell the truth about what you witnessed, as best you can. I'm only there to keep my eye on things. I like the guy, but sometimes police investigators can practice selective listening."

We decided on a time and she gave me directions to her place, easily identified by a sign on one of the main roads through Sagaponack, an incorporated village inside the Town of Southampton, and by some measures the wealthiest zip code in the United States.

"It's not what you think," she said, reading my mind. "You'll see when you get here."

By this time nearly all the roads in the area had been plowed, at least enough to allow one car through at a time. You could tell by the haphazard performance of some of the crews how unfamiliar they were with big snowfalls. It was made worse by continuing cold temperatures, which restrained the usual melt-off. On my way over to Dayna's I felt lost inside deep white valleys, peppered as they were with sand and gravel, making me fear for the Volvo's side panels should I slip or slide.

Harry blamed it all on global warming, and I made him explain how too much warmth caused the Hamptons to get too cold, but the explanation became so confusing I made him stop.

"By that reckoning, if they cool things down too much, we could turn into Ecuador," I said.

"Not necessarily," said Harry.

"Okay. Stop."

As promised, a tidy little engraved sign at the end of Dayna's driveway announced SPECIALTY HARDWOODS. SALVAGED AND PLANTATION GROWN ONLY. It was a long driveway, thoroughly plowed, past a field to the right and a stand of naked oaks, maples, and dogwood to the left. As she'd told me, the house and a barn where she stored and prepped her products were toward the back behind the woods. Both the house and barn were painted a deep, rich red. Scattered throughout the setting were mature maples, oaks, and one towering evergreen that turned out to be a cryptomaria, some sort of gargantuan cedar from Japan. Gates, fences, and pergolas like Tad Buczek's testified to various garden areas currently buried beyond recognition in deep snow.

A black-and-white border collie met me at my car door.

"Well, hello there," I said to the dog. "Are you the official greeter?"

The collie let me pet her head, then turned and ran toward the barn, stopping after about twenty yards to look back at me. When she saw me following, she ran on. I had yet to reach a side door at the end of the path when the collie ran back again to make sure the dumb human hadn't gotten lost.

"I'm coming, I'm coming," I said.

The door opened and Dayna stepped out.

"Good girl, Misty, you brought me another one," she said. "You probably didn't know I cooked up people in the barn," she said to me. "This wood thing is just a front."

"Wait'll you get a hold of Joe Sullivan. Feed you for the whole winter."

Inside the barn was nothing but wood. The structure itself was hand-hewn chestnut post and beam, as was the floor. The planks between the posts were wide-board hemlock, all original from the eighteenth century. Dayna told me the outside was sheathed in another layer of new western cedar, stained red.

Along every wall were racks filled with thick slabs of wood in various stages of refinement. In the middle of the floor were massive olive drab machines used for cutting, planing, and joining the planks. These dated back to the thirties and forties, Dayna said, when her husband's grandfather first started in the lumber business.

"Jeffrey's dad bought all the spare parts he could get when they stopped making these things," said Dayna, brushing dust off a pair of coveralls. Unlike the ones she wore the other night, these were bright red and made of lighter-weight material. Her hair was pulled back in a ponytail, and under the golden incandescent light inside the barn, her face looked younger, her bright blue eyes kindly and vaguely amused. "Otherwise, I'd never be able to keep them going. Better than new, of course. A lot heavier and truer once they're set up. That's the hard part."

"Jeffrey's your husband?" I asked.

"Yup. He inherited all this."

"Cool. Does he work here, too?"

She smiled at me like women do when they're about to fill you in on their husbands, boyfriends, or lovers—current and ex.

"Jeffrey doesn't work," she said. "His only job is surfing, at present somewhere on the north coast of Oahu."

"Interesting gig."

"Five years ago he sold Southampton the development rights to the farm and announced he was going to travel around the world and surf for the rest of his life. I could come along if I wanted, though he couldn't guarantee he'd stay faithful, what with all the surfer chicks hanging around all the time."

"Sure. What's a man to do?" I said.

"To his credit, he agreed to stay married so I could still live here. The town has to wait till we're both dead before they get the place, which I'm responsible for keeping up, so it works out for everybody."

"Except you're out a husband," I said, as much of a question as a statement.

"Like I said, works out for everybody," said Dayna, her blue eyes somehow catching a glint of light from the surrounding ruddy glow.

We retired to her office, where I gave Dayna my five-minute briefing on "How to Talk to Cops" (look them in the eye; keep your answers short, to the point, and unwavering; always tell the truth, unless you can't, in which case shut up and don't lie). During all this Misty had me lobbing her a sawdust-encrusted tennis ball, which she caught in her mouth despite the close quarters, only to bring it right back and drop it in my lap for a repeat performance.

"Does she ever get tired of this?" I asked Dayna.

"What do you think?"

Sullivan showed up soon after that. He was wearing camouflage pants tucked into paratrooper boots and a black sweater. A black baseball hat covered his blond crew cut, completing the look of a Special Forces commando recently returned from behind enemy lines. I resisted the urge to salute.

He introduced himself to Dayna, then ruffled the fur on Misty's head before ordering her in a calm, firm voice to go lie down, which she instantly did. Dayna looked impressed. She offered coffee and we accepted.

After she left the office, Sullivan said, "Nice to see you."

"I'm sure," I said. "And no, I won't go lie down in the corner."

He took off his hat, scratched his head, and put it back on again.

"That thing yesterday that Ross had me do," he said. "I told him, never again."

"Understood."

"He's really got a bug up his butt about this one."

"Ross was born with a bug up his butt," I said.

"Ross takes everything that happens in Southampton personally. You know that. He read the case files and thinks you did a disservice getting Franco an early release."

Southampton is actually a pretty big place, encompassing as it does villages like Quogue, Water Mill, Bridgehampton, Sagaponack, Hampton Bays, and Southampton Village itself. In a bad winter like this, though, it could really start to feel like a small town. With only two or three degrees of separation between the full-time locals, it was a fine line between intimate and claustrophobic.

"I didn't know that," I said. "And even if I did, it wouldn't have changed what I did. It was clearly self-defense."

"It was a sword fight between a kitchen knife and some barbecue equipment wielded by Franco, a former fencing champion at Duke University. But who's keeping score?"

I scowled at him.

"Okay," said Sullivan, taking a coffee mug from Dayna, who'd just returned to the office, "let's move on to the current situation."

The first half hour was easy for everybody. Sullivan put on his just-here-to-help-ma'am, regular-guy performance, which Dayna gladly soaked up. He didn't challenge her on the facts as she knew them, resulting in the same story he'd heard from me. But then, at the end of the interview, after he'd already thanked her and seemed to be headed for the door, he stopped and looked back at her.

"Oh, just one more thing," he said. "How did Franco seem to you? Was he nervous, jumpy, that sort of thing?"

"Dayna's not an expert on Franco's state of mind, Columbo," I said.

"This isn't a courtroom," he said, then added, "Did he look furtive, you know, shifty, like he was hiding something?"

"We've already stated that Franco was agitated and concerned," I said. "You'd be, too, if you'd just found your boss with his head bashed in."

"That's right," said Dayna with an upbeat voice, "agitated and concerned. Though I'd never met the man, so I wouldn't know what he's like normally."

Good answer, I thought.

"And what about Ms. Swaitkowski?" he asked. "What about her state of mind? Was she agitated as well?"

"Hold it right there," I said.

"You're not just Franco's lawyer," he said. "You're also a witness. Did you think she and Mr. Raffini showed excessive concern about calling the police?" he asked Dayna. "Did you feel they were worried about certain information being revealed?"

Dayna answered before I had a chance to jump in front of her.

"Ms. Swaitkowski seemed annoyed that Mr. Raffini had yet to call the police and insisted that he do so immediately. She instructed Mr. Raffini to tell the officers arriving on the scene the complete truth and to leave nothing out. She said he could trust you completely, that you were good guys," she added matter-of-factly.

I just sat there and tossed the ball for Misty, rousing her from her sleep and ignoring Sullivan as he said a second farewell and left Dayna's office.

7

Crime on the East End is probably no different from most of the country. It's mostly petty, stupid stuff committed mostly by people in various states of cognitive disrepair. Aside from the occasional flimflam—a con man posing as a European count, say, fleecing both bankers and benefactors—it's all the usual stuff. Fistfights over parking spots, kleptomania, secret vendettas gone awry, public urination, purloined Pomeranians, et cetera.

The only police matter of genuine local interest that winter, and much more interesting to the cops than anyone else, was a string of exotic car thefts. For the last three winters, person or persons unknown were boosting Porsches, Aston Martins, Bentleys, and expensive collectibles like Packards, Morgans, and Cords from where the wealthy had left them in the garages of their summer homes, unneeded in the city and virtually forgotten until the start of the high season.

This was not a crime wave that engendered an outpouring of public sympathy. Most in town figured the owners were selling the cars to South American drug cartels and claiming the insurance loss. This is the type of loony conspiracy theory indulged in by our locals when discussing the wealthy city people, about whom they knew next to nothing. I knew enough to know city people had far more lucrative and efficient ways of acquiring ill-gotten gains than anything as ridiculous as that.

So unless it was the peak of the season and celebrities were out and about flashing their summer plumage, the Hamptons rarely attracted the interest of the outside media. The last event to make national news was a car bombing in East Hampton, which everyone assumed at the time was an act of international terrorism. It wasn't, as it turned out. So the interest quickly died down. Except on my part, since I was there when it happened, getting nearly blown up along with the car.

As in most places, however, sensational murders were rare, so despite our off-season obscurity, the death of Tad Buczek prompted a call to my office that morning from *The New York Times*. I hadn't heard from these folks since the car bombing, so I didn't completely believe it at first.

"Come again?" I asked.

"Roger Angstrom, *New York Times*," he repeated. "I'm looking for a comment on the Buczek killing. This guy Raffini worked for him, right? Have the police established a motive yet?"

"There is no motive."

"There isn't?"

"There's no motive because Franco didn't kill him," I said.

"What makes you say that?"

"I'm his defense attorney. I only defend innocent people. And I don't comment on active cases."

"You sort of just did. You said Raffini was innocent."

"Okay, but that's as far as I go."

"I was thinking about driving out there this afternoon. Could you meet with me for a few minutes?"

"Probably not," I said.

"I'll have other people's opinions. You might want a voice if you disagree with what they said."

"Why are you interested in this?"

"I'm a crime reporter. It's what they pay me to do. I write about the innocent and the guilty, but I try to be as fair and accurate as I can. Defense attorneys generally like that."

Why does the fear of being manipulated always cause me to spur the manipulator on to greater effort? It's like I step out of my body and look back at myself diving for the obvious bait.

"What little I've experienced with the press has rarely featured both 'fair' and 'accurate' in the same story," I said.

"That's because you've never worked with me."

"We'd be working together? I thought you just wanted to talk."

"Fairness and accuracy are hard work. That's why I need to talk face-to-face. To get it right."

No way am I doing this, I said to myself while hearing my voice giving Angstrom directions to the Japanese restaurant below my office that often served as a conference room when conferring with people I didn't trust. The owner, Mr. Sato, took a protective interest in me, which I nurtured and reciprocated with free legal advice for his employees, all of whom he'd brought over from his hometown in Japan. Thus adding a glancing familiarity with immigration law to my scattered résumé.

"Hope you have four-wheel drive," I said to Angstrom. "We got a whompin' mess of snow out here."

"Snow? Really? That's exciting."

I said something lame and rushed him off the phone. I'd have plenty of chances later on to make a bigger ass out of myself.

———

My plan was to work at my desk for a few hours, catching up on my other cases and pretending not to be worried sick about Franco Raffini. The plan held firm at first, but then I found my attention drifting toward the window, which had a great view of a big windmill across the street. I did that for a while until my eyes were attracted by the security monitor glowing at me from the table next to my desk. It wasn't a very scintillating video. I could switch from two views of the hallway to the area immediately beyond the outside door, which was a nearly undifferentiated field of white. I continued to look anyway, flicking between the cameras until assured of the senselessness of the pursuit. Then after going back to work for another half hour, it occurred to me I hadn't reviewed the recordings made from the security cameras. It was good policy to review and delete the material to date to avoid running out of memory. It was an even better policy when I needed a break from busywork, which was most of the time.

The people who sold me the system wisely included software that let me scan the recordings on my computer at high speed, automatically stopping at any important change in the image. These changes were then assembled into a thumbnail menu that you could sample all at once, drastically reducing review time.

I fired up the program, then went back to my drudgery until a little ping told me the menu was ready to go. I clicked on the icon and the screen filled with fourteen static images labeled by time and date. Twelve of them were me coming and going, one was the FedEx guy dropping an envelope in a box I kept by the outside door, and the other showed the two guys I'd just missed seeing the other day. I checked the time code—they'd come back when I was over at Dayna's.

It was unmistakable; they were the same guys. And now I had their faces, clear as a bell, looking directly up at the camera. One was substantially shorter than the other. The taller one looked African American, though light-skinned, suggesting mixed heritage. The other was all white, with a round, brutish face, his mouth set in a semipermanent sneer.

I pulled my robe tighter at the throat as if to shield myself from their staring eyes. Then with an unsteady hand I clicked on the static image. The video started with them walking into camera range. They looked from side to side, then at the door, feeling around the trim, but avoiding the doorknob. One of them finally looked up at the little hole that held the camera, pointing at it and saying something to the other guy. He nodded, and they left again.

My breath caught in my throat as the implications settled in. I went back to the still image and downloaded it as a JPEG. I also downloaded the video segment of the two guys and disconnected the laptop to bring along with me before heading across the hall and diving into the shower.

While I owed my current job as a full-time defense attorney to Burton Lewis, I owed my initial transition out of real-estate law to Sam Acquillo, my first client in a criminal case, who'd hired me on the strength of nothing but deluded trust and a dollar he'd paid me as a retainer two years earlier. We won the case, which had more to do with his complicated brain than my dazzling professional skills, but the equally complicated friendship we'd developed by then was thoroughly cemented, and a new path for me all but decided upon.

I could go to Burton with most questions related to legal niceties, but when it came to a pair of creeps doing threatening things at my back door, Sam was definitely the go-to guy.

Among his less impressive credentials, Sam had been a partially successful professional boxer, earning enough to put himself through MIT, proving a hardheadedness rarely matched in my experience. Though he was now pushing sixty years old, you could do a lot worse than having Sam by your side in a street fight.

He lived in a small house at the tip of a peninsula that stuck out in the Little Peconic Bay in North Sea, an area directly north of Southampton Village. His girlfriend, Amanda, had her own house next door, and "complicated" wouldn't even begin to describe their relationship. His mutt, Eddie, probably the only being who could live with Sam full time, had been feral for the first two years of his life, and consequently only did what he wanted to do, to everyone's satisfaction.

I tried calling in advance, but Sam rarely answered his phone, usually absorbed as he was in some woodworking project in his basement shop. Like me, he'd gone through a serious career evolution, moving from the head of R&D at a giant corporation to semi-suicidal beach bum to skilled cabinetmaker. During that time he'd been in and out of trouble with the law, which is where I came in handy, though along the way he'd done a lot to help the cops do their jobs, whether they liked it or not. So, like me, he'd become close friends with Joe Sullivan. Ross Semple, not so much.

When I reached the end of Sam's driveway, Eddie was there, standing on top of a big heap of plowed snow with the wind off the bay stroking his fur, making him look like Fabio on the cover of a bodice-ripper.

He jumped down and followed me up to Sam's house, where he led me to the basement hatch. I scratched his head and told him he and Misty could start a guide-dog service for visiting attorneys.

"You could work for tennis balls. I'll write the contracts."

No interest, apparently, as he quickly left me, diving back into the snow, through which he swam off toward the bay on a secret mission. I cleared a spot to bang on the hatch door and waited for the usual friendly greeting.

"What the fuck," said Sam, pushing open the hatch and sticking his head out. "Don't you ever call first?"

"I would if you'd ever answer. What're you doing down there, anyway? How come you're not out skiing?"

I followed him down the steps into his brightly lit, somewhat orderly, dust-covered workspace.

"My ex-wife tried to get me to ski. Until she realized it was a good way to spend time with her boyfriend at his chalet."

"I take it you found out."

"I did."

"What happened to the boyfriend?"

"I don't know, but the chalet had a bad day."

He looked at the briefcase that held my laptop.

"There better be a bottle of wine in there and a couple of glasses," he said.

I looked at my watch. "It's not even eleven in the morning."

"Shit, really? Then let's make some coffee."

I followed him upstairs to the main part of the house, which boasted the decorative extravagance of a Shinto temple run by a blind monk.

"You should get my mother-in-law in here to doll this place up a bit," I said. "You'd be amazed at what she can do."

Eddie barked at the back door, knowing with that sixth sense of his that we were in the kitchen. I let him in so he could fuss over me, as if he hadn't already. Sam worked at a French press that had processed more coffee than all the presses in Paris and Montreal combined.

"You could get a new one," I said, pointing to the poor exhausted thing.

"When I need a lifestyle consultant, I'll call in my daughter. Everyone else gets to shut up and enjoy the ambience."

After pouring the coffee, Sam gave Eddie a biscuit and we all went out to the winterized screened-in porch that looked out over the Little Peconic Bay. I use the term "winterized" loosely. We went out to a glassed-in icebox that required a raging blaze in the woodstove to be rendered moderately habitable. I was the only one who seemed to care.

"So what's the problem this time?" he asked when we settled down.

"Why do you always think it's a problem? Okay, I've got a problem. Let me boot this puppy up and you'll see what I mean."

Sam stoked the stove as I sat at a small table and worked the laptop. I also gave him an edited briefing on the Buczek case, assuming he knew the rough outlines of the story from the news, which was a mistake.

"Somebody finally killed that son of a bitch?" he said. "There's a surprise."

I'd forgotten that Sam ignored the news—local, national, or international. Likely he was holed up in the wood shop the last few days, so no one had a chance to give him the word.

"He was Pete's uncle. He served me barbecued ribs at family gatherings."

"He was still a son of a bitch. Big guy with big hands. Would take a lot to put him down."

"How about a big chunk of ice?"

I told him what Ross had told me. He nodded like he was listening, but I could see unspoken thoughts whirring behind his eyes. Sam lived life with a permanently installed poker face, though by now I could read it better than he thought.

"What're you thinking?" I asked.

"I'm not thinking. I'm listening."

"No, you're not. You're thinking."

"Okay, I'm remembering. Not exactly the same thing. There was talk around the bar that Tad could be a bit dirty."

"Meaning?" I asked.

"You know what I mean. Into things he shouldn't be into. Illegal things."

"Like?"

"What's on your laptop?" he asked.

"Are you evading me?"

"No. I'm trying to remember. I guess the talk was vague. Nothing specific. Just a little dirty."

He set down his coffee mug and cracked his knuckles, as if that would free up his long-term memory. Eddie looked up at the sound. I watched the laptop as the photo of my unknown visitors filled the screen.

"There's my problem," I said, turning the screen toward Sam.

He leaned in my direction and looked hard at the image for a few moments. Then his face morphed into a smile, if you can use the word "smile" about a face that looked more like a granite outcropping. He actually almost laughed as he sat back in his chair.

"Those fucking meatballs. That's just great," he said, enjoying a private moment.

"You know those fucking meatballs?"

He nodded.

"I do, after a fashion. They used to work as muscle for Ivor Fleming. Maybe still do. We had some lively times together a few years ago."

"I think I remember him. Didn't you have me do some research back when I was stupid enough to do that for you?"

He sat farther back in his chair and closed his eyes, collecting his memories, or thoughts, or both. Then he reminded me that Fleming was a scrap-metal merchant with a big operation up island. He gathered metal from all over the northeast part of the country, squeezed it into solid blocks, then sold them to processors in the U.S. and abroad, mostly China these days like everyone else.

Unlike Buczek, there was nothing vague about the rumors surrounding Fleming. The whole world seemed to know he was dirtier than stink, but even after a series of indictments for money laundering, drug smuggling, prostitution, bribery of a federal official—even dumping toxic waste in protected habitats—nothing had stuck.

Sam said most of this happened years ago, and either Ivor had gotten smarter or more honest, because even when Sam had dealt with him, his profile had slipped well below the horizon.

"So how did it turn out between you and him?" I asked. "I forget."

"We agreed to stay out of each other's way. Which until now has been the case."

"Until now?"

"Ike and Connie paying you a visit is inconsistent with the agreement, however tacit."

"Ike and Connie? Sounds like a lovely couple."

"Ike's the skinny one, Connie's the other. Not as tough as they think they are, but tough enough."

I didn't know whether to feel terrorized that a known gangster's thugs had been at my back door or relieved that my own personal thug knew who they were. I decided to feel a little of both.

"This can't be good," I said. "What does Tad Buczek or Franco Raffini have to do with a shady scrap-metal baron?"

"Correlation doesn't always equal causation," said Sam—the kind of thing he said a lot, which could be annoying. "What else have you been working on?"

I hadn't thought of that, leaping automatically to the most pressing case at hand. I went through the other things on my plate, but none seemed likely to attract the interest of a guy like Ivor Fleming.

"So what do I do?" I asked.

"Keep your security system running and the Glock close at hand. When you have a minute, we'll go pay a call on Ivor. See what's what."

A wave of comforting warmth washed through me. I walked a fine line with Sam. I knew he'd do almost anything I asked him to do, but if

I asked too often, I'd lose his respect. Worse, I'd lose respect for my-self. On the other hand, there were debts between us, an unspoken sense of reciprocity that would make disengagement feel like a viola-tion. Like I said, complicated relationships are my specialty.

I accepted the offer without a lot of fanfare and went back out to the kitchen to pour another cup of coffee. Eddie followed me in the hope of getting another biscuit, a hope well founded. As I drank the coffee I looked out at the snow heaped around Sam's backyard and was struck by the oddness of it all, the state we'd been thrust into by such a sur-prising display of enraged nature, something almost not of this earth.

I tried to shake the feeling that the world had changed on me when I wasn't looking and I would only know the true significance right at the moment it would be too late to do anything about it.

8

As it turned out, Franco's bail became a nonissue. He didn't get any. The ADA charged him with premeditated second-degree murder, which made it easy to convince the judge that no amount of bail money warranted the risk posed to public safety by releasing a wanton killer like Franco Raffini.

I wouldn't say my counterargument was feeble, exactly–merely hopeless. I was glad Franco took it as well as he did.

"Not your fault, Jackie," he said as we sat together in a conference room at the Suffolk County Jail. He looked lost inside his orange jumpsuit, almost collapsed into himself with despondency. "I did it to myself."

"You haven't helped yourself, that's a cinch," I said. He slumped even farther in his seat, a portrait of pure misery. "But we can start to fix that. From here on out, we can make things better."

He looked up at me without raising his head. "How we gonna do that?"

"Why were your fingerprints on that big chunk of ice?" I asked.

"It was sitting there next to Tad's head. I just tossed it to get it out of the way. I tossed a bunch of ice out of the way."

"You told me you had your gloves on the whole time."

"I had to take the right glove off to check Tad's pulse, right here on his neck." He demonstrated on himself. "That's an easy thing to forget."

"What else did you forget?" I asked.

"I don't know. I'm not trying to forget anything."

My experience told me that people didn't have to try very hard to forget things they didn't want to remember, but I put that aside.

"Tell me about Zina," I said. "How did she and Tad get along?"

He winced at her name, but it also seemed to open him up a little.

"Just because everybody thinks something is true doesn't mean it isn't," he said. "Sometimes the obvious is the obvious."

"Zina and Tad weren't exactly lovebirds," I suggested.

"To be honest with you, I don't know how he felt about her. I just knew how she felt about him. Which wasn't that great. Come on, just look at her, then look at Tad. The man was a big ugly bull."

"He mistreated her," I said, a question in the form of a statement.

"That's not what I mean," said Franco. "I never heard him say anything unpleasant to her, much less smack her around or anything. It was just the way he was in the world. Intense, busy all the time, in a way just this side of crazy. Zina's nothing like that. She's subtle, and likes things calm and steady. And she's kind of refined." He looked slightly embarrassed, as if caught betraying his own romantic illusions. "Ah, hell, I don't know what I'm saying. It just didn't make sense, the two of them, that's all."

"A number of people saw Zina's motives as purely mercenary," I said. "That she was only in it for the money, and the American citizenship."

He frowned. "Of course they'd say that. And I wouldn't blame her if it was true. But I never heard her say marrying Tad was just a scam to get into the country."

"She said there was nothing for her. That she had nowhere to hide. What's that about?"

He rubbed his goatee and sighed. "I don't know, except she always seemed a little lost and alone. Resigned, maybe? I tried to get more out of her, but to be completely honest with you, not that I haven't been honest in this particular conversation, we didn't speak that much about anything. It wasn't what you'd call a speaking kind of relationship. I tried, you know, to make something more out of the situation, to get to know her better, but that wasn't what she had in mind."

I struggled with the image of Franco Raffini as the beautiful Katarzina's boy toy—to be felt but not heard—but that was what it sounded like.

"Everybody can get lonely, Jackie," he said. "Doesn't mean they always want to become your soul mate."

I allowed how that could be true without copping to any experience in the matter. The thought of Harry leaped involuntarily to mind. Soul mate? I shoved the thought back in its hole.

"If Zina didn't marry Tad out of expedience, why did she marry him? It doesn't sound like she liked him, much less loved him."

Franco took some time before answering the question. It wasn't evasion; he seemed to be working hard on the answer. Then he gave up.

"I don't know. Honest, Jackie. I don't know. There's something really distant about Zina. I never got the feeling she was completely there—more that she was mostly somewhere else. 'Distracted' is maybe a better word? She didn't try to hide it, at least from me. This is going to sound really strange, but I think one of the reasons she liked me was I never pressed her on anything. That's why we didn't talk that much. When the most obvious thing about her is off the table—that most of her mind is off on some other planet—there's not much left to discuss. I don't think I'm making any sense. Sorry."

Quite the contrary, I thought. I bet he had it nailed perfectly. That was Franco's secret with women. He had the one quality we all crave over every other. He could sense the subterranean frequencies, the subtle undercurrents of mood and state of mind. In a word, he was sensitive.

Then another swarm of unwanted feelings about Harry surged into my mind. Harry had a similar gift. He'd learned from the tumultuous and infinitely variable nature of our early relationship how to calibrate the exact amount of air I needed between us at any given time, and had somehow accepted that I was the one who set the shift in parameters, however capricious and unpredictable.

This made Harry a man of inestimable tolerance and generosity. But was that the same as Franco's sensitivity? And if not, so what?

"I get what you're saying, Franco," I told him. "I really do."

"You do?"

"Who knows what's going on with Zina, and you likely did her a kindness that some may condemn, but that doesn't make it less kind."

"So you don't think I'm just a depraved, philandering monster?"

"I don't. I think you're a good man who'd be well advised to restrict his romantic entanglements to single women going forward."

Something approximating a lift in spirits showed on his face.

"Going forward," he said. "There's a nice thought."

When I was back outside, the sky had managed to transition all the way from deep, limitless blue to surly gray, and the wind had died down, yet it felt colder in a way that defied respite. I shuddered, literally, and climbed stiff-limbed into the Volvo and made my forlorn way back down from Riverhead to the hoped-for refuge of my littered and congested yet warm and brightly lit office.

I'd barely begun to feel the soothing effects of my office when the phone rang. It was Mr. Sato from the restaurant below. He said there was a fellow from the newspapers who claimed he'd scheduled a meeting with me. Should he make the man comfortable or have Naoki-san, his three-hundred-pound sous-chef, escort him to the door?

"Shit, I forgot about him," I said. "Apologize for me and tell him I'll be there in five minutes."

"I'll tell him fifteen minutes. You don't want to look too eager. Besides, it'll tempt him to have a little more tuna tataki."

Any advice for me to show some restraint was usually apropos. I used the time well, getting back out of my recently donned bathrobe and figuring out how to dress for the press. I decided lawyerly. The guy's from the city; he'll be used to gray suits and conservative heels, silk blouse—light blue, buttoned to the throat. This took all the allotted fifteen minutes and then some, so by the time Mr. Sato guided me to the bar, Angstrom had already had two platefuls of sashimi and robota-grilled tsukune—duck and scallops wrapped in bacon.

I extended my hand and waited for him to drop his chopsticks and mop up his face with a white napkin.

He almost looked flustered, as if I'd caught him doing something untoward like stealing from the dessert tray or peeking at a girlie magazine.

"Ms. Swaitkowski," he said, sticking out his hand. "Roger Angstrom."

"You can call me Jackie, especially since you can't pronounce Swaitkowski."

"Thanks for the correction. Do you want to grab a table?"

"The bar's fine," I said, climbing up on the high stool and not mentioning that I'd spent a fair amount of quality time on that very stool. "You obviously managed the roads."

"You're right. You got a whompin' lot of snow out here. What the hell happened?"

"It's the beginning of the apocalypse. But I'm ready. All stocked up with fresh drinking water, cabernet, and eyeliner. Just the essentials," I said, and immediately regretted it. Why am I joking with this person who I actually fear is planning to make a fool out of me?

When he smiled, big creases formed in his cheeks, too grand to be dimples but with the same effect. His hair was curly, not unlike Sam's, but in a looser weave and more fitting to his age, which I guessed to be early thirties. His teeth, also well exposed by the smile, looked too straight to be real. He was only slightly taller than me and thin—even his down vest and bulky flannel shirt expressed a pervasive slightness and delicacy. On his nose perched a pair of silver wire-rim glasses, round, like John Lennon's.

"I appreciate your taking the time to talk to me," he said, gently bringing things back to the appropriate level.

"I'm not sure what we have to talk about. I can't discuss anything about the case or the police investigation that isn't already in the public record."

He held up a small recorder in his right hand and a little notebook in his left, and looked at me inquiringly. Without hesitation, I pointed at the notebook.

"Got it. Had to ask," he said.

"Indeed."

"I understand the limits of your discretion in regards to an active case, but I'm also interested in some of your prior involvements. In particular the Windsong bombing, where you were seriously injured."

Ah, I thought, Roger's been digging around the archives. Which these days means doing a Google search of all the names connected to Tad Buczek's murder. His own paper would have the richest repository of information on yours truly as a result of the Windsong thing. The strategy was clear. Get me talking on safe ground, then slide me unexpectedly into forbidden territory. Nice try, Roger, I'm hip to you wily reporters.

"That's hardly breaking news. The case was firmly closed years ago."

"I'm not thinking about the case. I'm thinking about you. What about being terribly hurt in a car bombing motivated you to leave a comfortable practice in real-estate law and become a crusader for criminal justice? For the defense, no less. Why not join the District Attorney's Office, or the Attorney General's? Why jump immediately to the dark side?"

Oh no, I thought. Not that.

"I'd argue your characterization of criminal defense as the dark side," I said. "There's darkness in the justice system, no doubt, but it's not reserved for one side or the other. There's plenty to go around."

He started writing in his notebook. Oh crap, I thought. What am I doing?

"Listen, Mr. Angstrom," I said. "If you're thinking of writing a story about me, you've made a sadly misguided decision. First off, I'm so constrained by confidentiality, even regarding past cases, that there's precious little information you can glean, even if I wanted to provide it, which I don't. I won't cooperate at all. I'd rather stick a hot poker in my eye than show up in the newspapers. And that's off the record. The hot-poker part."

"After reading about your injuries from the car bombing," he said, "I was, frankly, braced for some disfigurement. Scarring, at least. And here I am looking at you, and actually, there's nothing of the sort. You're really quite attractive."

I checked my watch and saw that it was a little past three, outside the time zone for scotch on the rocks, but well within white wine territory. So I ordered some. Angstrom responded with a vodka martini, asked for both shaken and stirred. I waited until both glasses were on the bar.

Here's the thing. The plastic surgeons on the Upper East Side of Manhattan who put my face back together did a stellar job. So stellar that I look better than I had before, despite the freckles, which for some reason they felt worth preserving. That doesn't mean I think I look good in a general sense. My nose is too small, my blue eyes too pale. My hair's an unruly mess on the best of days. Okay, figure not so bad, though it's getting harder to keep it that way. So when men say I'm attractive, my automatic thought is, What are you trying to get from me?

"What are you trying to get from me?" I asked.

He drew back into his stool.

"What do you mean?"

He looked genuinely taken aback, which gave me pause. So I tried a different angle.

"I spend a lot of time with police detectives and prosecutors. It may not surprise you that they use a variety of tactics such as misdirection, empathy, emotional bonding, even flattery, to extract information from people who might be a little reluctant to give it up. I'm guessing guys in your business do approximately the same thing. So, let's skip all the manipulation and cut to the chase. Tell me what you want."

He lit me up with another of those dimpled grins.

"I want to write a story about you. I think you're really interesting. And I think you're a lovely woman. Sorry if that sounds manipulative. It's really what I think."

I'd already checked to see if he wore a wedding ring. He didn't. So all I had to do was smile back at him as I climbed off my bar stool.

"I'm sorry, too. But I can't do this."

The weather had decided to change again while I was in the restaurant. The gloomy gray sky had turned blue again, and the breeze was coming in off the ocean, so it was both noticeably warmer and seasoned with a light touch of salt. The surrounding snow was a blinding white under the hard light of the sun, low in the sky and threatening to turn into an azure sunset. I had to put on my sunglasses for the short trip from the front door of Mr. Sato's place to the rear of the building and the door that led up to my fortress, a place where I could convince myself I was safely locked away from all intrusion, from the outside world and my own impulsive and benighted heart.

9

As soon as night had thoroughly fallen, my crisp, professional outfit propelled me out of the office, down the stairs, and into the Volvo, which I drove east down Montauk Highway.

Too lazy to change, too uncomfortable to just hang around in a tight skirt and pantyhose, too unsettled to spend more time by myself, I followed the urge to escape into what I thought was a sheltering anonymity.

I knew a place. It was a tiny French restaurant run by a real Frenchman who honored the Gallic custom of treating paying customers with haughty disregard (mostly an unfair stereotype—when actually in France I've rarely had a rude moment). The restaurant was in Amagansett, the last village on the South Fork before reaching the terminus in Montauk. I'd been there only once before, hoping to practice my language skills, and instead got into a duel in which I said something in French and the owner either corrected my pronunciation—favoring Parisian inflections—or answered me in English.

This time I merely sought a dark place where I'd fit in dressed as I was, far from familiar surroundings, where I could waste some money on overpriced, underproportioned tasty food and pretend I was in a foreign country where there was no danger of anyone wanting to strike up a conversation.

The owner directed me to a small table in the corner and promptly left before I could ask for a menu and the best pinot in the house.

"Puis-j'avoir le menu et votre meilleure bouteille de pinot noir, s'il vous plaît," I said to him when he finally found the energy to walk the few steps from where he stood indifferently by the kitchen door.

"It is an expensive bottle," he said.

I refused to take the bait.

"Je m'attends a rien de moins," I said to him. I would expect nothing less.

Ignored after that as expected, I was forced to linger interminably over the menu, which was all in French, nibble on sliced baguette, and kill about half the pinot, which, as advertised, carried a breathtaking price tag. After two-thirds of the bottle was gone, I didn't care so much.

"Would Madame like anything translated?" asked the owner when he finally buckled under the suspense and came back to my table.

I ordered the weirdest stuff I could pick out, something like snail livers on toast and pickled boar brains, and another bottle of wine.

"Cette fois, emmenez nous votre pinot noir bon marché."

"Our least-expensive wine? We have a mediocre blend from a struggling vineyard who we'll likely not source from again. I'm sure it will suit Madame perfectly."

The rest of the night went as hoped. The food was actually very good as long as you didn't dwell on the details, and that mediocre pinot tasted better than the first bottle, though in fairness, it was launched from a less critical plateau. Most important, my mood, generally a jumbled mix of cheerful goodwill and heart-seizing anxiety, was fully restored.

I sailed out to the car and took the measure of my mental and physical acuity. It wasn't too good. It wouldn't be the first time I called

Harry and asked with abject apology if he could please come and save me from a vehicular manslaughter charge. There was even a time I couldn't reach Harry and had to call Sam. He acted like I'd given him the greatest gift in the world just to get out of bed and drive twenty miles to retrieve me and get me home in one piece. I know he did that so I wouldn't hesitate to ask him again if necessary, which only cemented the odd grip he had on a remote but exclusive piece of my heart.

Part of the night's strategy was to leave my cell phone in the car, the most certain way to ensure a complete disconnect from electronic nags. I fumbled with my keys, confirming the need to call in reinforcements, but eventually got the door open. I closed the door and meant to toss my purse on the passenger seat, but instead it landed on a man's lap.

I shrieked and went for the door handle, but two hands from behind wrapped around me and gripped the silken folds of my nice blouse. They were strong enough hands to hold me in place, even with an errant little finger that took the opportunity to stroke the top of my right breast. I grabbed the finger and started to bend it back when another player entered the scene, the round muzzle of a big semiautomatic held by the guy in the front seat, pressed into the side of my head. All motion stopped.

"Let go of me," I forced out. "I won't go anywhere."

"That's a cinch," said the voice next to me.

"Let go of me or I'll snap off this finger," I said, pulling it back another notch.

The owner of the finger loosened his grasp, but not all the way.

"Break it and you'll be dead," said the voice behind me.

"How do I know I'm not dead anyway? Might as well take a finger with me."

"That's just stupid," said the same guy. I countered by pulling the finger back to near breaking point. He yelped. "Jesus, let go."

"You first."

He complied, helping himself to a semi-feel along the way. Once his left hand was all the way gone, I let go of his pinkie. He quickly pulled it away. The gun, however, was still stuck to my temple.

My heart fluttered in my chest and fear squeezed off my breath. The fuzzy, slightly happy wine buzz was now a blanket of semi-anesthesia of dubious benefit, as my mind furiously sought a way out.

"What's the deal, boys?" I choked out.

"Does there have to be a deal?" said the one with the gun.

I tried to turn my head toward him, but he told me to look straight ahead and keep both hands on the wheel.

"There's got to be some reason why you're risking twenty years at Sanger for assault, unlawful restraint, and use of a deadly weapon in the commission of a crime," I said.

"I hate smart-ass lawyers," said the guy in the back.

"You've got a lot of company," I said. "I hate some myself."

"I told you she had a reputation," said the guy with the gun. "The original smart-ass."

I risked a quick look in the rearview mirror. In the darkness of the parking lot all I could see was a shadowy form in the backseat. It was a bulky form, which was the best I could tell.

"How about putting down the gun," I said. "Those things can just go off."

"Is that so? Maybe that's why I'm holding it to your head in the first place."

My mind iced over and I felt my hands going numb. I'd been threatened before, but never in such tight quarters, my Volvo now a metallic and glass box closing in on me.

"You've got to tell me what this is about," I said. "Talk to me."

"Do we got to talk to her?" the guy with the gun asked the other guy.

"I don't think so," he answered, as if genuinely considering the question.

"I've got a thousand-dollar limit on my ATM card," I said. "There's a bank right across the street."

The guy with the gun made a soft whistle.

"A thousand bucks. Now that's some real money."

"I can get more."

"I bet you can."

No less terrified, I began to feel the stirrings of inchoate rage. At this evil cruelty, at my own foolishness to think I could work in a world where things like this could happen. Suicide by career choice.

"If your intention was to frighten me, you achieved that," I said. "Now tell me why or pull the trigger and get it over with."

The man pushed the barrel more forcefully into my head. I pushed back, gripped the steering wheel with my deadened hands, and conjured an image of Harry, to whom I silently said, *I love you and I'm sorry to have put you through so much, but at least I saved the worst for last.*

A thousand years of silence went by and then the guy pulled the gun away. The pressure was gone, but I still felt the outlines of the round tube as if it had burned a brand into my skull.

"Okay," said the guy with the gun. "Maybe we can work out a deal. You think?" he asked the guy in the back.

"Up to you," said the other guy.

"You believe we're serious," asked the guy with the gun.

"I do," I said, with as much sincerity as I could put into my voice. Not a hard task. "I am convinced beyond the shadow of a doubt."

"That's a good starting point. So here's the deal: You give what looks like a world-class defense of Franco Raffini, but unfortunately, there's nothing you can do to save the man from life in prison. We're thinking maximum security—say, Pendlefield, outside of Buffalo."

I nodded. "I can do that. He doesn't stand a chance anyway. Their case is too strong."

"Exactly," said the guy cheerfully. "Like fallin' off a log."

"But that's not all," said the guy in the back.

"Oh, right," said his partner. "We never had this conversation. It was all just a bad dream. Too much booze. Based on how you smell, that should be easy to cop to."

"Don't worry, boys. I know the drill. I've already forgotten."

"Smart-ass can be smart, too," said the guy in the back.

"They don't let dummies practice jurisprudence," I said.

"Whatever the fuck that is."

The guy in the back told me to keep looking out the windshield as the doors opened and they got out of the car. The guy with the gun had one last piece of advice for me.

"The day Raffini walks through the doors at Pendlefield is the day we stop watching every move you make. We'll be your guardian angels, only like in reverse. And the next time there's no chitchat. It's just bang-bang, lights out. Got that?"

"I got it."

Even without the gentle encouragement, I continued to hold the steering wheel and stare out the window. As my throat loosened, I heard myself making little wordless sounds. And then, at some point, the enormity of simply being alive caused a torrent of gratitude and joy to flood my mind, and not until I'd exhausted myself of massive, gasping sobs did I allow a proportionate sum of murderous wrath to set up lodgings; whether they were permanent or not would have to be seen.

I spent the next two hours of the following morning shooting the heads off black silhouettes clipped to an overhead cable system used to retrieve your targets and determine the degree of carnage. The operation was privately owned but had become the de facto Southampton police firing range, since the town didn't have one of its own. To that point, there were cops in the shooting booths to either side of me, one whose clusters were so tight it looked like a single big hole. The other could barely hit the paper. I took note of their name tags.

Like the French restaurant in Amagansett, this was a good place to hide from conversation. Secure inside a pair of ballistic glass panels, with earmuffs on and concentration fully focused, it was a soothingly solitary pursuit. I don't know if that's true of all firing ranges; this was the only one I'd used since I was a kid. But I think the coppish nature of the clientele also lent a professional atmosphere that I always appreciated, especially that morning.

I would never win a sharpshooting contest, but my aim was slightly to the plus side of average. Along with snow driving, tire changing, circuit-breaker switching, and other manly arts, my father had also taught me how to shoot a pistol well enough to carry a license my whole adult life. It was only since I'd drifted into my current practice that the license and training had taken on some utility—up to and including shooting a guy who was trying to kill me with a hammer. This is a major advantage, to know you're capable of such a thing. It makes the target shooting far less abstract, and thus a more meaningful endeavor.

I'd started out on my father's Smith & Wesson 39, a 9mm semiautomatic, and had evolved to the even lighter, more powerful .40 caliber Glock, the official firearm of the Southampton Town Police. Since Joe Sullivan had reintroduced me to gunfire, it was easier to use the same weapon for practice and training. This was why, when I was at the back of the room at the bench set up for cleaning your guns after practice, the cop with the good aim took me for another officer.

"Were you at last year's PBA conference?" he asked. "You look familiar."

I didn't look up from the bench.

"I'm familiar because I'm a defense attorney in Southampton."

"Oh. Sorry. I'm stationed in Sag Harbor. I thought by the way you handled that thing . . ."

"Thanks, but I'm not in a good place to talk right now."

"That's okay. Your two-shot pattern is smart, but I wanted to suggest you pause maybe a half second longer after the first discharge. Your second shot is going high because the barrel hasn't settled back down."

He walked over to another bench and began disassembling his gun. I knew he was right. I'd been given the same advice before. What he couldn't know is why I was rushing the second shot. It was anger getting into the process, bypassing the required cool judgment and directly pulling the trigger. It was the worst possible state of mind to be in when shooting a gun, but God forgive me, it made me feel better.

Burton Lewis had an office on the top floor of the building he owned on Wall Street, but he was just as easily found at his house in Southampton, where he spent at least half his time. Not that Burton was a man of leisure. In fact, Burton was one of the hardest-working people I'd ever known, even though he was the third generation of his family who technically didn't have to work at all.

In the twenty years since he inherited the building on Wall Street and the big law firm that went with it, he'd quadrupled his personal fortune while still finding time to replace shingles, cut out dead limbs, lay down stone patios, build a pool room into an unfinished area on the third floor, and undertake countless other tasks at his rambling seaside mansion.

Not directly seaside. His great-grandfather thought having a house directly on the ocean was an absurd risk, so he built his slightly inland. That all but one of the neighboring houses built on the ocean had either been moved back or allowed to wash into the sea during the intervening years confirmed the man's skill in establishing an enduring fortune.

Though he was as gracious and genial as a man could possibly be, Burton the Fourth was fundamentally a very private person. There were practical reasons for this, since anyone with great wealth can be wary of the dangers envy can present. But more than that, Burton was simply shy, and being gay even in these increasingly enlightened times seemed to reinforce that predisposition.

So it was fitting that if you wanted to visit Burton in Southampton, you had to pass through a solid wooden gate at the head of his endless driveway. And to do this, you had to get past the mansion's second-in-command, Isabella Torres, Burton's Cubana assistant.

"*Jacquelina*," she said through the intercom speaker next to the gate when I announced my presence. "How is my favorite *abogado*?" She meant lawyer. "He told me you were coming by."

"I thought Burton was your favorite *abogado.*"

"Okay, favorite female version of the same. Except when you come with that smart-aleck carpenter. He's a bad omen, that one."

Isabella liked me, which was not an insubstantial accomplishment. Most people she disliked on principle, and no one more than Sam Acquillo. That Sam was also Burton's best friend complicated matters.

"Just me this time, Isabella."

The driveway ran in a straight line between two tall privet hedges before curving into the final stretch that emptied out onto a broad turning circle. It was odd to see the house surrounded by piles of snow, most of the lush and sculptured landscaping lost beneath the mounds. It looked diminished somehow—still massive, but humbled. Isabella had the door open before I crossed the front porch.

She had that ageless look of a person carrying too much weight and too many difficult memories. She and her husband, another *abogado*, had made a terrifying escape from Cuba to the Florida Keys in an open powerboat, after which he found work with Burton as an investigator in his tax practice. Soon after that, he dropped dead of a heart attack. Burton took Isabella in as a housekeeper, and that was that.

"He's with Arlon, installing the new dryer," she said, motioning me to follow her. We passed through the cavernous foyer and slipped through a narrow door that was built into the wall paneling, literally a secret entrance to a hallway that served as a shortcut to the kitchen area. I said "area" because it was comprised of several rooms specialized for storage, prepping, cooking, and serving. Connected to the storage room was a laundry, where Burton and one of the staff handymen, a skinny little African American named Arlon Chapin, were struggling to retrofit a big commercial-grade dryer into the more modest space left by the old appliance.

Arlon was a former client of ours, who, with two other successful graduates, lived in quarters above Burton's five-car garage. Which probably explained why the local exotic-car thieves hadn't tried to boost the Gullwing Mercedes that once belonged to Burton's father that also resided there.

All I saw of Burton were his khaki-covered legs sticking out from behind the dryer where it was pulled away from the wall. Arlon was leaning down with his hands on his knees, watching whatever Burton was doing.

Isabella told him I was there.

"Goddamn thing," Burton swore, uncharacteristically. "Who would put a vent hose with a nonstandard diameter on a brand-new piece of equipment?"

"Don't know, Burt. You sure it's nonstandard?" Arlon asked.

The room shook with the sound of some sort of power tool Burton was operating behind the dryer. Arlon smiled at me, acknowledging the pleasure Burton took in tackling home maintenance, no matter how challenging.

"If the vent don't fit, make the vent hole bigger," Arlon said to me, his smile broadening.

More clattering noise and dust ensued, followed by the rest of Burton as he crawled out from behind the dryer.

"Got it, the bugger," he said happily.

Wood chips festooned his straight brown hair and weathered but preternaturally youthful face. He shook his head like a terrier and brushed debris off his denim shirt as Arlon pulled him to his feet.

"We're so glad," I said. "We know you hate defeat."

"Not true. Defeat is a healthy thing. In small doses."

He helped Arlon push the dryer into place, then left him to tidy up the job site. Burton told Isabella we'd be retreating to one of a half-dozen sunporches—a fairly long journey through a continuum of large rooms, each appointed in a different fashion though all in fine taste. Eluding the dual stereotypes of gay and rich, Burton's house had a worn-in quality, clean and neat but roughly maintained. Not unlike the man himself.

He stopped at a powder room along the way, cleaned up, then led me to the Ice Palace.

It was half of an octagon, about twenty feet at the extremes, and all glass—walls and ceiling. The furniture was iron, painted a dove gray except for the tabletops, which were clear glass. The slate on the floor matched the furniture, and the seat cushions were the whitest of whites. Beyond the glass walls was a sea of pure snow cover, but for the slight azure tinge courtesy of the sunlit blue sky. The field was dotted by a small flock of fidgety little gray birds, its vastness constrained only by a distant, nearly leafless privet hedge.

"What do you think?" said Burton, dropping into an iron love seat and looking around the room.

"Could use a little color."

"My thought exactly. But which?"

Somehow Isabella had managed to follow directly behind us with a rolling tea cart, transporting tiny sandwiches, bite-sized pastries, and a large coffee urn with matching creamer and sugar bowl.

I waited for the spoils to be distributed before lousing up the pleasant mood.

"I was assaulted last night by two guys. I thought they were going to kill me," I said, then took a bite of my wheat-bread-and-tuna-fish sandwich wedge.

Burton asked me to elaborate, and I did at some length, starting with a review of the Raffini case and including my brush with *The New York Times* and subsequent escape to the French restaurant that almost worked out as well as I'd hoped.

"And you'd seen them before at the entrance to your office," he said.

"At the outside door, though I only got a good look at one of them last night. I didn't see his face, but the body type lines up."

Burton looked at me over the top of his coffee mug. "So how are you doing?" he asked.

"Fine. I can't afford to be otherwise. I need to save Franco Raffini."

"You're not his savior. You're his attorney."

"Technicalities," I said. "Do you know Ivor Fleming?"

"Only by reputation. Though I thought he'd retired from the crime business."

"That's what Sam said."

"Sam would know," said Burton. "They've had dealings."

"Any guesses?" I asked.

He thought about it, then shook his head. "Not a clue. Though I fear for your devotion to Mr. Raffini. I have my doubts about the man."

"So do I," I said. "But they can't get in the way."

"By all means; he deserves the utmost effort, which I know you'll provide. I just want you to be guarded from disappointment. He may have had the misfortune of two false accusations of nearly identical character in a row, but that doesn't preclude the possibility that he's guilty of something."

That wasn't what I wanted to hear. I put up my hands as if to ward off the thought.

"I can't think that way, Burt," I said. "Not now."

"Of course not. You're right. Though it would be a simple matter to hand the case over to another of our attorneys. Your relationship with the victim could raise questions. You could withdraw on ethics grounds."

I hadn't thought about that, obvious though it was.

"I guess that's your call, Burt."

"It would only be an issue if they convict. Franco could appeal on the basis of ineffective assistance of counsel. That you gave it less than your all."

"But that's not going to happen," I said, with far more confidence than I felt.

"Of course," said Burton, and then changed the subject. "What should we do about Fleming? Approaching you is unacceptable."

"I'm subcontracting that one to Sam."

"Splendid idea. As long as he confines himself to legal means. You don't need another front opening in the midst of the current battle. More coffee?"

We sipped in silence for a few moments, then he said, "You seem unusually discomfited."

"I'm not comfited, that's for sure."

There are plenty of times when I feel my emotions are a lot smarter than my brain. The trouble with feelings, however, is they're mute. They just sit there, somewhere between your throat and the pit of your stomach, agitating for some cause, grousing away, resisting some belief held firmly by the rational mind upstairs. Your mind, unfortunately, has all the verbal chops. It natters at you in your own voice, trying to convince you that those subterranean grumbles are meaningless, or imagined, or both.

"What if I prove him guilty," I asked. "To myself. Beyond a reasonable doubt. What then?"

Burton's handsome face, ever kindly and vaguely amused, warmed another few degrees. He opened one of the tiny sandwiches and studied the interior. Marginally satisfied, he closed the two slices of bread back up and wolfed it down whole.

"Keep it to yourself, and when the time comes, you'll know what to do."

The sun must have found a cloud, because the crystalline room and the sterile desolation outside suddenly turned a surly dark gray. A gust of ocean wind stirred up the powdery snow and sent a spray against the tall glass walls. Burton turned in his seat to look over his shoulder, and together we waited for the breeze to recede and the sunlight to reassert its dominance over the day. However tentative and irresolute.

10

After I briefed him over the phone, Sam made a feeble attempt to persuade me to stay home and let him handle the situation on his own. I didn't dignify that with a response.

"When do we go and who's driving?" I said instead.

"Wheels up from my place at two P.M. We'll take Amanda's pickup. Four-wheel drive."

"Isn't that truck an inconspicuous fire-engine red?"

"You can't have everything."

"Though you do have a plan."

"I do. We'll discuss it on the way. Wear something dark and bring the artillery."

In an interesting about-face, the wind had shifted to the southeast overnight, bringing in much warmer temperatures and a steady, soaking downpour of rain. Even under the best of conditions, the drainage in the Hamptons is barely adequate because we're at sea level and municipally disinclined to make big investments in crucial infrastructure. With the ground still frozen and natural spillways clogged with snow, the only place for the rain to go was into spontaneously formed

ponds and improvised rivers, some more like torrents cutting off streets
and highways and turning basements into indoor swimming pools.

Luckily, I anticipated the chaos on the roadways and left early for
Sam's, choosing a rolling back-road route through open fields and
sparsely developed rural habitats. This actually took me within spitting distance of Tad Buczek's place, and I caught a glimpse of one of
his gnarly sculptures through the naked tree limbs and sheets of rain.
I'd made the right choice, however, dodging excess traffic and fording
only a few shallow streams, thus landing at Sam's driveway ten minutes
ahead of time. He was ready with a thermos of coffee and a little soft
cooler filled with cheese and fruit prepared by his girlfriend, Amanda.

"I never let him ride off on dangerous missions without sustenance,"
she said, handing me the cooler.

"Who said anything about dangerous?" asked Sam, tucking in his
battered canvas shirt as he walked into the kitchen.

"No one said anything," said Amanda. "I just assumed."

Amanda was in many ways my morphological opposite: dark, slim
as a wisp, and sharp-featured, as if her face had been sculpted out of a
chunk of mahogany. By a very good sculptor. At least six years older
than me; it didn't show. Sam loved her, which to me was her greatest
attribute. Me, she tolerated, as you would a troublesome stray your
partner had indulgently let sleep in the toolshed.

"We're just going for a little look-see," said Sam. "Be back before
daybreak."

Eddie walked stiffly into the kitchen from the screened-in porch,
saw it was only me, wagged his tail for a few languid seconds, then
walked back the way he came.

"Nice to see you, too," I called to him.

"There's plenty of fuel in the truck, though I imagine you can find
more along the way," said Amanda.

"Thanks for letting us borrow it," I said.

"Not at all. Sam has extended me the use of his '67 Pontiac. Not a bad exchange when you consider weather conditions."

Those conditions had no intention of letting up as we drove west on Route 27, the four-lane artery you picked up around Hampton Bays. From there you traveled through Long Island's pine barrens. Far smaller than the ones in New Jersey, but enough to convey the sense that there was a natural buffer between the twin forks and the rest of the island, saturated as it was with rampant and haphazard development.

Neither of us felt like talking, the silence filled in by the wind noise and chattering rain. I occupied myself with my coffee and bites of fruit and cheese from Amanda's provisions. It wasn't until we were nearly at Fleming's plant in Massapequa that I asked Sam to lay out his plan.

"Not much to tell you," he said. "It's simple. We wait in the visitors' section of the parking lot for Ike and Connie to leave the building, which they do at around five o'clock. We follow one of them home. My suggestion is Ike. We can get his take on things before pestering his boss. He's the brains of the operation, meaning he's got about two-thirds of normal mental capacity. Plus he lives alone in an apartment. Connie's got a wife and a bunch of kids, unfortunately. Think of the impact on the gene pool."

"You know an awful lot about these guys."

"Known them for years. And I was over here yesterday freshening the data."

"That wasn't the deal," I said flatly.

"Just reconnaissance, Jackie. Save the umbrage for better things."

I would have pushed harder, but I was distracted by the view outside. Though partially obscured by the veil of rain, the congested, chaotic terrain of Nassau County was now distinctive for an unexpected reason. Almost no snow. The weather people had emphasized that the storm that hit the East End had come up from the southwest and largely spared the rest of New York State. But it was still a shock to see clear roads and sidewalks and the occasional patch of grass, mostly brown and disheveled though it was.

Ivor's business, called General Resource Recovery, blended in well with the local ambience. The parking lot was inside a rusty chain-link fence. Sam drove right to his preselected parking spot with the perfect view of the front entrance to the plant's office complex. Behind us was an area dedicated to staging giant heaps of tangled metal, which were fed into the plant by hooks riding on overhead conveyors. According to Sam, after going through a sorting process, mashed-up cubes of raw scrap came out the other end, where they were stacked and loaded into shipping containers.

"Turning lead into gold," said Sam. "Fleming finally figured out how."

"So why risk it all with bad behavior?" I asked. "And are you sure we're safe just sitting here?"

"I'm not sure, but I've done this twice now, and no one's ever bothered me. I think it's the audacity factor. Everyone assumes you'd have to be out of your mind to pull any crap on Ivor Fleming."

"Oh, good. Comforting. And the first question?"

"Birds gotta fly, fish gotta swim," he said.

"Sociopaths gotta lie, cheat, and steal?"

"And sell drugs, murder people, and listen to public radio without contributing a single dime."

Before leaving the office I did a quick search on Ivor and his company. From the first page it was clear. Press reports of endless accusations, charges levied and overturned. Alleged association with conspiracies and organized crime. Countering denials, belligerent silences, and affronted protests of innocence. Blah, blah, blah. The net of it all was that Ivor exhibited the same genius at thwarting prosecutors as he had for drawing their attention in the first place.

Then a few years ago things changed. The only hits connected to

Fleming involved employees at General Resource Recovery. One guy rushed by helicopter to the city after being injured at the plant. Another pitching a winning game in the softball league. Others were pictured at Rotary events or proudly greeting dazed-looking exchange students. No mention of Ike or Connie.

The clock hit five, and a few minutes later people started coming out of the building. It was a thin and steady stream, ideal for scrutinizing possible candidates. Sam spotted Connie first, striding out with a woman about his height and girth. I was relieved to see him peel off and head for his car, for no good reason. Maybe his wife would be better off if he pursued other options.

Soon after that, Sam tapped me on the forearm. "There he is."

And he was. A tallish guy in a long, unbuttoned raincoat over a suit with a dark blue shirt and silver tie. His features were decidedly African, though his skin was more a diluted orange and his hair, tightly curled, was sandy red.

When Ike reached his car, Sam drifted out of his parking space and pulled up to the end of Ike's row. We saw him back out, and were able to slide in behind him as he turned right out of the lot.

Sam's philosophy on tailing a car with only one vehicle: it's better to lose your quarry than get caught. So he stayed well behind and allowed cars to get between us. Ike was in a white 3 Series BMW, which was easy to keep in view as long as he didn't feel like exercising the car's performance characteristics.

And this is how it went for about ten miles, before Ike turned into a little town house complex called Ocean Highlands. I looked around the flat, landlocked location and thought, Right . . . how about Strip Mall View, or Toxic Waste Court?

Sam waited until Ike was parked before driving into the lot and zipping into an empty spot. He shut off the engine and put his hand on the door handle.

"Timing is important here, so stay close and keep your hand on the gun."

"In case something goes wrong?" I asked.

"If something goes wrong, shoot me for being stupid enough to let it happen."

"Okay. I can do that."

"Don't enjoy it too much," he said, then jumped out of the truck and walked fast toward one of the town houses. Ike was in front of us, searching through a jam-packed key ring. Sam slowed a few steps until Ike selected a key and moved with confidence toward the door. Sam broke into a remarkably quiet run, given all the puddles on the sidewalk, so Ike had no idea what was coming when he turned the lock and started to open the door.

Sam flat-handed Ike's head into the door, sounding off a crack I could easily hear ten paces behind. The momentum of Sam's approach propelled them both into the apartment, Ike falling forward and Sam landing on top of him. I raced to close the gap, and slammed the door behind me. It was dark inside the apartment, but light enough to see Sam gripping Ike's curly sand-colored hair and twisting the guy's right arm behind his back. Ike yelled something, but his words were muffled, his face stuffed into the carpet. Sam told him to shut up while he patted him down, eventually coming up with a stubby little chrome-plated revolver and a slender knife inside a leather sheath, both of which he stuck in his pocket.

"Any other goodies I need to know about?" Sam asked the pinned man.

Ike shook his head and said a muted version of "And fuck you," unmistakable words, even if you didn't catch every consonant.

I found a light switch and turned it on. I pulled out the Glock and pointed it at Ike's head, being careful to keep my index finger along the barrel and well away from the trigger. Sam told Ike he was letting go but not to make any sudden moves that could spook the girl holding the gun. Sam rose slowly and Ike followed, slower still.

When they were both on their feet, Sam slid off Ike's raincoat, then pulled his suit coat partway down his arms, yanked him over to a couch, and sat him down. We stayed standing.

"You still got a death wish," Ike said to Sam.

"As yet unconsummated. You guys build up expectations and then just disappoint."

Ike leaned down and used his limited mobility to touch the egg that was beginning to form on his forehead.

"You mind telling me what this is about?" he said.

"Recognize my colleague here?" said Sam, pointing at me, the afore-mentioned girl with the gun.

Ike looked, then shook his head. "Never seen her."

"You've seen her back door," said Sam. "We got you on video."

He dropped the printout of the video capture on Ike's lap. Ike looked at it, then up at Sam.

"There're easier ways to have a conversation," he said.

I had to agree with Ike on that one, though I had much more important information to convey. I gestured for Sam to move closer. When he did, I whispered in his ear.

"It's not the guy," I said. "In the parking lot at the restaurant. Totally different voice."

You had to know Sam well enough to interpret the little "huff" sound as a laugh. As usual, it was both comforting and a little annoying that he found the current situation amusing.

"No shit," he whispered back in my ear.

"Not even close. This guy sounds like an alto in the boys' choir. You could break down doors with that other guy's voice."

"Okay. Not a problem. Ike was still at your back door. We can stick with that for now."

"Excuse me," said Ike. "Can I get in on the conversation?"

"We're talking about you," said Sam. "You should be honored."

"Yeah, right. Fuck you again."

"We want to know why you were at Jackie's back door. And didn't ring the bell. How come?"

"That's Mr. Fleming's business to tell," said Ike. "We just follow orders."

"So he sent you there," I said.

"Oh, she speaks," said Ike. "I thought she was just the only one of you pussies who could handle a gun."

"A more respectful tone would be in your interest," I said to him.

Ike shrugged. "Listen, we work for Mr. Fleming. He tells us to pay a call on somebody, we pay a call. All he wanted was to scope out where you lived, get a bead on you. Soon as we saw the security shit, we backed off. That's it." He looked at me. "I don't think Mr. Fleming was aware you were friends with Charles Bronson here. Otherwise he might've taken a different approach. I don't know, I'm just saying."

"Why the interest in Jackie?" asked Sam.

Ike enjoyed saying what he said next. "Oh, so you think Mr. Fleming says to himself, I gotta project I'm thinkin' on, but I better not go ahead with nothin' till I consult with Ike, my most trusted adviser. 'Yo, Ike, you got time for me to give you a detailed briefing on my personal and professional business plans? If it ain't too inconvenient, of course.'"

"Okay, so both stupid and out of the loop," said Sam.

"Hey," I said to him, swatting him on the arm with the side barrel of my Glock. "We got our answer. No reason for insults."

Now, *there* was a weird dynamic. Me scolding Sam, my most valued physical and psychological protector, for possibly hurting the feelings of a guy I thought had threatened to kill me. Not just threatened, had convinced me that he was going to do just that. And now that all Ike had done was poke around my office, I was ready to establish a new relationship, make a new friend, maybe exchange Christmas cards.

Luckily, Sam knew my tendencies.

"Give me more than that," he said to Ike. "You're not that oblivious."

All he got from Ike was another baleful look.

"Yeah? And what are you going to do to me if I don't? Do you think it can be worse than what Ivor will do if I sell him out? If that's the case, then you're an even sicker shit than I thought you were."

There comes a time in every negotiation when you have to either push back on your opponent's position or recognize you have all you are going to get. I felt we'd arrived at the latter position, and was glad Sam felt the same thing.

"If there's anything to discuss," he said to Ike, "we'll meet with Ivor whenever he wants, at a place of his choosing. Otherwise, I expect me and Jackie to be left alone. Understood?"

"I capisce the English, motherfucker. I'll tell him. What he does after that isn't my concern."

"Fair enough," I said, still playing the reasonable guy to Sam's hard edge.

Sam nodded, codifying the agreement. "That wasn't so hard, was it?" he said to Ike.

Ike grunted and asked if we could get him some ice for his forehead. I said sure, and soon after we left him there, leaning forward, the ice in a ziplock bag pressed to his head, his body deflated, his urge for revenge likely fixed in place.

11

It snowed again on our way home from Massapequa. Not an all-out blizzard, just a lousy three inches, which in other years would have caused the governor to deploy the National Guard. Instead, the local weather people delivered the news with grim restraint and the island silently groaned and steeled itself.

As it turned out, I actually liked what the little storm did for the existing snow cover—glossing over the gritty surface and painting everything with a neat whitewash. My only worry was getting from my car to the back door without sliding on the frictionless surface, made more treacherous by my leather-soled cowboy boots, an equipment choice in desperate need of re-thinking.

I made it to the door unscathed and waved to Sam that everything was fine. He'd insisted on escorting me to my place, but I wouldn't let him come into my lair only to turn everything upside down in search of possible threats.

My security system was state-of-the-art back when it was installed, but I knew there wasn't a system that couldn't be breached by someone who knew what they were doing.

So as I moved from the keypad at the bottom of the stairs up to the hallway and then into my office, where the next keypad was buzzing, waiting for me to punch in the code, I retained that familiar nervy feeling. It would only recede to a barely noticeable level after I looked inside all the closets and behind the shower curtain in the little bathroom attached to the office.

With that accomplished, I snapped on every security device I owned and got into my robe, tying off the belt and sliding the Glock into one of the pockets. In the other pocket I found an unsmoked joint. I poured a glass of wine to complete the set, then snuggled up in front of my computer, stretched my neck, shook out my hair, and lit up the magic screen.

I started searching major newspapers for Tad Buczek, but little came up. I reminded myself that Tad might have been a major factor with Pete's Polish crowd, but he was barely a sidebar to the world at large.

The local papers had a lot more. I learned that Tad had been at Pete's funeral party. Not a big revelation. That was such a surreal experience, I wouldn't swear I was there myself. There were also lengthy reports on Tad's court battles with his neighbors, with plenty of colorful commentary from all involved. You could summarize it all by saying Tad never tired of pissing people off. But I knew that already.

I pulled up one of my search programs that specialized in court records. Unless you spent much of your life laboring in the legal trades, you probably wouldn't know that whenever anything's adjudicated in court, it becomes public information. It doesn't have to be a trial. A simple filing with some regulatory body is usually accessible if you know where to look.

And if that didn't work for me, there was always my magic software.

I got most of the way without help. It looked like Tad had followed the appropriate protocol by traveling to Poland to meet up with Zina, spending almost a full month with her before receiving a fiancée visa and bringing her home with him. They were married a month after that.

Her maiden name was Katarzina Malonowski, and she had lived in Kraków, where she was born thirty-two years ago. Her parents, Godek and Halina, were native-born Poles, both deceased. I tried to search more on the parents, but everything was in Polish, so I backed out of that application and wandered down another hallway.

The last time Tad had tried to hire me to fight one of his neighborhood battles, I passed him along to another lawyer, a pretentious windbag named Sandy Kalandro, who was nevertheless a capable attorney. More important for Tad, he was politically and socially well connected and might even have known some of the opposition.

I searched recent filings in area courts and quickly found what I was looking for: Kalandro's petition to start probate on the Buczek estate, which his buddies at Surrogates Court immediately granted. This meant I could read Tad's last will and testament in the comfort of my office workstation.

I scrolled quickly through the antiquated legal language and found the list of assets. When I rolled through the pages and reached the bottom line, I was in for a jolt. Twenty-three million dollars in stocks, bonds, gold, and art. And another fifteen in real estate and general belongings, including a '65 Maserati Sebring Coupe I never knew he had. Also wisely left alone by the exotic-car thieves. I hoped Freddy knew to take extra measures now that the big watchdog had left the scene.

I went back into the body of the will to dig out the details. Zina, interestingly, only got a lousy three million, all of it from the investment portfolio. Saline and Freddy were named, and the will specified the estate should continue to fund their positions, including housing and health care, for as long as they wanted them. No mention of Franco Raffini.

The rest, including the property and everything on it (that last part a dubious accomplishment), was to be distributed among Tad's sprawling family. I was happy to see a half million earmarked for Paulina. Taxes were likely to take a bite, but no effort was made to reduce that with charitable gifts. Family's one thing. To hell with widows and orphans.

Even though Zina was in line for only a small percentage of the estate, the similarities between Franco's first adventure and this one were way too close to escape the notice of the DA any more than it escaped Ross and Sullivan. In most cases, it's very difficult for the prosecution to admit prior crimes into evidence. All the judges I knew looked at such things as far too prejudicial. They rarely allowed it, as long as you kept your client off the witness stand and beyond cross-examination. But it was possible they could prove to the judge that the Pritz case contained facts that went to motive, or that the first event aided in the planning of the second (just proving a certain criminal propensity wasn't enough). However, even if they failed to win that point, it was going to light a rocket under the prosecution, a pattern of two being pattern enough for them.

Was it enough for me?

I moved back into Google and searched for Franco Raffini. Remembering Sullivan's crack about his fencing skills, I dug into his time at Duke, where he was an accomplished student and active participant in sports and campus activities. He starred in fencing and soccer, though by graduation had focused solely on swordplay, having won the league championship and done well in national university tournaments.

I had all the court records from Franco's manslaughter conviction still on my hard drive. For the heck of it, I pulled them up and started digging around. The facts in the case were never in dispute: Franco and his lover are at her house in the belief that her husband was away on business. Franco is cooking for her on the family barbecue when the husband suddenly appears, grabs a carving knife, and tries to stab Franco. He succeeds in cutting Franco's forearm before Franco pulls a skewer out of a rack on the side of the barbecue and fends off further swipes of the knife, which goes on until Franco manages to impale the guy with the skewer.

I contended in court that the husband had become suspicious and faked the trip in order to catch his adulterous wife in the act. This helped frame the situation as attempted murder, lending greater justification to Franco's claim of self-defense. And since he'd already spent a few years in prison, the ADA put up a flimsy fight and the judge found it easy enough to shorten the sentence.

I'd forgotten their names. The husband was Don Pritz, and his wife Eliz. Like Franco, Don was in the financial business, some sort of a dealmaker, broker, go-between, whatever. I know nothing about any of those things. Although I knew at the time that Don traveled a lot, more than three-quarters of the year, which Franco told me had driven Eliz to seek intimacy outside the marriage. That hadn't been my issue when I busted Franco out of stir. Now I wondered. Especially since Eliz never showed her face or contacted any of the players when I first took up Franco's case.

I looked around Google for more information on Mrs. Pritz, but found nothing. Then on impulse, I drifted into a look at the Pritzes' family finances, and of course hit a wall of confidentiality. Yet what I love about the Web is there're so many ways to skin a cat. I went back to the court records from Franco's first trial. Franco's lawyer, a guy named Art Montrose, had subpoenaed the Pritz family financials and got part of his wish—current bank accounts and retirement funds. Included were the names of Don's investment accounts, but no numbers. The same with life insurance. I had the name of their insurance agent and carrier, but no death benefit. There was no indication that Montrose had pushed for more information, which surprised me. He was no longer part of Burton's firm, which I noted and stored away for later.

I confirmed that Eliz was still living in their house in Remsenburg, a hamlet on the western edge of the Town of Southampton. I checked on the market value of the house, which was estimated at 3.5 million dollars. This was as far as I could go using entirely legal public search engines, so somewhat reluctantly (and somewhat gleefully) I opened another search application program that was anything but. I got it from a former client, now devoted friend, who used to be in the cyber-intelligence business for the U.S. Navy. I had intense mixed feelings about using the program, varying from wretched shame to heart-racing euphoria. It didn't tell you everything, but it told you a lot. And since my friend had sent me the latest version on a thumb drive dropped into my mailbox, there were now things it could do that I had yet to try.

As exciting as the results can be, it's pretty boring to get dragged through the process, so I'll cut to the chase. I only cracked two out of five investment accounts, each worth a little north of two million dollars apiece at two hedge funds (who could use a little advice on cyber-security) but got nowhere with the banks. Not surprising, given their justifiable bank-vault mentality. With the insurance, I hit pay dirt. They had a mix of term- and whole-life policies Don had taken out when they were first married, while both were in their twenties. These were relatively affordable, though the payouts didn't amount to much. It was the one he took out only a month before he died that was a bit of a shocker.

Seven and a half million dollars.

Hm.

I woke up the next morning knowing what I wanted to do, I just didn't want to do it by myself. Not that I didn't like being by myself. I did.

What I needed now was someone large and fun to have around no matter what the circumstances.

"Tell me you have cabin fever and are just itching to get outside for a while," I said to Harry when he picked up the phone.

"How dangerous a criminal are we going to see?"

"She's a rich widow. Don't know how dangerous."

"Where does she live?"

"You're on the way. I'll pick you up in fifteen minutes."

Harry lived on the fringes of Southampton Village in a converted gas station. This wasn't apparent from the outside, since it had been a very old gas station and the prior owner had done a nice job on the landscaping and architectural cues, including a fireplace and chimney, to blend it into the surrounding residential neighborhood. He was an artist who specialized in big pieces that he could assemble in the garage bays and extract through the big doors. All of that was still there, partly filled with racks Harry occasionally used in his transport business.

I parked next to Harry's Volvo, which looked almost exactly like mine, because I bought mine to allay the envy I felt over his. He greeted me at the door wearing an impressively voluminous down coat with the fur-lined hood pulled up, ski pants, and black goggles.

"I didn't know what to expect," he said.

"You'll probably survive the walk to the car," I told him. "From there we'll have to rely on the heater."

He put the coat in the backseat, revealing the under layer, a fluffy chartreuse fleece with his company's logo on the breast.

"They gave it to me as an incentive to buy a bunch of them for my employees. Since I don't have any employees, I sent my regrets. And kept the fleece."

"Where'd you get the coat? Admiral Perry's closet?"

"Catchy name. Would go well in these parts," he said.

"These parts are a famous summertime retreat where you expect to sweat and develop skin cancer. These times are the issue."

"These times are here to stay."

"Don't start," I told him, pointing a gloved finger.

"I spend all day communicating with people all over the world. Everyone has weather like they never had before. Floods, fires, blizzards, cyclones, tornadoes—I think you're allowed to throw in locusts, since there's an agricultural component. It's Armageddon."

"Whatever happened to Mr. Optimistic Glass-Half-Full-Sunny-Side-of-the-Street Goodlander?"

"I'm optimistic that we'll find a solution before we're devoured by nature. As a matter of fact, climate change will become the great unifier of humanity. All wars will come to an end as our collective genius becomes obsessively focused on bringing carbon emissions down to barely traceable levels. Massive job-creating corporations will rise up as science and technology bend all economic activity toward developing alternative energy sources, and the subsequent wealth will be plowed back into an innovation-based economy. Our children's children will live in a world of infinitely sustainable energy and world peace."

"Don't start on the kid thing," I said. "I've got plenty of minutes left on that biological clock."

"I'm not sure I like children that much. One trip to McDonald's cures the urge."

"Where did you learn to say exactly the right thing at exactly the right moment?" I asked.

"Years of doing exactly the opposite. There's a theory of learning that says the more you screw up, the smarter you get."

"Then I'm a genius."

"Tell me about the widow."

I conveyed as much information as I could about the case during the drive from Southampton Village to Remsenburg, which was about twenty minutes away. Harry was like a human tape recorder when it came to the essentials of a narrative, so I knew none of my babbling was a lost effort.

The only thing I left out was the little episode in the parking lot at the French restaurant. There was no reason to awaken Harry's hyper-protective impulses, fully dormant now for some time. It would only put a warp in the relationship right when I most needed it to be straight and sure.

Remsenburg is the westernmost outpost of the Hamptons, although location snobs would likely argue over that distinction. Status debates aside, it's a serenely beautiful place, almost entirely residential, and adorned with lots of sumptuous and dignified beachside estates. Eliz Pritz lived in one of them.

Harry navigated to the address with the GPS built into my cell phone. Even so, we had the usual back-and-forth when we got there: You sure this is it? I'm sure. You sure?

And that was just approach avoidance on my part. I'm always hell-fire on approach right up until I reach my destination, then the avoiding kicks in.

"I'm assuming you didn't call ahead," said Harry.

"Never."

"So now you're wondering if you'll get a warm reception."

"Always arrive unheralded. Forewarned is forearmed."

"Which is why we're sitting here at the end of her driveway," he said.

"I'm assessing local conditions. That driveway is covered in snow."

Harry leaned closer to the windshield. "Maybe an inch," he said.

"Okay. Thanks for that. We're going in."

Her driveway was half the length of Tad's, but more elegantly land-scaped. I wished we were in the warmer months so I could see what was really there. Then again, I wished for a lot of things that were basically impossible.

The next decision was one I'd often faced. To bring or not to bring Harry with me to the door. On some occasions, the sheer mass of him had caused some unuseful consternation. On the plus side, he was such a distraction that people often let us into their homes before realizing what they were doing.

I chose the second tack but asked him to stand at the bottom of the stoop while I rang the bell, putting us approximately at the same level.

"I'm sorry, I don't accept solicitations at the house," said a tinny voice out of a little speaker, well camouflaged, next to the door. It startled me.

"I'm an attorney. I need to ask you a few questions in relation to an important case."

It was quiet for a moment.

"I can give you the name of my attorney. That is all."

"I'm defending Franklin Raffini. He's been accused in another murder. I could use your help."

Another pause.

"Do you have a pen and paper?" she asked.

"I do."

"Dinabandhu Pandey is the name," she said, spelling it out and giving me a phone number and address in Hampton Bays. "You may approach him if you wish. If I don't see you leaving immediately, I will call the police."

I looked around the door frame and saw a pinhole camera, just like mine. Damn.

"That went well," said Harry as we strode in a purposeful, dignified way back to the car.

"The unheralded approach is not foolproof," I said, a hint of warning in my tone.

"I have only admiration for how successful it usually is. So now what?"

"Dinabandhu Pandey?"

"East Indian. Hindu. Don't ask me more than that. Names get complicated over there."

"Let's go see him. We're over here anyway."

"Unheralded?"

"Absolutely."

It wasn't much of a trip back east to Hampton Bays, which we'd passed through on the way to Remsenburg. Harry once again used my phone to navigate to the attorney's office. It was a tiny converted house with a coat of fresh white paint over ancient, poorly-scraped clapboard. There was room in the semi-plowed parking lot for three cars. We took the last two spaces, pulling in next to an ancient white Honda Accord that looked perfectly harmonized with the frozen ground. An enormous maple, subspecies unknown, spread its naked canopy over the entire property.

"What's the strategy this time?" Harry asked.

"Frontal assault. Lawyer to lawyer. Mano a mano."

"This mano will be right behind you."

"I know that, darling," I said. "This is one of the things we love about you."

"We? When do I get to meet the other chick?"

"In your dreams."

We got an entirely different reception from Attorney Pandey. I pushed the buzzer next to the door and it opened soon after.

A dark-skinned guy in a rust-colored shirt, flowered tie, and what must have been gold silk pants answered the door. His top button was undone and tie loosened, and he wasn't wearing shoes or socks. A strong aroma flowed out of the door with him, and after a second, I realized it was taco sauce.

"Hey, wazzup?" he said. I handed him my business card, which he barely glanced at. "Swaitkowski," he said, with perfect pronunciation. "Is that Polish?"

"It is. Can we meet with you for a few minutes?"

"Sure. About what?"

There was not a trace of accent in his voice. Friendly welcome and abiding goodwill shone across his face.

"The murder of Donald Pritz and subsequent events," I said, wanting to cut to the chase.

It didn't deter him.

"Absolutely, dudes. *Entrez-vous,*" he said, swinging open his door and ushering us in. "You can call me Pandey. Even I can't pronounce my first name."

The place was a shambles. He had an ancient, oaken battleship of a desk, though the workable space amounted to only about ten percent of the surface. Most of the floor was also covered in boxes, loose files, and magazines. The decorative motif was a brainlessly chaotic twentieth-century jumble and the windows hadn't been cleaned in years. A bulldog slept on a Persian throw rug and hardly budged on our arrival.

My kind of place.

There were two unencumbered club chairs near the desk, which I took for client seating. Harry joined me. Pandey sat behind the desk.

"You're an enormous guy," he said to Harry, who'd heard that before. "It must be hard to move around with everything geared to us little people."

"I've traveled every continent, including Antarctica, and yes, it's hard to get around," said Harry graciously. "The leg space is the real issue."

"Try looking like me." Pandey pointed to his dark face. "I've been frisked so many times, my crotch is growing calluses," he said, enjoying his own joke. We enjoyed it, too.

"We tried to talk to Mrs. Pritz, but she refused in no uncertain terms," I said. "I'm defending the guy who killed her husband. He's mixed up in another murder case. Maybe that explains her reluctance."

He disagreed. "She's reluctant about everything. Truth be told, she's a bitch. Can't stand her. I was Donny's lawyer. He was my college roommate. I don't know why she kept me on. Easier, I guess. You want water? I have a bunch of bottles in the fridge."

He jumped up from his desk and dug three bottles of water out of a small refrigerator in the corner of the room. He poured part of his into the dog's bowl, which failed to excite the dog. I looked at the degrees hanging on the walls. Undergrad at Princeton; master's in international affairs, Georgetown; law degree from Stanford. I still couldn't figure out where the taco smell was coming from.

"Sybil's actually very good company," he said, pointing down at the bulldog. "But she needs her beauty rest. Sweetest thing in the world. Hard to believe these guys used to tear the throats out of bulls. So Franco's in trouble again. What's it this time?"

I briefed him on the outlines of the case, staying within the bounds of public knowledge. He listened carefully, nodding along the way.

"I read about that. Skimmed it, obviously. Didn't notice it was Franco. Guy was born under a bad sign."

"How so?" I asked.

"Bad luck and trouble's been his only friend," he said, smiling, waiting for me to pick up on the reference.

"Been down ever since he was ten?" Harry asked, ending the suspense.

"Never knew what he saw in Eliz. Had a perfectly lovely wife of his own and a successful career. Like they'd paved the fast track just for him. I have a guess on the problem Eliz might've had with Donny. Not sure it's shareable."

He tapped out a snappy beat with a pen on his desk. Then he swiveled his chair to the side and put his feet up on an empty computer stand.

"None of this came out at the trial. Wouldn't have helped him, so don't get mad at me. Might've hurt. Donny confided in me that he and Eliz had some compatibility issues. You know, of that kind."

"You're right. I think their marital problems were a stipulation," I said. "Hard to exclude it given the overall circumstances."

"If you roomed with Donny like I did, you'd understand the issue."

"He was a little guy?" asked Harry, catching on before I did.

Pandey shook his head. "The opposite. A horse would neigh in envy. And he was such a klutzy dweeb. Had a bitch of a time getting a date. I wanted to put an ad in the *Daily Princetonian*—'Hey girls, you don't know what you're missin'.' It warped him a bit. Had wicked bad jealousy issues. Just a theory, I'm no psychologist, God knows. Though getting dates was never my problem. It's the ongoing-relationship bit that eludes me. Are you two an item? You introduced him as your friend," he said to me.

"We are," I said.

So maybe I was wrong about Franco. Maybe the only appeal was having right-sized equipment. I forced the images out of my mind.

"I've read all the transcripts of the trial," I said. "Is that how it all went down?"

He shrugged. "Frankly, I didn't follow it all that closely. I was extremely bummed to lose Donny. Goofbucket that he was, Donny was a really good friend. My only official job was to get Eliz through probate, which was a slam-dunk. Husband to wife, you know Surrogates Court. They save their powder for the generational transfers. That's where the big tax bucks are."

"But they did have a fight. With handy cooking implements?"

"Oh yeah. The skewer was part of a barbecue setup that was just delivered that day. It was supposed to be a surprise birthday present. There's your irony for you."

"You don't seem to hold much animosity for Franco," I said.

Pandey dropped his feet back to the floor. "I hold animosity toward no one, for starters. Except maybe Eliz, try as I might to suppress it.

I'm a Buddhist. Converted from Hinduism when I was at Georgetown studying famine, pestilence, and war. Broke my mother's heart. Until I got the law degree and started paying her rent. My father died when I was just a kid. He would have killed me, and I'm sort of not kidding. Those traditional people take religion really seriously. So no, I knew better than anyone that Donny was capable of jealous rage. Preceded by paranoid delusions, which in this case weren't so paranoid after all. Killing him did seem a little extreme, but I've never had somebody come at me with a carving knife."

Sybil chose that moment to rise to her feet and shake herself out, the ripples in the loose folds of her skin starting at the neck and moving to her nonexistent tail. She came over and stuck her massive muzzle between Harry's legs. He gripped her head with his knees and pet her. She wiggled her butt.

"See what I mean?" said Pandey. "Loves everybody. The ideal Buddhist dog."

"So Donny pretended to be on a trip so he could catch Eliz in the act?" I asked, hoping he'd say yes, since that was what I'd asserted in court.

"Not exactly. He called me from O'Hare in Chicago, where he was supposed to connect to Seattle. 'She's with him right now, Pandey,' he says to me. 'Go over there and kick the bastard out of my house.' And I say, 'No way, man. I can't do that. And what makes you think this is happening?' He said he couldn't tell me. He just knew. Then he said not to worry, he'd take care of it. The rest you can read in the transcripts."

"None of this was admitted?"

"I told the prosecutor. I guess he didn't feel it helped the case. If you came across it during discovery, you also chose to let it go. Not really material to the actual fight, which was the crux of the whole matter."

"It wasn't me," I said. "It was Art Montrose. Same firm. Art's moved on."

"Fired, I hope. Did a lousy job for your client. His cross of Mrs. Pritz was pathetic. That's when I stopped paying attention to the trial. When I started feeling sorry for the guy who killed my best friend."

Sybil, done with Harry, came to visit me. I scratched the top of her head and tried to gently keep that slobbery muzzle away from my nice new jeans. Pandey leaned up from his chair and gazed lovingly at the bulldog.

"How does she feel about tennis balls?" I asked.

"She's never retrieved anything in her life. First time I tried she looked at me like, 'Hey, you want that ball so bad, go get it yourself.' Just wondering," he said to me, "what does all this have to do with Franco's current situation?"

Harry looked at me as if he was wondering the same thing. So that made three of us.

"I don't know," I said.

That explanation seemed fine to Pandey. We exchanged names of other lawyers we knew in the area, a professional ritual. We uncovered several common acquaintances, including Sandy Kalandro.

"Kind of a douchebag, we're agreed?" he said.

"We are, but I'll deny saying that."

"Me too. Though a douchebag with impressive connections."

With that, I relieved Harry of the tedium he was likely experiencing and let Sybil and Pandey get on with their day. Once back in the cold, Harry felt free to repeat the question apparently on his mind.

"Like Pandey said, why all the interest in a case that won't even be part of Franco's trial?" he asked.

"I'm not entirely sure, but something's eating at me," I said, holding his arm tightly as we walked side by side down a poorly shoveled walkway more suited to single-file. "Though it's also true that the cops and the ADA both believe Franco's a serial seducer of married women, whose husbands he subsequently kills. They can't use it in court, but it'll dominate their thinking and behavior. I'd like to disrupt that if I can. Am I making sense?"

"You are," he said convincingly. "You usually do. Eventually."

I let the "eventually" part slide and climbed into the Volvo. "Okay, handsome. We always do what I want to do. What do you want to do? I don't care what it is, I'm doing it."

Even without all the extra padding, it was no small thing to have Harry sitting next to you in your car. When he spoke, you not only heard it, you felt it through the car seat.

"A little surfing off Flying Point?" he asked.

"No freaking way. We'll die of exposure."

"Get married."

"We've already tabled that discussion. What else you got?" I asked.

"This open invitation has a lot of restrictions."

I gripped him by the fluffy fleece and shook with all my strength, to little effect.

"Come on, surprise me with something doable on this planet at this particular time," I said.

He turned in his seat far enough to almost fully face me, his considerable bulk pressed against the passenger-side door.

"Helicopter ride into New York. Limousine. Box seats at Metropolitan Opera—*La Traviata*, with dinner, back home in time to catch Leno."

"Yeah, yeah, big talk, Mr. Logistics."

It's what we ended up doing. And a lot more. It was perfect. I lavished appreciation in every form I could imagine, which he acknowledged. And I thought, What else can any man do to prove his wonderfulness? What is wrong with me?

12

I specialize in exaggerated men. Sam isn't overly tall, but he's solid as a Roman statue. You know about Harry. Randall Dodge, my favorite computer geek, the provider of the double-secret, not-remotely-legal search application, wasn't as tough as Sam or as tall as Harry, but you'd never call him a shrimp. I'm guessing a lick over six three in height, broad-shouldered and lean, but wide, so he could be imposing straight on but almost disappear when turned sideways. He had enough Shinnecock Indian in his blood to earn a spot on the Southampton reservation, but boasted other stuff in the genetic mix, including African American and Irish, which he always enjoyed reminding me, being born Jackie O'Dwyer and happy for it.

His shop was called Good to the Last Byte and was located off the big parking lot behind the main shopping district in Southampton Village. Like me and Dinabandhu Pandey, he was a complete slob, which made us completely compatible.

His main source of revenue was sourcing and supporting digital gear for the confused and inept, serving both the summer hordes and year-rounders, local and imported. But his talents far exceeded that, which I gladly exploited and he gladly let me, in return for free legal assistance at a few critical junctures and bottomless supplies of latte and croissants, or pizza, depending on the time of day.

Just inside the door of his shop was a counter piled high with keyboards, CPUs, monitors, and arcane boxes bristling with ports, knobs, and toggle switches. This barely foreshadowed the staggering jumble beyond, which I accessed through another door after alerting Randall by pushing an enormous red buzzer in the middle of the counter that read WE'RE BIG ON SERVICE. PUSH HERE AND DISCOVER!

Randall wasn't much on sharing facial cues, but I wanted to believe he looked glad to see me. He pointed to the bag in my hand.

"I hope there's ham and cheese in one of those croissants," he said.

"How do you know they're croissants?"

"The last three times you brought ham and cheese. I'm developing a dependency."

"Ta-da," I said, whipping out the desired product. "Though pierogis stuffed with ground beef and cabbage would be more fitting to the matter at hand."

"I've got a table suited to all forms of matter."

We wound our way down a narrow cavern walled with towering racks crammed full of electronic equipment, most of which was utterly unidentifiable to me, and I think partly to Randall, though he feigned otherwise. The other thing you needed to get used to at Randall's was the mood lighting, which spawned the type of mood you'd expect from sitting in Stygian darkness relieved only by LCD screens and blinking LEDs.

"What's it like spending your days and nights on the flight deck of a Klingon warship?" I asked.

" 'Tis a consummation devoutly to be wished."

"What have you got there?" I asked, pointing at one of the screens that showed an image of his storefront. "Security cam?"

He looked over and shook his head. "Google Earth. It's a street view of the shop. Hard to believe they went to the trouble of driving around the parking lot. I've also got the aerial."

He slid his chair over to the keyboard and brought up an image of his roof, which he zoomed out of until we could see the whole village. It was dumbfoundingly cool to look at.

"What a world," I said.

"And this is just what's publicly available. I can also access a geosynchronous weather satellite that monitors this part of the world in real time. Or go back about a year, if I want. I got access from a buddy of mine from the Navy. Highly unauthorized. Most people know these things exist, but actually seeing it work is pretty spooky. Orwell's probably spinning in his grave."

After we finished our croissants he brought up the program and we messed around for a while. First we zoomed down on top of my Volvo, then Randall went outside and ran around the parking lot waving to me. Truly freaky stuff.

Eventually tiring of the fun, Randall came back inside and gave me a look that said, *Okay, why are you here again?*

"If you wanted to do research in Poland via the Internet, how would you go about doing it?" I asked.

"Learn to speak Polish or get yourself a Pole."

"I tried to learn Polish as a defense against my in-laws. They used it as a secret code. I'd hear this long string of incomprehensible jabber, with the name 'Jackie' in the middle. But I just couldn't. French is hard enough."

"Try Algonquin. Almost nobody can talk it, and that's the easy part. If you're asking me if there's some sort of translation program that would let you access Polish sites, there isn't. You need to find a guy."

"You know a guy?"

"I do. Only it's a girl."

"Is there anything you don't know?" I asked.

"You don't have to know. You just have to find."

Randall's girl turned out to be UB45JK, a long-term partner in a virtual online game called Dystopriots, in which a band of plucky computer hacker/warriors in a postapocalypse America are battling to restore civilization. He was pretty sure she was actually a she, that she had been raised in Poland, immigrating to the U.S. ten years ago for college and never leaving. She lived in the basement of her grandparents' house, where in the country he didn't know (never asked, because it was irrelevant to the virtual experience). He showed me her avatar, which looked like an even more elfin, waiflike version of Zina Buczek, but he reminded me she probably looked nothing like that in real life. He showed me his, a bearded, bald-headed Caucasian dwarf with the handle Gyro.

"Sometimes people pick their opposites," he said. "Let's see if she's home."

In a few minutes we were looking at the inside of a destroyed building, roof gone and only three walls still standing. Rubble was everywhere and fires burned in the distance. It was a stereotypical vision of an urban war zone, but compelling anyway because of the startling realism. I commented on that.

"They're getting better at this stuff. It won't be long before you'll be able to jump right in there, or anywhere else you want, and maybe not come back out."

"Is there a game where a band of plucky gourmands are forced to eat their way through all the restaurants of the Côte d'Azur?"

Responding to something Randall typed on the keyboard, his dwarf pulled an iPad out of a big holster on his belt and tapped something on the screen. We swept up and turned in the air, gaining a position where we could read over the dwarf's shoulder.

"UB45JK, you in the neighborhood, pretty girl?" it said on the screen.

"I am, big boy. Not sure I can play today," came the quick reply.

Randall played the keys with lightning speed and perfect accuracy.

"Just have a quick question. I've got a homey here who needs to do some research on Polish sites and only knows about two words of the language."

"Maybe three," I said. "Tell her I'm defending a guy charged with murdering a Polish artist / potato farmer, whose widow is from Kraków, and the investigation is carrying me in that direction. Might as well get it all out on the table."

He did, then we waited while she absorbed the information.

"Cool," came the response. "Give me her e-mail and I'll get in touch maybe tomorrow when I'm out from under all this work. Need the day job to keep the computers running."

"You da best, UB45JK. The bee's knees. The straw that stirs the drink."

After she signed off, I swatted him on the shoulder and said, "Randall, you were so nice to her. I could swear you were flirting."

With unshakable poker face in place, he said, "You can also be a different kind of person in there if you want."

It was particularly jarring to emerge from the embracing murk of Randall's shop and out into the shimmering winter whiteness. While not quite overcast, haze filled the sky, dulling colors and eliminating shadows, flattening the world into two dimensions—cold and weary.

I've heard that a person's greatest asset is also their greatest liability. That's sure true about me. I'll put my powers of dogged concentration up against the best of them. The trouble comes when I try to turn them off again.

I think it's called obsession.

Since I was already in the Village, I decided to get another cup of coffee at the place on the corner and maybe read the paper. Look at other people come and go, uncomfortably and uncustomarily bundled and clenched against the steadily darkening day. Clear my head of all the clamor of the Buczek case. Or at least give it a try.

My favorite table, buried in the farthest corner, to my delight, was available. I used my hat and briefcase to stake my claim, then navigated the chaos at the coffee stand. I snuggled into the spot and was just starting to feel a slight lift in my mood when all was destroyed by Roger Angstrom of *The New York Times*. He came in the door, picked up a copy of the *Post*, and instantly spied me staring at him from across the room.

"Mind if I join you?" he asked, approaching with a coffee and bran muffin.

I thought, Are you kidding? You might be absolutely the very last person in the universe that I'd want bothering me at this very moment.

"I guess, sure. Have a seat," I told him.

"You're not an easy person to investigate," he said, sitting down. "Your friends are pretty tight-lipped."

"I have friends?"

"I started with Sam Acquillo. Well, that was scary. Next time I'm bringing a bodyguard."

"Bribery works better. Think vodka."

"He's a very interesting guy himself. But to borrow a legal analogy, he's a hostile witness," he said.

"You have no idea."

"The Swaitkowskis are friendlier, but no more forthcoming. I feel like Virgil Tibbs—outsider in a hostile town. I thought this was the Hamptons. All blabbermouth New Yorkers."

"You're workin' the wrong side of the street, ace. I could help you with that, but I'm not going to. Rather, I'm going to finish my coffee and do a little work. If you want some excitement around here, there's a zoning hearing with the board of appeals this week. That's the real bloodsport on the South Fork. You want drama? Shakespeare would be envious. You don't believe me, but I'm really not kidding. When five feet of setback, a squabble over adverse possession, and a right of way through the middle of Buffy's tennis court are in contention, it could mean millions of dollars. And when everyone can afford the best of my colleagues money can buy, and all of them are used to getting their way, the playing field can get pretty bloody."

He listened to all this with his mouth open, poised to take a big bite out of his bran muffin. When I stopped talking, he did, having missed nothing.

"You're doing a bad job of convincing me you're not the story," he said.

"If you be the paragon of modern reporting, the fourth estate teeters."

"Was that a paraphrase?"

"Not sure. I was an English major. But only fragments stick in my head. All this talk about Shakespeare."

"I was an English major, too. You have a boyfriend?"

"I do. More than twice your size. Flies me in helicopters and takes me to *La Traviata*."

"Oh, sure. Rich guy."

"Logistics guy. Even better. No prospect there, either. When you get back to Manhattan, tell me how much warmer it is. I can live vicariously."

He left before my mood had a chance to fully collapse, and over the next hour, I made a full recovery. I'd switched from coffee to herbal tea, avoiding the onset of caffeine poisoning, and bent all my energy into a game plan for the Buczek case. Sam once tried to teach me how to create a schematic that gathered up all the known details of a case and also defined the unknowns, expressing them both in a tidy timeline and exposing the key voids in the narrative, in descending order.

Being an engineer, he was really good at this. Me? No way.

I'd adopted none of his techniques, though I'd cobbled together my own approach, which I thought captured the same spirit. I called it WTF, and essentially, it was a rambling description of the case, enhanced with other things going on around me that may or may not have any relationship to the situation. Consequently, a detailed analysis of the crime scene might include a lament over Clinique discontinuing Zero Gravity Repairwear Lift Firming Cream (they still have it, I think, so don't panic).

The most important outcome of this effort was a list of questions, categorized under "Things I wish I knew," "Things I'd know if I was a better human being," and "Things I must know or else go back to mortgage closings and septic permits."

If I'd learned anything, it was to be sure you know what you don't know. It's too easy to think you know everything, because then you fill in the blanks of knowledge with supposition and convince yourself that it's the same as hard fact. I couldn't afford to do that. There were too many people in my business bent on casting even your hard facts as fantasy, much less your silly guesses.

Before I assigned them categories, I started listing things I didn't know. What really happened the night Tad was killed? Why did Ivor Fleming send his goons over to my apartment? Who were the other goons at the French restaurant? Was Tad really into criminal activities? And if so, what? What was Zina *really* doing with him? Why do I care about the Pritz case? Why is that Angstrom dude interested in me? Why can't I commit to Harry Goodlander?

I wrote down another ten questions of varying importance, then instead of assigning categories, circled the ones I felt needed the most prompt attention. Felt, not necessarily thought. Meaning, the questions that were itching at me the most, not necessarily the most in need of answering.

The question about Eliz Pritz got a circle and a star.

I took out my cell phone and called our office in Nassau County, which had handled Franco's first case. I asked if they knew how to get in touch with Art Montrose, Franco's lawyer at the time. They did, and as much as I disliked the idea of talking to another damn lawyer, it was where my strongest impulses led, and as Burton had recently pointed out, there was no controlling those things.

East Marion was a tiny hamlet near the tip of the North Fork notable to me mostly because there wasn't a Marion. Or even a West Marion. Just East Marion.

It was also apparently home to Art Montrose, whose exact location was represented by a red dot on my phone's touch screen. Normally, a journey up to the North Fork felt like a pleasant outing, even when on business. My favorite route, though arguably more time-consuming, involved two short ferry rides on and off Shelter Island, the landmass that sat securely between the North and South forks. Though I didn't know how it would be in this horrible weather, which was making every trip feel like a Shackleton expedition.

Because of this, I broke a long-standing custom and called ahead to see if Montrose would be home. My contact in our Nassau office said he had an office there, so the odds were good I'd catch him, and I did.

"Yes, I'd heard that Mr. Lewis opened an East Suffolk branch," Montrose said on the phone in a low, slow voice. "You seemed a surprising choice for the slot."

Oh, thanks a lot, I thought. And aren't you the one who blew the Pritz case?

"You may not be aware that I've transitioned away from my real-estate practice," I said. Then I described how I'd spent the first year reviewing back cases and cleaning up messes, not pointing out that several belonged to him, including Franco's.

"Ah, nicely done," he said. "I applaud you."

Bully for you, I thought.

"Before you get too happy, let me brief you on the latest," I said.

Which I did, sharing just enough of the story to give him adequate context. He listened with little comment.

"A hell of a thing," he said when I finished. "Out of the frying pan and into the fire. Is there something I can do to help?"

"You can tell me more about the frying pan. Or more precisely, that rotisserie setup."

Before he had a chance to demur, I told him I was planning a trip up his way and would love to drop by and discuss things in person. I could tell this was not a thrilling prospect, but I dropped Burton's name a few times—or, more accurately, used his name and all the influence that implied to bludgeon Montrose into acquiescence. He started to give me directions to his home office, but I told him I already had it locked on my GPS.

"No one can escape the red dot," I said.

The first leg of the trip is straight up Noyac Road through North Sea, past Sam's house, through Noyack itself, then up the fat peninsula called North Haven, home to the more privacy-inclined summer people and herds of deer, the latter of whom were busy stripping the bark off specimen trees and trampling shrubbery, knocking off the snow to get at the evergreen leaves.

As the only way to get on or off Shelter Island, the ferries ran year-round, the stoic young guys who crewed the boats seemingly inured to any and all conditions, be they tempestuous or idyllic perfection. That day was no different. Though the quieter waters along the shore had frozen over solid, the tide-driven channel itself was clear. The water at the docks, defined by several rows of tall piers, was kept liquid by bubblers just below the surface.

They'd already loaded a pair of cars and a big box van when I pulled up to the ramp. They waved me on, and the Volvo crunched over the layer of salt and sand spread on the vehicle deck. When we pulled out into the channel, I got out of my car, as I always did, despite the bitter wind. The sun was still bright, and from the water the wooded coastline, dotted with an occasional private dock leading up to a waterfront home, was a beautiful thing to behold. The ice and snow made it feel even more entrancing, alien not just to our watery world but to the earth itself.

I pulled my Russian fur hat tighter on my head and wrapped my arms around myself, containing the warmth of body and mind within.

There are more than two thousand permanent residents on Shelter Island, and every one of them was indoors when I drove across, following the white box van whose painted sides showed a beach chair and palm tree and asked the question, ISN'T IT TIME TO COOL YOURSELF BY THE POOL?

There were too many answers to that to even start.

The voyage across the north channel was longer, but I held out all the way to Greenport. From there, it was another fifteen minutes to East Marion along Sound Avenue, which was no better plowed than our main roads down south—only far less traveled, the principal traffic heading to the big ferry to Connecticut that left from Orient Point at the bitter end of the North Fork.

Art's house was technically in an area of East Marion called Oysterponds, a throwback village clustered next to a harbor protected by a natural breakwater from the ocean swells of Gardiners Bay.

Montrose owned one of the older homes, which meant he had a nice water view between similar buildings across the street. I rang the bell.

"Now I remember you," he said upon opening the door. "You were involved in that nasty subdivision out on Oak Point."

He was neither tall nor short, but a large belly overflowing a pair of plaid pants, and a matching double chin, made him more imposing than he deserved. His hair was thin and red, fading into gray. He wore tortoiseshell glasses and a blue Oxford cloth shirt that strained at the buttons.

"I was," I admitted. "Probably what gave me a taste for nasty things. Can I come in?"

He stepped out of the way, then led me through the welcome warmth of the house to his office, which was also comfortably heated, although its small size put me in uneasily close proximity to Art Montrose.

The office decor expressed the standard-issue golf/sailboat/fox-hunt motif, as if purchased through a catalog geared specifically to pretentious professionals. There were two colonial-style chairs padded with red leather in front of his desk. I took the one that let me look at the water over his shoulder.

"I had to pull out the file to reacquaint myself with the particulars of the case," he said, holding up a thick folder. "They do tend to blur."

"They do. My mission here is to achieve some clarity." I took my little notebook out of my briefcase and clicked open a ballpoint pen. "I'm just going to ask you some things, in no particular order, okay?"

He nodded solemnly. "Ask away."

"Did you know that Eliz Pritz was the beneficiary of more than seven million dollars in life insurance benefits?"

"I did. With house, investment accounts, 401(k), and some valuable tangibles, the total estate was a little north of twenty million dollars. But remember, Donald Pritz was a successful investment banker, whose yearly income frequently exceeded a million dollars. His potential lifetime earnings were significant, justifying life insurance coverage at that level."

He'd given that speech before, though it was likely refreshed by a look at the file.

"So you thought it was irrelevant to Franco's case."

"Hardly. I thought it was central." He sat back in his own red leather chair, which squeaked and took him a little farther back than he wanted, causing a slightly panicked return to upright. "Damn chair's nearly worn out. Gonna kill me one of these days."

I must have looked perplexed, which gave Montrose the first opportunity since we met to display some pleasure.

"Okay," I said. "I'll bite."

"I believe beyond the barest shadow of a doubt that Mr. Pritz was killed for his money."

That quieted the room for a few moments.

"Is that in your file?" I asked.

"Hell, no. The only thing in the file are the stipulated facts in the case, some documents acquired during discovery, and notes to myself and our office on defense strategy. The real facts, and hence the real story, are all up here." He pointed to his head. "Where I intended them to stay in perpetuity."

"You still do?"

"No. Given what I read about your case, I no longer care what happens to Mr. Raffini, and since you're bound by the same obligations that oblige me, there's no threat to confidentiality. I'll tell you anything you want and enjoy the relief to my conscience."

Now I wasn't so sure I wanted to hear it. Though as he said, we were still in some ways on the same team, and I felt like I'd never be able to eliminate all the questions circled or uncircled in my notebook without the information he might provide.

"Okay," I said.

He leaned back again, only more gingerly, and put his hands, with knitted fingers, on top of his prominent belly.

"I felt as if the entire story could be told through the phone records. When you went back three years, you saw the beginning of the relationship between Franco and Mrs. Pritz. The initial calls between her home phone and his cell, at first spaced far apart, increased steadily until they became more than a daily occurrence. Since Mrs. Pritz handled all the household finances, including paying the bills, evidence of this should have been easily concealed. However, Mr. Pritz was a very jealous man. As soon as he began to suspect her of having an affair, the first place he'd look would be the family phone records, which were conveniently in his name. According to Mrs. Pritz, Donald first began confronting her with his suspicions at least three weeks before his death, and yet the calls continued unabated."

"She didn't care if he found out."

"Wanted him to. I only met twice with Eliz, but there was nothing about her suggesting naïveté. Quite the opposite. A woman like that would not have unwittingly used a credit card she shared with her husband to buy drinks at the bar in a hotel where on the same night Franco Raffini had rented a room."

I knew now where he was driving to. And I really didn't want him to get there, but it was too late to stop the car.

"By the way," he said, "the last call Donald got that night was from a familiar number. Franco's cell phone. Right at the moment he was at Chicago's O'Hare about to connect with another flight to the West Coast."

"It was a setup," I said.

"Very much so. Something about that call alerted him that his wife's lover was with her at their house. You know the rest."

"No, I don't. Not really."

"I think it happened as described by both Mrs. Pritz and Mr. Raffini.

Donald came through the doors to the patio, where he picked a large carving knife up off a table near their gas-powered barbecue. Mr. Raffini snatched up a rotisserie skewer, which he used to great advantage in warding off Donald's attacks, though one swipe of the knife opened up a deep gash in Franco's forearm. That was when Franco finished Donald off with a lunge straight through the heart. Literally the coup de grâce."

He pronounced "grâce" properly, which earned him a few extra points.

"You said 'their barbecue.' I thought it was a birthday present from Eliz."

"Not the barbecue, the rotisserie. It's a separate piece of equipment. Brand-new, delivered just that day. What a coincidence. From what others told me, Donald didn't even like to grill. That was usually a job for Mrs. Pritz."

I thought about what he was saying, tossing the information around in my head like salad in a salad bowl.

"Okay, even if the moment was contrived to end in Donald's death, there's nothing that directly implicates Franco beyond having an affair with Eliz and killing Donald in self-defense. Both of which he freely admitted to from the start."

Montrose held up the fat file. "You can look for yourself. I went to see Franco's firm, just a routine visit. I ended up in a conference room with their CFO and corporate counsel, who both looked like they were about to heave or pass out from the stress. The counsel started by saying they were hoping 'to get ahead of this.' I was smart enough not to ask, 'Ahead of what?' Then he handed me this"—he shook the file again—"a complete accounting of Franco's trading history in the months leading up to the murder. Franco's career as Wall Street wunderkind had recently made an about-face. Rather dramatically, over a huge, unauthorized bet on oil futures that locked in a colossal loss. That's all it takes, one deal, if it's bad enough. The firm avoided a run on its assets by keeping everything hush-hush, which included holding on to Franco until they could cover the loss and withstand the bad press. A decent arrangement for both, since Franco had not only bet the firm's funds, he was so confident in the trade he tossed in his own. All of them. As long as the ADA didn't specifically subpoena the information, there was no reason for it to come out. And that's how it went."

Damn, damn, damn, I thought.

"Motive," I said.

"In spades. Even the slipshod defense Franco got from me would only result, at worst, in a conviction for negligent manslaughter. I made it such a slam-dunk that the ADA just had to go through the motions, with no good reason to think beyond the obvious. All Franco had to do was cool his heels at Sanger for a few years, a chore you graciously truncated, and then join his co-conspirator in well-funded bliss."

"That's not what happened," I said.

"So I noticed halfway through the process. Franco became steadily more dejected as the trial went on, looking around the courtroom whenever we first came in and mumbling things like, 'Dammit, Eliz, where the hell are you?' I know from a contact at the county jail that he tried to call her several times, but never got through. So we had a real catch-22 on our hands. I could try leveraging his disappointment into implicating her, but there was no way he could do that without exposing himself to a much more serious charge. So I didn't ask, and he didn't tell, and we marched our way in silence to the conclusion of the case."

"And you kept all this to yourself."

"I did. I sullied my professional reputation with Mr. Lewis, who was very disappointed in my performance, which led to my resignation. Though I did manage to save our client from a charge of intentional second-degree murder, which carries a life sentence."

"You should have come clean. Burton's an honorable man."

He sat back up and put his elbows on the desk. "I know. That's why I kept my mouth shut. All the truth would do was throw him and his worthy pro bono enterprise into the same moral and ethical vortex. Better to take the hit and move on with my life."

So who's honorable now? I asked myself, actually feeling my throat clench a little, like it always does when contemplating noble self-sacrifice. Suddenly Art Montrose became genuinely imposing, his outsized midriff in full relief before the faux-antique desk.

13

As further proof that my emotions, and by association, my instincts, were the smartest part of me, I drove on autopilot back toward Southampton. I bypassed the ferry rides, driving west to Riverhead, at the crotch of the forks, and then back east again to Southampton. I didn't know what the weather was doing at the time, since I hadn't the wherewithal to notice it.

It might seem silly to feel crushed over a situation that amounts to the central dilemma of criminal defense—how do you defend a person you know is guilty of the crime? I believed without reservation in the principle that every person deserves the right to a vigorous and thorough defense, if for no other reason than to protect the integrity of the system for the sake of the innocent. It just makes the job a lot harder when they're not.

Technically, Franco had confessed to nothing, so in the eyes of the law, presumption of his innocence was still my official obligation. Intellectually, I got that. Emotionally, it was another thing.

I knew other people on the job—sincere, decent people—who had no trouble accepting the overwhelming odds that their clients had done the deed or worse, and could still give their utmost to the task. Not me.

I really, really wanted to believe in my clients. To believe their words, to cleave to their explanations, their perspectives, with unwavering devotion. For me, the effort needed more fuel than a simple, rational calculation could provide. When my heart isn't in the game, I'm nearly worthless.

Still driving in a trance, I snapped out of it only when I realized I was parked in front of Harry's house. The day had nearly petered out by then, and I decided twilight was no time to be operating heavy machinery like a Volvo station wagon. I got out and knocked on his door.

He looked glad to see me.

"What do you have that treats existential crises?" I asked.

He looked at his watch. "Gin and tonics, though they only take effect after four P.M. We're in luck; that's only ten minutes away."

"Ten minutes is a respectable head start," I said, walking through the door.

He brought me to the living room and sat me down, then went to prepare the drinks. I spent the time wishing I wasn't alone and watching tiny birds flit around a raised bird feeder through a big pane-glass window. The birds were joined by a squirrel, who had apparently mastered the art of walking upside down on the underside of the platform and maneuvering over the edge, his tail fluttering fast enough at one point to blur and his hind legs running in thin air. But he made it.

The birds didn't seem to mind. I asked Harry when he came with the drinks if feeding the squirrels meant a drag on the birdseed supply.

"I only feed those ambitious and clever enough to reach the platform. That guy's the acrobat. There's another one who leaps from a branch all the way over there." He pointed at a fairly distant maple tree. "I call him Rocky. They're the only two. I'm trying to breed a super race of squirrels."

"Why would you want to do that?"

"Ask them."

He dropped down next to me, we toasted, and I slurped down half the drink. I started to tell him about my conversation with Art Montrose but had to stop after a few minutes to cry. Not a big bawling kind of cry, but bad enough to force Harry to wait patiently, his arm around me, his yellow chamois shirt a convenient sponge to sop up all the tears.

"I bet that felt good," said Harry when it looked like I was thoroughly finished.

"It did. You should try it sometime."

"I will. Might help get me through the basketball season."

I finished off the gin and tonic and handed him the glass.

"Good preview," I said. "Now bring me the show."

When he got back, I took a gentler sip and renewed my story. Harry listened carefully, with only a few clarifying interjections and the occasional response to one of my rhetorical questions that he never failed to properly answer.

I often poured out my feelings to Harry, but rarely just to unload all that emotional crap. I also valued his opinion and his logistics-wizard, problem-solving skills. So he knew he had license to probe a little, to challenge my assumptions. Which he did.

"You haven't heard Franco's side of the story and he hasn't confessed to anything, so it's still all just supposition," he said.

"You're right. Though it's supposition with an odor of legitimacy."

"Around the Pritz case, sure. Everything hangs neatly together. Not so with the Buczek thing. That's a sloppy mess. I could think of a thousand ways he could have knocked off Tad Buczek with far less criminal exposure. He put himself directly in the crosshairs with no chance to plead self-defense."

"You can't ignore that Zina is another unhappy wife who could win a fat inheritance," I said.

"Well, that gambit didn't work out so well the last time, did it? Why would Franco try it again with a far less credible scenario? Go to prison for a couple decades, then expect Zina to pay for his golden years? Doesn't make sense."

My heart began to lighten, not entirely from the gin and tonics.

"Why did he move the body?" I asked.

"He's telling the truth. He panicked. Whatever he planned to do with it suddenly seemed more trouble than it was worth."

That was still an unsatisfying answer, but it didn't undermine Harry's essential thesis. If this was another murder pact between Franco and his married lover, it was a pretty shabby operation. It didn't fit.

"Something went wrong," I said. "There was a better plan, it just went off the rails for some reason. What we're looking at is the confusing residue of improvised damage control."

Harry pondered that.

"Reasonable scenario," he said. "You're so smart."

"You're not supposed to say that. You're supposed to have a convincing counterargument."

"If I did and didn't mean it, I'd lose all my credibility."

I still felt a lot better than I had when we first started to talk, for reasons as obscure to me as those that pushed me to the brink in the first place. But I didn't fight it. Instead, I got a little more looped and messed around with Harry, and later we went out to dinner, came home, and messed around a little more, which effectively anesthetized me against further questions on the meaning of life, at least until the next day, but I was grateful for the reprieve.

It wasn't the first time I'd woken up at Harry's with a bad headache. And no change of clothes. As usual, he was already up and at his workstation, and had breakfast waiting for me in the kitchen. I put on one of his shirts, which translated into fairly modest loungewear, and poured myself a big girl's cup of coffee. I interrupted his work by asking if I'd said anything stupid in the time before we passed out that I couldn't quite remember.

"You said I was the most fabulous Harry Goodlander who ever lived and that you'd love me for all eternity. Was that stupid?"

"No. I stand by it. Even in broad daylight. How long have you been up?"

"A few hours. Gave me time to go get you fresh socks and long undies, your cream, toothbrush, and that four-million-watt industrial blower in case you wanted to tackle the hair. You've already got the insulated jeans, but I brought a clean shirt and matching sweater."

I held his head between both hands, cheek-to-palm. "I'm going to take a shower before the force of my appreciation gives me a heart attack."

"That would defeat the purpose."

After showering and eating, I left fully restored and filled with a renewed sense of mission. My existence had meaning, and my vocation a true purpose on earth. I would not be a punching bag for my capricious emotions or a sap for my conniving brain. Rather, I'd press the whole team into a unified effort to answer every goddamned question in my little notebook, driven by a belief that however many possibilities may present themselves, there can only be one truth in the world.

It was my job to get as close to that as humanly possible.

I drove over to Sagaponack under pale, overcast skies. I'd gotten used to the narrowed roadways by this time, and played the "You go first, no I'll go first" game with oncoming traffic almost by reflex. I listened to public radio and let the Volvo find its own way to Dayna Red's place.

I'd barely turned into the long driveway when Misty appeared out of nowhere and chased alongside the car all the way to the red barn. I got a nice greeting when I opened the door. Actually, she jumped up into my lap, then into the passenger seat, where she stood and looked out the windshield. I asked her if she wanted to go for a ride, then regretted it when she looked back at me with unrestrained enthusiasm.

"Maybe later, kid. We'll have to clear it with your mother."

She followed me to the side door of the barn. Dayna answered my knock with a look that said she was almost as glad to see me as Misty was.

"Hi, there. What a treat," she said.

"Not so fast. You haven't heard why I'm here."

"Come in, come in," she said, waving me through the door. Misty slid along in my wake. "I can't imagine anything bad. You're always such fun."

We sat in her cozy office, scented with the aroma of sawdust and greased machinery. Misty immediately presented me with her tennis ball but relented without complaint at a single word from Dayna.

"Maybe you could toss it a few times before you leave," she said to me. "It's her raison d'être."

"Totally there," I said. "I've been grappling with that myself recently."

"Is that why you're here?"

"Sort of. I was hoping you could tell a lie for me."

"Depends on the lie."

"Of course," I said. "I want to go to the Buczek place, but I've already been back once, and I'm afraid if I go again, I'll get a lot of resistance. I can force them with a subpoena, but that's way too heavy-handed at this point and I'd rather not turn Tad's widow into an enemy."

"You said 'them.'"

"She's got two hired hands living there, a married couple—handyman and housekeeper. Longtime employees of Tad's. I don't know what they think of Zina, but they have a proprietary air about them."

"So what do you want me to do?" she asked.

"Tell a tiny lie. That you lost something the night you were over there and want to come look for it. What kind of thing, I don't know, but I bet you can come up with something."

Do you know people who sometimes shake their head when they really mean to nod? Dayna was one of those people, sinking my heart before sending it aloft.

"Absolutely. No problem. Happy to do it. When?"

"Now?"

She reached over and slapped me on the knee.

"Why not? All I got scheduled is ripping about a million board feet of seven-quarter poplar, not even a real hardwood, much less an endangered species. Let's do it. Can I bring Misty? She'll stay in the truck."

I followed Dayna to the commercial strip on County Road 39, where I left my Volvo in the parking lot of an electrical supply company and joined her and Misty in the truck. The cab smelled like her shop and a little like wet border collie, both of which were pleasing to the nose. Otherwise it was clean and well-kept, distinguishing it from other tradesmen's trucks I'd climbed into.

An iPod was jacked into the stereo, playing Alison Krauss.

"Girl was like a child prodigy, nationally ranked fiddle player," said Dayna, pointing to the stereo, "and all anyone knows up North is she's cute and can sing."

"Too many of us labor in the shadows rather than be called to greatness."

She looked at me. "Damn, that's good," she said.

"Thanks. I was an English major. That's the kind of thing they teach us to say."

"I majored in the hippie arts and the testing of illegal substances. Cured of that now, but sometimes I miss it."

Once I get to know you a little better, I thought, we can fix that.

"How about you?" I asked Misty.

"She's strung out on tennis balls and kibble, so don't ask her."

"What are you going to tell the Buczek people you lost?"

"My retractable plow-blade stabilizer. Everyone knows you can get by without those things, but it's sure a nice-to-have," she said.

"So they exist."

"Of course not. Where'd be the fun?"

On the way to Tad's she took me through a condensed version of her life story, which included a lot more than counterculture zest and excess. She and Jeffery had traveled the world for three years, touring every continent and living by their wits and tolerance for discomfort and insecurity. I marvel at stories like this, having spent nearly all my days in Southampton, minus college and law school and those rare weeks in Europe, mostly France. It made me feel stolid and fixed, like a tree stump or the village war memorial.

I shared that with her.

"Nah," she said. "I've barely read a book in twenty years. What the hell do I know?"

On the way there, I partially broke my call-ahead rule by calling to say we were on our way. Saline had answered the phone and I explained to her the situation. She seemed unhappy with the request but gave us the go-ahead.

"I'll tell Fred. He gets agitated when people wander around the property like it's the town park," she said.

"Understand that. We'll make it quick."

When we reached the entrance to the compound, Dayna stopped before pulling into the drive.

"So what are we looking for, in reality?" she asked.

"I don't know." It was the honest answer. "I just want to take another look. If you put in the effort, places will tell you things."

"I know some indigenous peoples who could help with that. Consciousness expanding–wise," said Dayna.

"Let's see how standard consciousness works first."

I directed her down the long drive, around the hairpin turn, and over to the cleared space next to the pergola. We got out of the truck, leaving Misty behind, who watched us move away with a stare that could have bored holes in the glass. I led Dayna to the picnic table where Franco had laid out Tad like a side of beef, then up the path to Hamburger Hill, where all the action apparently occurred.

The contours of the disturbed snow and footfalls had become even less defined as the weather continued to erode the snowpack. I'd seen it plenty, yet now would have had a hard time pointing out any important features. The crime scene was evaporating before our eyes.

"What am I missing?" I asked Dayna. "Is it gone forever?"

"I don't know," she said. "What was here before?"

"There were a bunch of footprints between here and where the staff has a house and storage barn. That night, I counted them, and they added up to Franco's claim that he came here, went back to the barn, then returned. This area here, the main crime scene, was too covered in tracks to make anything out, though all the bloody ice, and the chunk heaved over there"–I pointed to a nearly nonexistent depression–"proves Tad was killed here. Franco says he dragged him from here down to the pergola"–I pointed down the hill–"where we saw him on the picnic table."

"So no footprints from here to the pergola," said Dayna.

"No. There wouldn't be any. None had been made, and if they had, dragging Tad down there would have wiped them out."

I looked down the broad swath of snow flattened by the sliding tarp, weighted by a two-hundred-plus-pound dead body.

Dayna was looking at me like she was reluctant to say something.

"You think there might have been footprints," I said.

"If Franco found Tad by approaching from this direction," said Dayna, crossing the crime scene and stalking a few paces toward the staff housing, "how could there be footprints on the other side? Did someone coming from the pergola meet him up here?"

"And why cover them up," I said, then let myself come back to earth. "Of course, this is all rank speculation. There's absolutely no physical evidence to support it whatsoever."

Dayna kept looking around.

"This is definitely not my gig," she said. "But I think there's something to this."

I told her she'd come up with an intriguing insight.

"Brilliant, really," I said aloud, and then to myself, Even if it's true, where does that leave us? Any closer to an explanation?

Dayna was clearly pleased by this, but she had the good graces to leave it at that and not try to launch another round of speculation. We poked around a little more, then drifted back to the truck. Misty was glad to see us, spinning around on the bench seat as Dayna unlocked the doors. She had a chance to pee before we took off again, our progress cut off by Fred Lumsden, whose own truck approached from the road. We both stopped and he got out of his truck and walked up to my door.

"Hi, Fred."

"Saline told me you were looking for something. Find it?"

I shook my head, sadly.

"Nobody's finding anything till spring, I'm afraid," I told him.

"Maybe you could describe what it is," he said to Dayna. "I'll keep my eye out."

"That's good of you," she said. "But it's a pretty unusual beast. If you got an e-mail address, I could send you a picture."

He rummaged around his jacket pockets until he came up with a piece of paper. He wrote down his address and handed it to Dayna.

"Saline and I share the same e-mail," he said, looking at both of us as if warning not to write anything indiscreet, the world's least likely possibility.

"Got it," said Dayna, tossing the card onto her dashboard. "I'll be in touch."

And then she drove away, heaving her truck around Fred's by riding up high on the snowbank, fighting to keep the wheels in sync as they coped with the different angles and surfaces. Fred stood and watched us go, hands at his sides and inner thoughts enclosed within layers of canvas, flannel, and quilted down vest and fur-lined parka.

14

When I got back to my office, there was a bag of cabbage and komatsuna on the stoop and an envelope stuck to my door with a piece of duct tape. I used my teeth to pull off my glove and opened the envelope, handling it by the edges. The note said, "We're still watching. Signed, your reverse gardian angels."

I was incredulous.

"That may be, geniuses, but now I'm watching you," I said out loud, banging in the code, dashing up the stairs and through the next door to the office. I plopped down in front of the monitor and rewound the tape. I booted up the computer and started downloading the last twenty-four hours into the editing program. The little dialog box told me to wait while it transferred the files, which was a mighty task. I jumped up, got out of my coat and hat, and grabbed a bottle of water from the fridge, just to burn the time.

Could it be, I asked, that those jerks are even stupider than Fleming's boys, that they didn't realize there was a security camera trained on the door? They did spell guardian wrong. That was an encouraging sign.

As I sat back down, the screen filled with about a dozen little windows, segments of the retrieved video that showed any change from the fixed background. Most were me coming and going, the FedEx guy, squirrels hopping through the snow, and Mr. Sato leaving me the bagful of leftover chopped vegetables. And then there were two guys who looked like they'd been hired by a casting agency to play the parts of Ike and Connie, though aside from body type it was a poor match. The Ike character was all Caucasian, with slicked black hair and a pale, uneven complexion. He wore a dark full-length coat that looked like wool. His eyes shifted from side to side while his partner wrote out the note and stuffed it in the envelope, then ripped off a piece of duct tape and clumsily stuck it to the door.

The lousy speller was heavy like Connie, but much taller, with a round head covered in gray buzz-cut hair. Neither looked at the camera peering through its pinhole just above the doorjamb, confirming their oversight.

Professionals plying the crime-and-punishment trades knew this fundamental fact: Most criminals, especially hired muscle, were pretty stupid. You met the occasional Franco Raffini, or an entrepreneur like Ivor Fleming, or a street kid who could have run Harvard had life's lottery put him in the right household, but on the whole, they're mostly dumb as stumps.

I think I was actually whistling with excitement as I selected the clearest shots of their faces and converted the images to JPEGs and saved them to my laptop's hard drive. I even started singing a little song that went something like, *"Gonna getcha, gonna getcha, look out you dumb bastards, we're gonna getcha now . . ."* but then stopped, disturbed by my lousy singing voice.

I pulled out my cell and called Joe Sullivan.

"You're ready to start plea bargaining?" he asked when he picked up the phone.

"No. Confessing. Not Franco, me. But I need to do it face-to-face."

"I thought we had Father Dent for that," said Sullivan.

"This is more your province."

"What did you do? How many times do we have to warn you about obstruction? What is it with you, a compulsion?"

"It's not like that. Just let me get off the phone and come see you."

He told me to meet him at the diner in Hampton Bays. He hadn't eaten since the night before, which was a shocking admission for a guy who required about two and a half times the normal person's food intake to maintain body mass, most of which was solid muscle.

"How come?" I asked.

"Let me get off the phone and I'll tell you when you get there."

The trip over to Hampton Bays was uneventful. Though if there had been events, you couldn't prove it by me. A herd of velociraptors could have run across the street and I wouldn't have noticed. As it sometimes is, my head was so full of noise a passenger in my car would have needed earplugs.

There was the steady, sonorous voice of Art Montrose, serving up an unrecognizable and thoroughly unwelcome portrait of Franco Raffini. There was Dayna's peppy enthusiasm, mimicking her dog's. The unpronounceable Buddhist Dinabandhu Pandey, with his own cheerful take on the sinister, as-yet-unmet Eliz Pritz, at this point just a reedy, clipped electronic monotone. It was all a cacophonous jumble in my mind, fighting for the floor, asserting positions that all seemed insightful and absurd at the same time.

I shook my head, trying to toss out some of the racket, and succeeded only in compromising what little control I'd managed to assert over my rebellious hair. This served a purpose, however, providing a distraction from the obsessive deliberations.

How's that for managing one's neurotic psyche?

———

Joe was at his usual spot in a booth facing the door, already with a plate of pancakes covered in strawberries and a side of ham. And a cup of coffee. And that was it.

"You're dieting," I said, sitting across from him. "Never thought I'd see the day."

He looked up darkly from his plate. "No appetite," he said.

Oh no, I thought, looking at him more closely, searching for signs of lethal disease.

"Don't look at me like that. It's not what you think."

"Not what?"

"I'm not sick. Not like that." He put down his fork and looked out the window. Then he let out an irritated sigh. "My wife threw me out of the house."

He looked back at me, not exactly defiantly but as if to say, *Okay, there, I said it out loud, to you. I shared a very intimate thing, but I'm not asking for sympathy and I refuse to show distress or weakness, so don't try to make me.*

I didn't. "That sucks," I said.

"It's been brewing. Not easy for a woman to live with a guy on the job."

He meant the cop's life, the one where you get to work long, odd hours for short money and struggle with all sorts of deviant behavior while entangled in an often rigid and irrational bureaucracy, with little in the way of sympathy from the people you're paid to protect, except in the abstract. Oh, and you also get to occasionally risk your life. If you endure all this with dedication and commitment, like Sullivan did, the odds were good there'd be someone miserable sharing your life.

"Buddy of mine has a mother-in-law apartment in Southampton Village. It's over the garage and I get one of the bays. It's a better neighborhood than I had before, I'll tell you that. Mostly summer people. Probably terrified to have a cop living among the hoity-toity."

"So it's, like, over, or is this a separation? If you don't mind me asking."

He shook his head. "I brought it up. You can ask me whatever you want. It's over. We never had kids, which she also blames on me, so that's not an issue. She's got some other guy, which in my experience with domestic situations usually seals the deal. She's scared to death I'm going to kill the idiot, but I couldn't give a crap. He's just a symptom. Having a relationship with my wife will be its own punishment. I'm just as glad."

"I'm still sorry," I said. "It's never cause for celebration, even when ultimately the right thing."

He bunched up his lips and gave a quick little nod. "You're right about that, Jackie. I haven't told anybody else, so if you wouldn't mind, just let it leak out on its own."

And then, of course, the worst thing starts to happen. I could feel the pressure as tears tried to force their way into my eye sockets. Not because Sullivan's wife left him. Because he'd picked me as the first person to tell. We spent so much time locked in professional combat that when we weren't in temporary periods of uneasy alliance, I'd forget the man's authentic heart was forthright and true. And at that moment I realized I might be one of a handful who actually understood that, and was thus worthy of his trust.

"Got it, Joe. Lips are sealed," I said as I stood up, claiming the need for an urgent bathroom run. Once there, I sat on the lowered toilet seat and dabbed my eyes until the moment passed. I pulled myself together, brushed the mop of hair away from my face, and went back to the table.

"So, what's this confession you're talking about," Sullivan said as I sat down.

I asked him to wait until I could boot up my laptop. After a few minutes, I had side-by-side, full-screen portraits of the Ike and Connie impersonators. I spun the computer around.

"Know these guys?" I asked.

He squinted at the images, frowning with concentration. "Not sure," he said. "Give me the whole thing," he added, looking up at me.

So I did, starting with the first visit by the real Ike and Connie and including my decision to drive out to the French restaurant and the subsequent conversation with the other two. I told him about visiting Ike, leaving out Sam's approach to initiating free and frank discussions. I told him I meant to bring him in as soon as I knew it wouldn't prejudice my client's case.

He listened through the whole thing without interruption, then when I was finished, he said, "Seems to me this could point the other way. These are the only elements of this case that have no obvious connection to the defendant. And the very fact that you've been warned off providing a proper defense would imply other players feel at risk, even if Franco was the one who actually committed the deed."

"That's my feeling," I said with vigor.

"I'd take the threat seriously. It's a pretty bad violation of the basic rules of engagement." He meant the unwritten agreement between criminals and law enforcement that cops, judges, and lawyers—prosecutors and defenders alike—were off-limits from threat, much less physical mistreatment. "Sorry you had to go through that," he said, running his hand along the edge of the computer screen and looking closely again at the images. "We'll be lookin' these guys up. Maybe go pay 'em a visit."

"You'll let me know, won't you, Joe? When you find out who they are?"

He smiled with half his face, which made it closer to a smirk.

"I will, but we'll be having no independent action here. I'll let you stay close on this as long as you stay close to me. There's a lot at stake, including your client's sorry ass. And your own."

"I'm sorry for any trouble I've ever caused you," I said.

"Then you can pay for breakfast," he said, standing up. "Best deal you've had in a while." He put on his coat, a pure white parka with a fringe of fur around the hood, likely surplus from Russia's Siberian Special Forces unit or something like that. "And you and Sam stay away from Ivor Fleming. We can handle him, too, without the aid of the civilian population."

"Roger that, chief. So you think there's a connection between Fleming and the Buczek case?"

"Just stay away from him. You poke at a snake, he's likely to bite."

I realized I hadn't ordered anything, so I got a yogurt and a coffee and used the diner's wireless connection to browse around on the computer, mostly in search of more cold-weather gear, which incongruously led me to sites with deals on winter vacations in the Caribbean, not that I'd be able to go. I kept looking so I could see photographs of couples cavorting in the surf in evening clothes, splayed on lounge chairs, or sipping a piña colada by the pool, backlit by the crimson setting sun, staring into each other's eyes in a way no one really does, but it doesn't matter. We're all eager to rent the illusion.

I arrived at the office just as the sun was going down. I rebooted the laptop and had an e-mail message waiting for me from UB45JK.

"Greetings from Dystopriot Land. My stubby friend said you could use a hand with the Polack-ski. Reply if you wish."

I checked the time. Four thirty. Cocktail hour! I turned up the heat and squirmed out of my clothes, down to the silk longjohns. I poured a chardonnay and lit a cigarette, which I finished by the time I'd reconnected and rebooted the laptop and checked the security camera record and my other e-mail. I poured another wine and clicked the Reply link on UB45JK's e-mail.

"Hi there, UB (hope you don't mind the abbreviation), I really would like some help," I wrote. "I don't know what time zone you're in, but I'm in for the night now. Love to hear from you."

About a half hour later, she came back.

"I'm in your time zone. I like UB, it's kind of cute. Never thought of it myself. You speak Polish?"

"*Nie*," I replied. "And that's about the only word I know. That and *Tak*." Meaning yes. "The last name's from my late husband. I was born Jacqueline O'Dwyer."

"Let's take this to IM," she wrote, meaning instant messaging, which would facilitate the back-and-forth. She gave me an IM site and instructions for reaching her.

"Same handle. Just ask for UB45JK."

When we made the connection she asked, "So what's the caper?"

"I want to do a background check on a woman whose maiden name is Katarzina Malonowski. She was born, and I guess raised, in Kraków. She's thirty-two years old. Her nickname is Zina and she claims to have a degree in economics. Her parents were Godek and Halina, also native-born Poles, I assume. They're dead. That's about all I know."

"Do you have a picture?"

I realized with some disappointment in myself that I didn't. I asked her to hold on and opened up Google to search for images of Katarzina Buczek. A slew of Eastern Europeans popped up, but only one was my Katarzina, which was all I needed. She had actually gone to a fundraiser, which in the Hamptons can put you in the crosshairs of a party photographer. There was no sign of Tad, no surprise. I copied the image, and after opening a separate e-mail, sent it to UB.

"Wow, she's really pretty. Those Mongol eyes. Probably descended from Kublai Khan. Are those lashes real?"

That's when I was fairly sure UB was a woman. I testified to their authenticity.

"She's better-looking in real life. Do you think you could get more on her?" I asked.

"Without a doubt. I have lots of BFFs in Kraków. But I can do a lot on my own."

"That's extremely good of you," I wrote.

"Happy to help any friend of Gyro's. I don't care if he's a dwarf. I'm definitely not a shortist. Is that the right word? English is a very difficult language."

Oh no, I thought. Another moral dilemma for our times. I knew damn well Randall was the opposite of a dwarf, but was she only referring to the avatar? What could I tell UB about Randall that didn't violate his privacy? Would he want me to anyway, to facilitate a better romantic connection? Luckily, she didn't ask.

"He thanks you back," I wrote. "Where do you live, anyway? I'm just curious."

"New Britain, Connecticut," she wrote back. "Throw a rock in any direction and you hit a Pole."

"So why not New Warsaw?" I wrote back.

"Good question. I'll take it up at the next town meeting."

We went back and forth for at least another hour, her comparing her life in the States with life in Poland, me rhapsodizing over Polish food, her complaining that her countrymen were too shy about touting Poland's international accomplishments, me agreeing, but attributing this reluctance to historical persecution and arbitrarily throwing in a dollop of complaint over the treatment of the Irish, her admitting she coveted the skin of an Irish friend of hers, me reflecting wistfully over the loss of my size 4 sometime early in college (I'm still a generous 6, for the record) and so on. All in all, we had a great time, and for all I knew, she was just an automatic-rifle-toting, computer-generated elf in futuristic combat gear.

After we signed off, I felt an odd mixture of loss and relief. Glad for the conversation, intimidated by the implications. I was only in my late thirties, and yet it felt like the world was whizzing by me into the future and I was already in its wake. And yet I had no fear of catching up. It wasn't that hard, if you wanted to try.

And that was the crux. If you wanted to try.

15

The concept of a memorial service for Tad Buczek was so incongruous that I was taken by surprise when I read the announcement on the bulletin board inside the front door of the church. It was going to happen in a few hours. Though officially called Our Lady of Poland Roman Catholic Church, it was naturally favored by the Polish community, but also people of other ethnic stripes who would never feel comfortable in the other, much bigger Catholic church across town frequented by our wealthier brethren.

I was there to see Father Dent, a man whose capacity for unheralded imposition passeth all understanding. I had an ambivalent relationship with God. I hadn't been to church since my father died, which left no one else to make me go, my mother being a declared but uncommitted atheist. Father Dent never once told me I should. In fact, he never told me to do anything. Never scolded or criticized or even chided me. Yet for some reason, I always knew where he stood on things. I'd been intruding on him since the first time we chatted, at my mother's funeral. My father had already gone kicking and screaming into that good night, leaving my mother in a state of shattered exhaustion from which she never recovered, dying shortly thereafter herself. I didn't think this was fair of God, and I told Father Dent just that.

"God might have different ways of regarding the word 'fair,'" he said to me, "though I'm sure He'd find yours among the approved definitions." And we'd been confabulating ever since.

"I think I might come to Tad's funeral mass today," I said to the Father, who was up on the altar leaning over a table filled with folded fabric.

"I have a terrible feeling that not all of the church's altar linens have found their way back from the kind women who offered to do the month's cleaning and pressing," he said.

"A carpenter friend of mine calls that 'growing little legs.'"

"I like the image if not the implications," he said with his soft, heavily Brooklyn–inflected voice.

"Did you know Tad?" I asked.

He stood up from the table and shook his head. "Never had the honor. Though I welcome his first visit to our church." I filled in the blanks—*Stay away if you want, young lady; we'll get you eventually.*

"I'm defending the man accused of his murder," I said. "The prosecution has a pretty compelling case."

"Though surely you're prepared with convincing alternatives."

I looked around at the wainscoting along the white walls and the stained-glass, gold-leafed altar and coffered ceiling, and felt the divine weightlessness of the place.

"I'm not. There aren't any."

"Can't win 'em all," he said, smiling kindly.

"Maybe some shouldn't be won," I said.

"I'm not entirely up on the legal system, but isn't that a judgment outside your purview as defense attorney?"

"Maybe not as a human being," I said.

"Ah. So we're inside my territory."

"And that is?"

"Crises of faith."

Man, we got there fast, I thought, not ready to admit my complicity in that. It was easier to just think of Father Dent as unusually gifted at getting to the point. Can't spend all day in the little wooden booths hemming and hawing.

"I guess I'm lucky," I said. "All my other guilty clients were unambiguously so, and my job was to simply make the consequences as endurable as possible. Parole in lieu of sentence, plea bargains, petitions for prisons close to the family, that kind of thing."

"So you're sure he's guilty," he said.

"No. I have my doubts. But they're hardly reasonable."

"So what are they based upon?"

I admit the answer didn't come as quickly as it should have.

"Faith?" I said.

He smiled. "If you still believe something deep in your heart, in the total absence of demonstrable fact, this is what faith is. Do you think it's an accident that everyone has these feelings?"

I looked at his small head, his delicate features, and his short-cropped white hair contrasting nicely with the black priest's shirt, and realized I had no idea how old he was. I didn't know what his past was like, why he became a priest, if he had a family, played sports in high school, or ever spent a night in jail. I knew absolutely nothing about him. I'd never asked.

"Father Dent, you're such a pisser, if I'm allowed to say that in a House of God."

"We maintain a wide latitude."

He went back to examining the table full of embroidered cloth.

"I'll be back. For the service," I said.

"I'll be here. Performing it."

"Do you care how I'm dressed?"

He looked over at me. "Everyone looks like an Eskimo these days. You'll fit right in."

I killed the next few hours at the nice restaurant on Main Street. I sat at the big U-shaped bar and ate lunch, washed down with ice water and green tea. No wine. I wasn't going to make my first appearance at the Polish church in years with half a buzz on.

The bartender was a friend of mine, a transported Brit named Geordie who'd failed to shed much of his Britishness.

"So we've taken the pledge, have we?" he said when I placed my order.

"I knew you were going to say that," I said.

"You did?"

"People who conspire in my routines always notice deviations," I said.

"Does that make them deviants?"

"Don't try that rubbish on a sober girl. Drunks aren't the only ones with a sense of humor."

"Then I'm doomed," he said, his evanescent smile belying the thought and proving it at the same time.

The church was filling up quickly when I got back. This part didn't surprise me. My time with Pete felt like a blur of huge family gatherings— all the official American holidays like Christmas and Thanksgiving, but also notable events like the Assumption of the Blessed Virgin Mary and St. Joseph's Day were all occasions for hordes of people, including swarms of children, to descend on one homestead or the other—often Tad's, the size of his property trumping the contentiousness of his personality. At first it was unsettling being thrust into intimate closeness with all these people I didn't know, but after a while, I grew to like it. I liked the instinctive sense of family unity, the strongest brand of community. I was sure the century and a half of immigrant struggle, and ethnic prejudice, played its part. You had to know which of your neighbors to truly trust, who would come to your aid without hesitation or hope of recompense.

I recognized most of them, usually remembering their names. My greatest worry was that I was now back on the outside, no longer a trusted member of the clan. Worse, I was the one defending the guy accused of killing the family member lying in the coffin in front of the altar. But those fears were unwarranted. I got nothing of the sort. In fact, all I got were warm handshakes and bright smiles.

I sat in the back pew and suffered through the service, fighting off distressing associations with my own family at church, a far tinier group that nonetheless managed to optimize the least engaging aspects of the religious experience.

I perked up when Father Dent walked down from the altar and stood next to the coffin to say a few words about our departed.

"Since everyone in this room knew our brother Tadzio Buczek, there's no need to gloss over the fact that he wasn't always an easy man to deal with. From what you all have told me over the years, his passions burned brightly, and a lot of people got caught in the flames." He paused for a moment and looked down, then looked up again, and said in his thickest Brooklynese, "But you got to admit, the man was never dull."

A soft murmur of laughter rippled through the congregation.

"It's been my experience that most people are good-hearted, hard-working, compassionate, and steadfast. All of you fall into that category." Another pause. "Most of the time," he added with a warm smile.

Another titter ran through the church.

"These are fine qualities, and we wouldn't have a civilization without them. But there's a certain consistency that settles into a community of the responsible. Too much of a good thing can round over the corners, dampen the creative spirit. Maybe this is why God invented guys like Tad. To keep the edge on the blade. To poke our essentially conformist sensibilities once in a while. So we don't get too comfortable."

The deepest quiet descended over the gathering. Hundreds of men, women, and children, and not a sound.

"If this is a calling God assigns to some of us, then let's celebrate the fact that Tad carried out his mission darn well."

I remember at that point him looking directly at me, but I'm sure everyone there felt the same way.

Like all good Catholic funerals we had another robust round of ritual and commentary at the cemetery, where some of Tad's family bequests had been used to thaw out a sizeable piece of ground, his last chance to meddle with the earth. This was another place I thoroughly enjoyed spending a little time in, as necrophiliac as that sounds. Since the monuments were organized by size and extravagance, it was a person's last and best opportunity to jump social status, assuming he or she could scrape up the funds. My favorite was a grim, rough-hewn cross, in front of which was a white marble statue of an angel with wings spread as if just landing or about to take off.

And the names: Karvoski, Waskiewicz, Trzcilnski, Kochanowicz, Wasik. Sturdy, serious names to go with the owners—muscular, resilient men and women whose ingenuity and forbearance will never be fully known.

I became so engrossed looking at the gravestones that I wandered away from the funeral party. Being alone, it was that much more bizarre to come across another big memorial, this one with four names chiseled into the granite, including Peter Swaitkowski, beloved son lost too early.

There was no one there to hear the cry of shock that started in my chest and became much more one of sorrow by the time it left my lips. I'd shoved so much of that time out of my memory that even his spot within this community of the departed had been lost.

I knew then why I was drawn to Father Dent, but never into his church. It was far too fraught with poignant associations. It reminded me that people close to me had a hard time sticking around. I was only seven when my older brother was whisked into an oblivion as everlasting as death. I'd barely made it out of law school when my father suddenly disintegrated, forcing me back to the East End to stand by my beleaguered mother, who only lasted long enough to see my father dead and buried.

And then Pete hits that tree a half mile from our house, leaving a huge gash that I have to watch heal into a burled scar. See what happens, Harry, I said to myself, when people get close to me?

I looked back at the congregation, which seemed to be breaking up, with couples and small groups moving slowly back to the long lineup of cars. Tears had found their way into my eyes, but I wasn't really crying. It was all too enormous and awful and unfathomable. So I just mopped the wetness off my cheeks and walked back to join the caravan while it was still possible to be absorbed into the collective grief.

The last stop of the day was the senior center behind the church. Though run by the Town of Southampton, it was built on church property and the parish was its greatest patron. Partly to assure a ready facility for these kinds of events.

I got a chance to catch up with some of the family members I'd grown closest to, and finally had that deferred glass of wine. Even though I knew the welcome I received was genuine, I soon realized why defending Franco was a nonissue. They all thought I'd taken the gig to make sure some other lawyer from outside the family wouldn't get him off. They all assumed with me at the helm the bastard would fry for sure.

That put an interesting spin on my prior conversation with Father Dent.

I eventually worked my way around to members of the Buczek household once the lion's share of the family had had a chance to convey condolences. Zina was gracious and dignified throughout. She looked like a million bucks in her classic, conservatively cut black suit. Whatever the family ultimately thought of her, none of that ugly slander was then on display.

Holding to form, Fred and Saline were off in a deep corner next to a table full of food, avoiding eye contact by concentrating on little plates piled high with golobki—cabbages stuffed with some kind of spicy meat—almost as delectable as paluszki. I approached anyway.

"Hi, folks," I said. "How're we doing?"

"We're fine," said Fred. Saline said nothing.

I spent the next ten minutes or so trying to spark a legitimate conversation, and in return got a lesson on how to convey thoughts one syllable at a time. But they didn't know who they were dealing with. Persistence is my long suit.

The real break came when Fred was recruited by some other men to help set up tables for dinner, as if the endless flow of Polish soul food was insufficient sustenance. He left me with Saline.

"Got a job to do? Don't worry, Fred'll get it done," she surprised me by saying.

"Nice to be counted on," I said, not sure where she was going with that.

"That's what I call him. Fred'llgetitdone. Like it's all one word."

"Sounds like a handy guy to have around the house."

"You bet. My house, Zina's house, most of the houses these people live in. The family house servant."

Okay, I thought, now I get it.

"What's it been like with Tad gone?" I said. "If you don't mind me asking."

She used a piece of celery to stab a golobki and shoved it into her mouth. "It's harder for Fred. I was already stuck with Zina most of the time. To be honest with you, it's easier to deal with her without Tad around. They weren't exactly Mr. and Mrs. Compatibility. He had his ways of doing things, she had hers. Now it's all hers. With Fred, after being told what to do for twenty years, you can't expect him to always know what to do on his own. I've said 'What would Tad do?' probably a million times since he died."

Saline the taciturn and put-upon had apparently been replaced by an entirely different version, freed from her silence by the departure of her husband.

"So you guys are staying on," I said.

She looked vaguely alarmed. "Never heard anything to the contrary," she said. "Have you?"

I assured her I hadn't.

"I was just curious," I said. "Will you need to replace Franco?"

She leered. "The Italian swordsman? Exactly which of his roles do you think need replacing?"

I tried to apply my least worldly expression, eyes wide with curiosity. "I'm sorry, did he have a variety of roles?"

She cast her eyes to the side, leaned closer, and whispered out of the side of her mouth. "I work day and night at the main house and sleep in the staff house. There's nothing that goes on there that I don't know about."

I acted mildly shocked.

"You're suggesting that Mrs. Buczek and Franco were having some sort of liaison?" I said, also whispering.

She looked side to side. "Not suggesting. Telling. And it's not a guess. *I saw them.*"

"In flagrante?"

"Delicto. Tad was away. I thought Zina had gone with him. Apparently not. They didn't even know I was looking. Too busy. With what, I'll let you imagine."

I would have preferred she'd been more specific. My imagination had too hard a time limiting the possibilities on its own.

"Oh my," I said.

She nodded in that exaggerated way people do as a stand-in for "You know what I mean."

"How long ago was this going on?"

"Almost since the day the man arrived. I watched her watch him. She immediately started giving him the odd jobs Freddy usually did. Hey girls, gather 'round. I'm your handyman."

"So, I'm sorry to ask, but does that mean you think Franco had a reason to kill Tad? That he wanted to have Zina all to himself?"

Saline's pleasure in conspiratorial talk was flagrantly evident. It wasn't hard to figure out where the cops and Paulina learned of Franco and Zina's indiscretions.

"What do you think? Isn't that what he does? Kill off husbands? But I'm not worried," she said, literally winking at me in a broad, cartoonish way. "I've heard you've got everything under control. He won't get away with it."

This is the kind of thing they don't prepare you for in law school. Quite the contrary. Most of my professors would have you rear up in moral indignation and declare outrage at that sort of speculation. Instead, I asked, "Did Tad have any idea what was going on?"

She actually said "pshaw."

"That man never saw anything, never knew anything or suspected anything. If all you think about is yourself, you have no idea what other people are doing. Even if it's against you. Textbook Narcissistic Personality Disorder," she added, popping a piece of paluszki in her mouth.

That stopped me in my tracks a bit. I'd begun to realize there was a lot more to the lumbering woman than met the eye.

"I actually know what that means," I said. "It's an important thing to know in my line of work. But not many people do."

She displayed an interesting mix of smugness and resentment. "I'm a trained psychiatric nurse," she said, leaning even farther into me and using a voice now pitched almost to the inaudible, yet with an odd urgency. "It was the best I could do after leaving medical school. Ran out of money."

"I'm sorry," I said.

"You don't have to do what you're trained to do," she said, as if it were a mantra she'd chanted to herself so often it had lost the essence of its meaning. "You can do what you want to do."

"I agree with that completely," I lied shamelessly. "Some regrets are entirely misplaced," I also said, which I actually believed.

She stood straighter, recovering most of her slouching posture.

"Regrets are for fools," she said. "I've never wasted a second on what-ifs. Only what is."

I acknowledged this was a good philosophy.

"Kind of a short-form Serenity Prayer," I said.

"Prayer is for fools. Never was a God, never will be."

This time I looked around, hoping Father Dent wasn't within hearing range. Not that he couldn't have handled it. Would probably figure out a way to convert her on the spot. It just seemed discourteous to say things like that in a room full of devout Catholics. I also looked up toward the heavens, hoping that any lightning heading her way would avoid collateral damage.

"Anyway," I said, eager to shift gears again, "I haven't had a chance to offer my condolences to you over Tad. It must be hard after all those years."

She nodded, as if I'd cleverly uncovered a heretofore secret well of pain.

"You have no idea," she said, back in sotto voce, her stern face, inches from mine, plunging into abject remorse. "The void it's left. The absolute void."

I had a million things to ask her, to probe for, but what I heard coming out of my mouth instead was an offer to get her a drink, suddenly really wanting one myself. She took a pass, and even though I was probably blowing a priceless opportunity to record more unguarded commentary, I'd had enough. I had to get away.

It was far smarter for me to get back to Geordie's bar than to drink any more at Tad's send-off. I knew myself well enough to sense my own slow collapse into the kind of overwrought sentimentality I'd surely not want to expose to the Polish throng. He had a gin and tonic waiting for me on the bar before I had a chance to sit down.

"I saw you get out of your car." He pointed through the big glass doors to where the Volvo was parked. "I could tell."

"Why can't I just do my job without putting myself through all this damn emotional turmoil?" I said, sliding up onto the barstool and snatching up the G&T like it was a lifesaving elixir.

"If you didn't feel anything, luv, you wouldn't be much good at your job as it is, now, would you?" he said.

Priests and bartenders, I thought. Keep 'em coming.

16

Franco looked even worse than when I last saw him. His Italian face was paler than mine and hung so low it looked like it might slide off the front of his head and pour onto the table.

"Are you okay?" I asked him.

"Sure. I'm in some kind of hole for the rest of my life. It's really nice here in county jail, 'cause I've got my own cell. But it'll be even better when I get to prison and find out who my boyfriend's going to be."

"It's too early to go all defeatist," I said.

"Okay. I'll wait till after they convict. Till then, I'm happy as a lark."

"Fine," I said, annoyed. "Wallow if you want. I'm not giving up. Unless you want me to. I was related to Tad Buczek. By marriage, but related nonetheless. On that basis, the court would gladly assign you a public defender if you fired me."

That surprised him. He shook his head. "I don't care about that," he said. "I wouldn't have called if I thought Tad meant enough to you to mess up my case. You wouldn't anyway. You're not that kind of person."

"Thank you," I said. "Though you might not like me as much after I ask the next question."

He shrugged. "Ask away."

"Why do you keep lying about what happened that night?"

His eyes opened in horror, and it looked like he could start crying. "Jesus, Jackie, I'm not lying. Quit sayin' that."

"Somebody is. You told me you were in bed with Zina when Tad called to say he couldn't find her and was going out in the storm to look. But first he was going to check on the woodshed, after which he called you to come help. Why go check on the woodshed by himself and not bring along a hired hand? What, to give you time to wrap up things with his wife?"

"It's what happened," he said in a quiet whine.

"Zina told me *you* called Tad to say you were worried about the shed, and that Tad went out to meet you there to shovel off the roof. After he didn't return, she got worried and tried to reach both of your cell phones, with no success. The police and the ADA have certainly heard the same story, which means she'll be testifying to it under oath."

I suppose you can become so despondent there's no lower emotional rung, yet Franco seemed to find it.

"She's going to throw me under the bus," he said. "Big surprise. Don't they all?"

"Who's they?"

"You people. Women," he said.

"Like Eliz did?"

He looked down at his hands.

"I thought we'd already been through that one," he said.

"We're only getting started," I said. "You sure you want to stick to your Zina story?"

"Do you want me to make up a different one? Will that help with the case? I can do that if you want. If you want me to stick to the truth, then that's the truth."

"I want you to stick to the truth," I said, this time my voice lowered for emphasis. "Did you meet Tad at the woodshed?"

"No. I told you. I was on the way when I tripped over him. I cleared a bunch of ice out of the way and checked his pulse. The back of his head was covered in blood. He was dead. The snow was coming down so hard I thought I should get him under cover, which I admit was stupid. So I went back to get a tarp and rolled him onto it and dragged him down the hill to the covered part of the pergola. Then I picked him up, with great difficulty, and put him on the picnic table. Then I covered him with the tarp and called you. End of story."

I looked at him in silence for a few moments. He didn't like that, and he showed it by looking at the wall at the other end of the room.

"I reviewed the police photos from that night. The path created by dragging the body was at least five feet wide—more than you'd make by dragging a single body on a tarp in one direction, from Hamburger Hill to the pergola. How would you explain that?"

Franco's fallen face tightened with concern. For a guy who'd endured dozens of aggressive interrogations, he wasn't very good at hiding his inner turmoil.

"You drag a body as big as Tad's down a hill and see if you can keep a straight line," he said, almost convincingly.

"I'll do that if necessary," I said. "Though you know you can't double the width of the swath without retracing the path. So no. Don't buy it."

He went back to looking at his wringing hands. "I couldn't drag him back up that hill. I'm not that strong."

"Yes you are," I said. "You're a natural athlete. You just act like you're a pathetic hangdog. It's a good defensive ploy: Stay nonthreatening."

"It's not what happened," he said with a certain finality. "And I'm not a pathetic hangdog. I'm just a little depressed."

"A little? You'd drive Mary Poppins to suicide."

"I don't know who that is."

I whipped my little notebook at his face and he caught it with his left hand. I put out my own hand and he gave it back to me.

"Funny," he said. "Proves nothing."

"Why didn't you tell Art Montrose you'd been wiped out in a bad trade? Why did he have to learn on his own?" I asked.

He lurched back as if I'd hit him with a rock.

"He didn't know that," he said.

"Of course he did. He knew everything. The whole setup. Baiting Donald with constant phone calls between you and Eliz, credit-card tabs at hotel restaurants, the birthday gift of a rotisserie that her husband had no interest in, that last call to him from your cell phone as he was about to board a plane to Seattle, causing him to rush back to Long Island, perfectly timed to confront you at his house with his wife, and oh, how convenient, a sword!"

Franco slammed his hand down on the table loudly enough to cause the cop sitting outside to look in the door. I told her everything was okay, that we didn't have to move to where they could monitor us through a one-way mirror. She left reluctantly.

"She told me she loved me," said Franco.

"Yeah? When was that?"

"Before Donny was killed. After that, she said she couldn't be near the man who killed her husband. The husband she hated." He stretched out the word "hated" to attach emphasis. "Okay, I needed a lifeline. I didn't need what happened. What kind of crazy idiot would go through the shit I went through to get his hands on some rich broad's money? I know other rich broads who'd look after me just for the asking. Not as pretty as Eliz, but you take what you can get."

My perception of Franco had whipsawed back and forth so many times during the conversation it was giving me vertigo. I put my head in my hands to try to stabilize things.

"Sorry, Jackie," he said, misinterpreting. "I didn't mean to say 'broad.' I know that's disrespectful."

"What did you think when Eliz dropped you?" I asked, my head still in my hands.

"You know what I thought. I was the one who was set up. But if I try to take her down for it, I'm going down with her. Who'd believe I wasn't in on it all the way? Obviously not Montrose. Or you, either," he added with a touch of bitterness.

"You should have told me," I said. "I can't trust you if you withhold things from me. What else haven't you told me?"

He sat a little straighter in his chair and put both hands out on the table, clasped in front.

"That rotisserie was still in the box when I got there that night. She asked me if I could assemble it, that she'd tell Donny she'd hired a guy to get it ready as a surprise. So I did, but she told me not to put the skewers in the rotating thing, that she wanted to clean them first. So fine."

"They were loose," I said.

"I didn't grab the skewer when Donny came at me. She handed it to me. What a putz."

"Why did you call Donny at the airport?" I asked.

"I didn't. I'd lost that phone two days before. That was the last call it ever made. You can check the phone records. Look, what difference does all this make, anyway? That's over with. I've got a much bigger problem here."

Since I was so insistent on his candor, I felt it was only fair to share it back.

"It makes a difference to me," I said, "if you're really a killer or not. I know it's not a distinction that's relevant to the strict definition of my role, but that's tough."

He looked down at his clenched hands. "I'm not a killer, Jackie. I didn't even really stab Donny Pritz. He practically ran into that skewer. He'd lost his damn mind."

It might have been a less pure form of faith than Father Dent had in mind, but at that moment I decided the war between my head and heart would need to have a ceasefire and begin to approach the situation as a unified front. And it didn't matter which part of the team believed which part of the story. My entire being was going to believe what I wanted it to believe, and that would have to be good enough.

When I returned to the office I forced myself to read the e-mail piling up in my inbox and saw a recent delivery from rangstrom@nytimes. com. There was an attachment, which I downloaded and opened right away, seeing the opening line of an article: "The first thing you notice about Attorney Jacqueline Swaitkowski is her restless energy. Even when sitting next to her in a Japanese restaurant, you feel like you're in the company of a perpetual-motion machine."

And it went on from there for about five hundred words I couldn't bear to read.

"Crap," I said out loud.

I read the e-mail.

"Just a rough first draft," it said. "I don't usually do this—the *Times* would never allow pre-pub review—but I wanted to give you a feel for where I'm going with this."

"Crap, crap."

I read through the rest of my e-mail. There was nothing there relating to the Buczek case, which was good, since I could distract myself with work I owed all my other clients who deserved as much attention as Franco Raffini. This took me well into the evening to finish, and I was about to reward myself for the effort when a ping told me a new e-mail had arrived. It was from Randall Dodge.

"I connected with a source I used to have at Interpol," he wrote. "He can run a check on Ms. Malonowski if you still want."

"I definitely still want," I wrote back. "Haven't heard from UB, but the more checkers the merrier."

This was the point in the day when I normally went out to get something to eat, often on my own. I hated to be afraid of the dark, to have my freedom of movement compromised in any way. I decided I couldn't let it happen. That I couldn't let those sons of bitches ruin my life.

I was about to shut down the computer and head out when another ping sounded. Almost relieved that I had a reason to delay, I clicked on the e-mail.

It was from Joe Sullivan.

"I got something on your two boys," it said. "Call when you can."

I called him as fast as I could get out the cell phone and hit the speed dial.

"That took a long time," he said.

"I really want to hear what you have to say, but I have a proposal to make."

"I'm listening," he said.

I mentioned a restaurant around the corner from the one on Main Street in Southampton Village, more of a locals' joint that he'd likely favor.

"Meet me there," I said, "and I'll buy you dinner."

"You don't have to do that."

"I do. I'm afraid to go out at night and I owe you a favor. Then you can escort me home and I'll owe you another one."

He relented and I left soon after, surviving the walk from the outside door to the car with only an elevated heart rate to the worse. When I got to the place, Joe was standing near the bar inside a pack of men, most wearing baseball caps and heavy work boots, and all drinking beer out of the bottle.

"Who's the date?" one of them asked when I broke into the circle and Sullivan said hello.

"Not a date," I said. "Professional meeting. With burgers."

None of them saw the distinction. I was single, he was by himself, we were having dinner together, so it was a date. Since they all seemed to like the idea, why not. No harm was done.

"They know about your situation?" I asked as we sat down at a table in the back of the restaurant.

He nodded. "One of them's my friend with the apartment. None of them are cops, so it'll be another week before word gets to HQ. No biggie."

He reached into the inside pocket of the jacket he'd worn under his white parka and pulled out his casebook. So I pulled out my own notebook. Pages were flipped through and pens clicked and at the ready.

"Thought those guys were from Ivor Fleming?" he said. "Congratulations, you've now moved up to a higher grade of criminal."

The waitress came over and we ordered drinks and dinner at the same time to minimize interruptions.

After the drinks came, Sullivan referred to his book, then said, "It's nice to be living near New York City. It's such a melting pot of lowlifes representing every corner of the earth. Every ethnic group has its own organization and its own special turf. So how surprising is it that the Polish would have their very own mob?"

"Not surprising at all. Depressingly," I said.

"They operate sort of like an independent subsidiary of the Russians, who are a lot bigger but sometimes need to work through other groups with connections in different countries and ethnic neighborhoods in the city. Since, like everything else, the mob has embraced globalization, you need feet on the ground."

He turned around his casebook and showed me where he'd checked two unpronounceable names spelled with all the diacritics that make the words look like centipedes.

"Can we just call them Yogi and Boo Boo?" I asked, writing the real names in my own book, squiggles and all.

"Fair enough. They been a team for a while. As I thought, basic muscle used to handle the day-to-day, leg-breaking, window-smashing, head-cracking requirements of your average organized crime operation. It's not that challenging a career intellectually, but you get plenty of exercise and the opportunity to meet new people."

"So we don't know who sent them," I said.

He shook his head. "Could be any one of several Polish or Russian bosses working out of Brighton Beach and other parts of Brooklyn. There're a lot of scams going on, and a pair of neighborhood guys born in America would probably have plenty of work."

"So the Poles don't have a niche, a specialty like bank robbery or undocumented pierogis?"

"They're technically into everything our original Italian American–style organizations are into, but the international dimension tells me they'd like import-export. I'm just a humble country cop, but this is my guess."

"So drug trafficking, money laundering, smuggling, anything involving transport."

"Right. A lot of stuff goes in and out of there under the nose of the Port Authority," he said. "You can't expect them to search every container, check every manifest. You'd have to talk to somebody who knows a lot more about that stuff than I do."

"I have just the man. The bigger question is why muscle me over Franco's trial? Why would they want him put away so badly?"

Our food arrived, and he waited till the waitress left to answer.

"No idea, Counselor. Though we know just about everything in this case has to do with being Polish, with the exception of Ivor Fleming, who's the only Dutch-Filipino gangster I'm aware of. At least we don't have to waste our time with the Colombians or the Jamaicans, who scare everybody."

"You say 'we.' You and I can't do anything about a couple of jamokes in Brooklyn."

"You're right," he said. "We'll have to deal with them on our home turf. Which basically turns you into mobster bait. You should have protection."

"No," I said, so quickly I almost cut him off. "I need my freedom of movement. I appreciate it, but I can't be hamstrung like that."

He didn't push it. We'd had this conversation before and he knew where it would end up.

"But you do want me to escort you home?" he said.

"I do. Just this once. So I can take a little vacation from the twitchy nerves."

He toasted me with his beer bottle, noticed it was empty, and waved it at the passing waitress.

"You got it. Maybe we'll get lucky and they'll try to jump you again."

"Maybe we will," I said without questioning his definition of luck.

17

Knowing a cop is going to follow you home after a night out really puts a governor on the booze intake. All for the better. So we got through dinner sticking to safe, non-emotionally threatening subjects, and after Sullivan walked me to the outside door, shook my hand, and waited for me to wave to him from the top of the stairs, I still had plenty of vital energy left for another go at the computer.

To my delight, there was an IM message waiting from UB45JK.

"Our public databases are not as good as yours, but as far as I can tell there is no such person as Katarzina Malonowski. At least no one with that name who is 32 years old, born in Kraków the child of Godek and Halina, with a degree in economics. My friends over there who have friends who would know better than me say the same thing. I will try searching more, but have no high hopes. I have the pic you sent, which we can post to Facebook and other 'Do you know this person?' sites. That might work."

I wrote back, "Thanks so much for doing all that. One other place to look are chat rooms. Zina said that's how she met Tad."

"That's easy," she wrote, a few minutes later. "Natrafić.czat.net."

"That's easy?"

"It's nat.net for short. That's the only site they use over here to meet people in Poland. You can chat in English or Polish. There's a public forum for basic meet and greet, but as soon as things get going, you retire to a private room. Not my thing. No bunkers or cyborgs to blow up."

I thanked her again. "I owe you," I wrote.

"No worries. One thing you could do for me. Give Gyro a ham and cheese croissant. That's what he always orders in Dystopriot Land, but it's kinda hard to taste it virtually."

I assured her this would be easily accomplished. Then I took a chance.

"I can tell him where you live, what you look like? What you do for a living?"

It took a little while for her to write back, so I had plenty of time to kick myself for being so uncool and butting in where I didn't belong.

"Tell him to friend me. It's all there," she wrote, attaching the link.

I instantly clicked on the link and there she was, though it was hardly all there. Her avatar was the only photo and the only personal information was "Live in my grandmother's basement in New Britain, Connecticut." And her name, Urszula Bednarczyk. Maybe that's what she meant. As long as he had her name, he could get everything else. And she was probably right.

When I logged off UB's IM site, I called Burton Lewis on his secret cell phone, as always feeling privileged to have that access.

"Hello, Jackie. How goes the war?"

"You mean the fog of war? I have a legal question."

"I'll do my best."

"How do I get into a private chat room?" I asked.

"You don't without a subpoena. Assuming the site has the standard privacy policy. The police could also obtain a search warrant. If they choose to use the information in court, you could see it during discovery."

"I can't wait that long."

"Give me the particulars and I'll see what our central office can do."

I told him about nat.net, which a quick search had turned up in a town outside Chicago, one of the largest Polish American communities in the United States. I spelled out the administrator's unpronounceable name and told him I'd e-mail their privacy policy.

"Sounds like you're moving things along," he said after I finished a broader briefing.

"I wish I felt that way. It's more like I have this tangle of stuff that I'm just poking with a stick."

"Do you feel more certain about Franco?"

"Yeah. I'm certain he's lying. I just don't know what about."

After hanging up, I wrote to Randall and gave him the news on Zina, preliminary though it was. I asked if his man in Interpol could focus on identifying the photograph, something they should be a lot better at than UB's social networks. I also told him I had UB's name and did he want it.

"Shit, yeah," is the answer I got back about ten minutes later. So I sent it to him and suggested a trip on Facebook.

I spent the rest of the night Googling the names of the two Polish goons, yielding very little at first beyond a few arrests in and around Brooklyn for things you'd expect. Assault, threats of bodily harm, stalking, property damage, none making their way to successful prosecution, probably for lack of reliable witnesses.

Then I snuck in a back door of my own, unrelated to Randall's application—a document file I'd stumbled on once that cataloged a variety of things, including the histories and current circumstances of convicted felons. I dropped the names into the search box and waited.

Yogi's last name popped up. It was attached to a guy doing life at Pendlefield Penitentiary. I cross-referenced it with Yogi himself, and there it was. Brother to Yogi. Pendlefield was a big prison, divided into lots of discrete sections to reduce unwanted communications between inmates. That Yogi thought this would be a swell destination for Franco meant something. Probably the obvious. It would be his last.

After that, with my eyes burning with exhaustion, I went back to browsing travel and tourism sites, with an emphasis on anything displaying a coconut or attractive local people with open, welcoming arms.

The place where I now lived didn't look like it could be on the same planet as those other places. To reassure myself, I searched for summer scenes of the Hamptons and was rewarded by a flood of lush images of sun-burnt dunes, party tents, and greyhound-thin girls in bikinis, jewelry, and high heels. But even those seemed so fake. That wasn't even the Hamptons I knew. They were just the distorted clichés of out-of-town photographers. Or maybe it was all a hallucination. Maybe the searing cold and slog of snow-choked roads and sidewalks out there was all there ever was.

I checked the online weather report. Another big storm was on the way.

Maybe this was a good time to go to bed.

Sam woke me up the next day by leaning on the back-door buzzer and waving at the pinhole camera. I could barely see him on the monitor through his vaporous breath and my ravaged eyes. Eddie was there, too, looking up at the camera like he knew what it was.

I got out of bed and stumbled around the bedroom, finding whatever clothing was both in reach and suited to the purpose of modesty and warmth. The result was a T-shirt under a down vest, sweatpants, and fuzzy slippers. I cranked up the thermostat to help with the warmth part.

I buzzed him through the outside door and waited for him at the top of the stairs. Eddie got there first, alternating between saying hello and sniffing all over the floor. Sam clomped up the stairs and handed me a bagful of coffee and sugary, puffy things from the real Italian place in the village.

"The least I could do," he said.

"You're right. You could do a lot more."

I let them into the foyer that used to be the reception area when the apartment was an office full of surveyors, and then into the kitchen, which had a table where I made him sit until I'd extracted the coffee and dumped the pastries onto a plate. From there we went into the living room, where there were opposing chairs, which only took a few minutes to clear of junk so we could sit down. Eddie occupied himself sniffing at the boxes and stacks of printed matter littering the floor.

"Do you realize how little space you actually live in?" he asked, looking around.

"Don't start in, not at this time of the morning."

"Do you realize how much more life you'd have if you got up earlier?"

"Is this why you came over here and woke me up? So you could be an asshole?" I asked him.

"Nah, I could do that anytime. I got a note from Ivor. Hand-delivered to my mailbox. He wants a sit-down."

I took a sip of the cream-and-sugar-infused coffee, which remarkably was still quite hot.

"Interesting. Any other details?"

"That's all it said. A personal note from the man himself. Evil little gnome that he is."

"So how does that happen?" I asked.

"We sit down with him."

"Out in the open with lots of witnesses. A sharpshooter with his sights trained on Ivor the whole time."

"Don't know any sharpshooters."

"We'll just tell him there's one," I said. "Good enough."

"I have a much cooler idea," he said.

"One that couldn't wait until after eight o'clock?"

"No. The sit-down is scheduled for nine. You'll want to be better dressed. Though we can do it from here."

I almost choked on my latte. "What are you talking about?"

"Skype. The perfect solution. Voice and video, a face-to-face with no danger of anyone shooting anyone else. Twenty-first century, baby. You do have the application?"

I drew the collar of my shirt to my throat as if the camera was already on me.

"How do you know about Skype? You don't even own a computer. What happened to Sam the Luddite?"

"I don't need a computer. I've got a grown daughter. I Skype her once a week from a soundproof booth in the Southampton library. A little jerky, but clear enough. Very cool shit. Ivor was all over it. He doesn't want to get shot any more than we do."

I pointed the mouth of my latte at him.

"You've been cooking this up for a while," I said. "Thanks for the warning."

He squinted, the closest thing he ever got to a sign of regret.

"I probably should have told you, but you'd only just fret over it the whole time. This is better. No time for fretting. But you ought to take a shower and fix yourself up. You don't want Ivor thinking you're a slob," he said, looking around the room again.

I huffed loudly but did as he asked, keeping my hair dry under a shower cap but otherwise giving myself the full treatment. I emerged not only clean, but professionally suited up.

"That's what I'm talking about," said Sam. "We'll keep the camera at about waist up, so you can lose the pumps if you want."

We went across the hall to the office and my computer. With a little rearranging of the stuff on my desk, we were both able to sit in front of the screen and be inside the camera frame. Eddie did some more sniffing, then curled up on one of the few naked patches of carpet.

"This is too weird," I said. "Sit-downs are supposed to be in a private room in the back of an Italian restaurant."

A few minutes later a little box popped up telling us we had a Skype call coming in from General Resource Recovery. I accepted the call, expanded the window, and suddenly had a dark-faced, balding little guy in an open-collared silk shirt and wraparound sunglasses, with a Doberman pinscher sitting next to him, filling the screen.

"Hello, Ivor. Hi, Cleo," said Sam. "*Como estas?* Ivor's the one in the sunglasses," he added to me. I was glad Eddie was asleep on the floor, though who knows if dogs can see other dogs on a computer screen.

"Mr. Acquillo. I wish I could say it's a pleasure to see you again."

His speech had a Spanish inflection. I remembered from my research years ago that he was born in the Philippines, a mix of Dutch and Asian.

"Same here," said Sam. "It's only because we seem to have a situation."

"And you are Miss Swaitkowski?"

"Yes," I said. "I'm part of the situation."

"I think this can be easily resolved," said Ivor, putting his arm around Cleo, who continued staring into the screen. My appreciation of the Skype idea soared. "It seems to be on account of faulty information."

"Really," said Sam.

"I accept the responsibility," he said. "I sent my associates to call on Miss Swaitkowski, mistakenly thinking she was still in the real-estate business. I want to expand my home in Southampton, which will require a hearing with the appeals board. You came highly recommended, but now I hear you're into a different thing."

"I am," I said, temporarily losing all doubt over the career change.

"I'd like this to end here," said Ivor. "You'll have no further contact from us, and we'll forget about the manhandling of my security personnel."

All of us but Ike, I thought.

"Fine with me," said Sam. "We're not looking for trouble."

"We're not," I said.

"That's good. Then we're agreed. Let's make this the last time we need to have a conversation," he said, and with that, we saw him lean over his keyboard, and with a single tap, he was gone. I quit out of the application just to make sure.

"So that was easy," I said. "What do you think?"

"It was too easy. He's lying."

"That's too bad."

"No, it's not. It means something."

"To the Buczek case?" I asked.

"I don't know. But it's where I'd look."

"Sullivan told me to stay away from Fleming."

"It's not up to him," he said. "You've got your own job to do."

"That's the theory."

We talked some more while finishing off the fattening breakfast. Then Sam and Eddie left me to my own devices, which started with a quick change out of the nice clothes and into the ones that made me so thankful I worked in a one-woman office.

I kept the lipstick and mascara on, though. Why not.

Then I stared out at the windmill across the street and tried to read my own thoughts, conscious and otherwise. It wasn't a long deliberation, because the first impulse that seemed to have some sense attached to it found me at my computer keyboard writing to Randall Dodge.

"How's the Zina check going?" I asked him.

A half hour later, he wrote back.

"There is no Zina. No matches fitting the description. Interpol came up with zilch. I suggest we extend the search beyond Poland."

"Sure," I wrote. "You can do that?"

"As long as my friend remains my friend," he replied.

"So stay friendly," I wrote.

I hadn't allowed myself to react when UB first reported Zina's non-identity. UB was likely a clever cyber-warrior, but still an amateur. Interpol was different. Way different. You don't hide from those guys.

That was why I had to ask Randall. To hear that news. I knew it was coming, and though I didn't know where it would lead, from then on all things would have to be different.

"What do you know about Ivor Fleming?" I asked Roger Angstrom when he answered the phone.

"What do I know or what do I know that I can print?"

"What do you know."

"He has a very successful, legitimate scrap-metal business, collecting product from all over the East Coast, separating it by type of metal, more or less, and shipping it all around the world. His biggest customers have traditionally been sheet-metal fabricators serving the auto and appliance industries. Originally in Japan and Western Europe, now most of it goes to China, Brazil, and Korea."

"That's all printable. Tell me what's not."

"In return for what?" he asked.

A short list of options leapt to mind. "I'll give you an exclusive on the Buczek case. Once it's concluded."

"In your favor or not?" he asked.

"Either way is in my favor. All I'm striving for is the truth."

"I can't talk about this over the phone," he said. "We'll have to meet. Tonight?"

"You know where I am. Mr. Sato will ring when you get here."

Among the infinite number of things one can do with the computer is not only check the weather report, but actually see the weather bearing down on you in lush, representational colors. You only need to go to the National Oceanic and Atmospheric Administration Web site and look. These are the people who tell everyone else in the country what's going to happen, maybe, in the coming days. Unless something changes. That morning it was telling us on the East End that all the ferocious winter weather we'd been experiencing was just a prelude, a warm-up if you will, to what was coming later that week.

Of course, it also might miss us. Or it might hit us square between the eyes. No one knew for certain, breathless warnings from the attractive local newscasters notwithstanding.

Yeah, yeah, was all us jaded and irritable Long Islanders could think. Heard it all, seen it all before, and we're all still here. Wake us up when Armageddon is really coming to town and maybe we'll give it a little attention.

For my part, I had the outfit, finally. Everything warm, rugged, and resistant to overuse. My car drove like a snowmobile and there was limitless sashimi and green tea one flight down. We'd never lost power in the building, and even if that happened, there was always Burton's place, which was set up to live off the grid through anything short of thermonuclear war.

But I studied the giant Doppler radar map anyway and began to be impressed with all the green. Green, incongruously, meant heavy snowfall. At that moment, a lot of green was dumping on the western reaches of the South. As usual, the wind currents were projected to bring that monster over West Virginia, Maryland, and South Jersey, across a little scrap of the Atlantic Ocean, and then broadside into Long Island.

As far as I could tell from their projections, Southampton was predicted to be smack in the middle of the storm.

Oh, goody.

I noticed a little gadget on the site that let me zoom in on the projected center of the storm to see how it would be distributed across all the area villages and hamlets. It was driven by a version of Google Earth, so you could see all the real roads, buildings, and bodies of water.

It was at that moment I was seized by a revelation that had been lying dormant in my brain for days. The shock of it actually felt like a blow to the chest.

"Idiot!" I yelled into the empty office, and immediately called Randall Dodge, who by this time would likely devoutly wish he'd never met me.

"Yes, Jackie," he said, answering the phone.

"Dude, can I borrow your satellite application? The one we played around with the other day?"

"I can't give you log-in rights. The millisecond the system sees your IP address, it'll lock you out and cut me off. Forever. The deal is, you can trade, but you don't share."

"Okay, can I come over there and pretend I'm you?"

It took a while for him to answer, but not because he was considering the proposition. It always took him longer than most to respond to questions. I took it as a Shinnecock thing. Rapid responses were un-dignified.

"Sure. When?"

"Tomorrow in the A.M.," I said.

"Bring ham and cheese."

A mighty storm might have been roaring toward us, and I might have been totally unprepared for the consequences, and it was surely gray and cold and wretched outside, but for all that, my heart was warm with eager anticipation. I had a plan for the next day, one I could see unfolding in my mind's eye. I had a theory, and a track to run on until that theory was proven right or wrong, and that was all I needed to be a whole person—a cheerful, anxious, unrelenting person.

18

I brought five different types of croissant and enough coffee to float a battleship. Randall was ready with a relatively clear and well-lit workspace waiting for me, the satellite program booted up and hovering over Southampton Village.

"Does this thing work at night?" I asked, sitting down in front of the monitor.

"It's just a weather satellite," he said. "No night vision. That's NSA stuff. I wouldn't be sneaking into their servers. That's instant black helicopters overhead, commandos at the door. And then I disappear."

"We don't disappear people."

"We don't? Excellent news."

He gave me a quick tutorial on how to move laterally and zoom in and out by using a little joystick. It wasn't much different from Google Earth, just in real time. In a few moments I was up in Seven Ponds, and a few moments after that, I had Tad Buczek's place filling the screen.

It was disorienting, the proportions far different from how I'd calculated them on the ground. I reset my perceptions by starting at the head of the driveway, following it down the hill to the sharp turn, past the pergola, which was more sprawling than I realized, and then on to the main house. From there, I followed the drive to the staff house, which was farther away than I thought, and tucked up next to a stand of trees. Next to the staff house was a barn twice its size. At least I thought it was the staff house. There were other buildings nearby, rectangular boxes probably made of corrugated steel, and things I wasn't sure about but assumed were part of the Metal Madness collection.

"Can I jump out of this but keep it running, and go to another site?" I yelled to Randall, who was off in some other dark corner of the shop's back room.

He came over to me and tapped a few keys, then showed me how to get back again when I was ready. I went into Southampton Town's property records and fished around the tax maps until I had Tad's estate and the immediately adjacent properties, something I'd seen before, back when I was helping him torment his neighbors.

It took me a bit to figure out how to print it out, but I couldn't bear to bother Randall again. Now with the borders and existing structures delineated, I confirmed the location of the staff house and the storage barn. That was just the start, however. Using the satellite image, I drew the round Hamburger Hill on the tax map, along with two other large artificial mounds—one a rough square, the other S-shaped, like a fat snake. All were festooned with Tad's madcap sculptures, which were impossible to identify precisely looking down on them from above. Except for the big sprinkler on Hamburger Hill, which looked just like a sprinkler you'd have in your backyard, with three spokes sticking out from a round stand that looked far more uniform and refined from that distance.

But there was something missing, or I just couldn't make it out. I gave in and called Randall again.

"Can you identify other buildings," I pointed to the screen, "within these borders," and I pointed to the tax map.

He shooed me out of the chair and started working the controls, making me feel like we were in a flying saucer zinging above the property. He explained that the winter weather was both a boon and a curse. The leaves off the trees meant we could see under the canopy, but the dense snow cover smoothed out variation on the surface and hardened up shadows, reducing depth of field. I acknowledged all that without really knowing what he was talking about.

"I think that's it," he finally said, pointing to a blob on the screen. He continued to play with the resolution until there was no more resolving to be had. I looked at it with skepticism and squinted eyes. But then, magically, it was there.

"Don't tell me those little black dots are logs fallen off the pile," I said.

"That's nothing. The NSA satellites can see a zit on the end of your nose."

This time I shoved him out of the command chair and took over the controls. I zoomed back out.

"Son of a bitch," I said, pointing at the blob. "Do you see what I see?"

He leaned over me, his mass a little intimidating, his smell masculine and sweetly foreign at the same time.

"I don't."

"Here's the staff house," I said. "Here's the woodshed. Now, here's Hamburger Hill. What do you see, or don't see?"

"They aren't in a row?" he asked.

"Hardly. They represent points on a triangle. If Franco was going to see how Tad was doing with the woodshed, why travel forty-five degrees from the destination to get there? Focus in on the woodshed. What else do you see?"

Randall took over the controls and zoomed in on the rectangular building.

"The roof," he said. "It's crinkly."

"Which means what?"

"It's caved in."

"Why has everybody missed this?" I asked. "Why did I miss it?"

"Because it was cold and snowy, and thus too difficult to walk the scene, and even if it wasn't, assumptions trip you up every time," said Randall.

"Ain't that the truth."

I spun around in the chair and looked up at him, miles above me. "Didn't you tell me this was all recorded and you could go back about a year and look? Can I go back to before Tad was killed, and the days after?"

He stared at me with that damn Indigenous Peoples' poker face. I wanted to tell him, Don't you know that American women of European origin can't survive without immediate emotional feedback? Do you think virtual elves are any different? Do you want to live your whole life alone in a cave?

"You can't, but I can, though not without asking," he said. "I'm sure my friend will give me the links. It's very easy on his end. Everything's time-stamped. Write down the dates and times, and I'll give him a shout."

I wrote down a wish list, telling Randall I would be most happy with the dates I'd circled and starred. He watched me in silence.

"I admire your persistence," he said, taking the note. "I think I tend to give up at the first hint of resistance. Maybe that's why I spend so much time alone in the dark."

I pretended that he hadn't read my mind and went back to studying the Buczek compound. I wondered, if Franco wasn't heading for the woodshed when he tripped over Tad's body, where was he heading? Granted, it was in the middle of a raging blizzard, but Franco had worked there long enough to know the basic lay of the land.

I traced the line from the staff house to Hamburger Hill, then extended it forward in a straight line. The trajectory took me past the pergola, which was down the hill, and directly into another odd lump on the satellite image, one hard against the property line with the neighbors to the southeast. I zoomed in and saw what I thought I saw, though I needed Randall for confirmation.

"It's another building," he said, staring at the screen. "A little smaller than the woodshed, bigger than a bread box. You can mark it as a waypoint on your smartphone, which you can use to walk there from the road. It's only about fifty yards in. Though you might need snowshoes if this damn weather keeps up. "

"Sure," I said. "Why not. You're amazing. Did you contact Urszula?"

Another long, suspenseful silence.

"I did," he said. "She's a stimulating person. Thank you."

"Don't mean to pry."

"Yes you do."

"Does she know you're not a dwarf? Not that there's anything wrong with dwarfs."

"She knows my height. But I didn't tell her I'm red, white, and black."

"Who cares about that? You're a good-looking man. Send a pic. Did she send you hers?"

"I'm glad you don't want to pry," he said.

"What does she look like? Don't you want to know?"

"She looks like her avatar. Ears are just a little less pointy."

I slapped him on the shoulder.

"Wow, that means she's really pretty. I knew it," I said. "Did she tell you where she lives? New Britain, Connecticut. A hop, skip, and a jump."

"Four and a half hours by ferry. Less than that if you drive, without traffic."

"Could be a lot worse."

"You missed the part about Native Americans being very private, dignified people?"

"Pshaw," I said, my favorite word ever since I heard it from Saline Swaitkowski Lumsden, former medical student and psychiatric nurse. Proper preparation for a career in domestic service in the Buczek household?

I hadn't meant to call on Paulina again, but given the conversation with Saline after the funeral, it seemed essential. So as soon as I left Randall's, I headed directly for her condo. Even if I was a person who called ahead, it wouldn't have been necessary. Paulina was a homebody, and who wouldn't be with such a stunning home to be a body in?

"Jacqueline, what a pleasure," she said, though not too convincingly. I stood on her doorstep trying to look cold and in need of immediate shelter. After a brief hesitation, she let me in.

"Sorry to bother you again, Paulina." I wasn't. "But some new stuff came up and you're the only person who has the intelligence to help me."

This was a manipulative thing to say, given the inflated regard she had for her own brainpower. That I was using the word "intelligence" to mean hidden information meant I wasn't lying, though that probably wouldn't stand up under divine judgment.

I sat down in a chair on the other side of the room from the Clock before she had a chance to seat me. I pulled off my coat and tried to look fixed in place. She was forced to turn another battleship of a living room chair about forty degrees so we could talk to each other without spraining our necks.

"Wasn't it a beautiful service?" Paulina said before I had a chance to start grilling her.

"It was. I love Father Dent."

"As a priest," she said. Just making sure.

I refused to dignify that.

"You must have been pleased with the turnout," I said.

She obviously was. She leaned in toward me the way Saline did to deliver intimate information in a secretive way, even though we were the only people in the room.

"Did you see that the Chicago Buczeks were there? Flew into Islip. Five of them. They've done very well. Limousine service. Not as well as Tad, of course. They don't get along with the Long Island Buczeks, all of us with dirt under our nails and bad table manners."

"But it's nice they came to pay their respects," I said, hoping to keep things on an even keel.

"I suppose," said Paulina.

"I wanted to ask you about Saline's medical-school career," I said before the conversation trotted off in another direction. "What happened?"

Paulina adjusted her perch on the chair, which looked impossibly uncomfortable. Which it obviously was. This gave me some perverse pleasure watching her try to look otherwise.

"Who told you about that?" she asked.

"She did."

"Really."

Paulina looked offended that Saline had shared a key piece of suppressed information without her permission.

"Everyone knew the Swaitkowskis were a bunch of smartypants, including Papa, who could have been anything he wanted to but chose to take over the farm. He'd say, 'You can't walk away from a hundred years of tradition.'"

"Sounds like Saline gave it a try."

Paulina scrunched around in her seat and pulled at the hem of her skirt, which was at least a size too small.

"Papa's father didn't believe in educating girls. He said that every woman who graduated from college meant one less job for a man. This wouldn't be a very popular thing to say in these times." You got that right, I thought. "So she made it as far as she could on scholarships, first to SUNY Kings County, where she majored in agriculture, which was something her father at least understood. Then to New Amsterdam, which really set off a bomb. Even then, medical school was very expensive. Papa tried to help, but he was a young man just starting out with me and little Peter, darling boy."

The moment quivered over the vast empty pain that was our missing Pete, but she recovered just in time and went on. She leaned toward me again and lowered her voice, telegraphing the nature of what was to come.

"But then halfway through medical school, she moved back in with Papa's parents and got into bed and stayed there for an entire year. One whole year, with the shades pulled, and she didn't even eat, just drank fruit juice. I tried to get her to talk to me, but she'd just lie there. Her mother told me it was a nervous breakdown. Papa's mother died during all this, and she still didn't stir. She was such a big, strong girl, I thought she was going to wither away."

"That's horrible," I said. "How did she recover?"

Paulina looked around the muddled room for the right answer.

"I'm not sure. She just gradually went from eating to moving around the house to going outside. I was so busy myself in those days that I didn't keep that well in touch. Papa's father didn't know what to do with her, and with the mother gone, he had his hands full with the farm. The only thing I remember is her going to work at Tad's place, where she's been ever since."

"Really."

Paulina nodded. "You bet. It was a big farm back then, and he had a mess of hands. She was just one of a dozen. Wasn't till he built the big house that she started in with the housekeeping. Cooked, cleaned, did all that for Tad, who was a confirmed bachelor."

"She told me she trained to be a psychiatric nurse," I said.

Paulina looked amused.

"Never got to use it. Though it must've come in handy with this family," she said.

She got up from her uncomfortable chair and walked over to a big vase sitting on the floor. It looked like it had been poured into place, its glossy sheen and gaudy colors creating a tower of gelatinous concretions. She turned it a half turn, then went back to her seat.

"There we are," she said. "Just right."

"Thanks for doing that," I said. "It was bothering the heck out of me. So when did Freddy appear on the scene?"

"I don't remember, but it has to be about ten years ago, long after Saline started at Tad's. He was a hand on the farm, before it was mostly sold off. Wild drunk, was the story, but Saline made him give it up as a condition of marriage. Turned him into a better man."

She looked around the room again, in search of irregularities only she could detect.

"And she never took to her bed again?" I asked.

Paulina tried to recall.

"If she did, I'd have known it. We talk, you know."

Oh, yeah, I thought, you do indeed.

"How did she feel when Tad brought Zina back from Poland?" I asked. "Must have been hard after running the house all those years."

Paulina lit up with what you could only call an evil grin.

"The first he says to Zina after they walk in the door, was something like, 'This here's Saline. She runs this place. That ain't changing. You got issues with her, you talk to me.' Can you believe it? Though it was still a little hard, having another person to clean up after."

And I wondered how hard it was without Tad there to discuss any issues.

"Did she ever tell you what happened the night Tad was killed? Did she or Freddy have an opinion?"

This put Paulina in an awkward situation. Two forces pulling her in opposite directions: protecting things said in confidence, and the irresistible urge to spill the beans. It was a short fight.

"Saline swore me to secrecy," she said.

All well and good, I thought, until she has to swear to tell the truth, the whole truth, and nothing but the truth.

"I won't tell anybody if you don't want me to," I said, telling about as big a whopper as a person could tell.

She looked from side to side, just to make sure no one was standing nearby trying to listen in. It was so serious an effort, I almost looked myself.

"Tad wasn't really out there to check on the woodshed, like Zina told the police. He was out looking for her," she said, nearly whispering. "He was in a rage. Just a rage. He'd found out about her and Franco the Casanova, finally, and was yelling and screaming and saying he was going to kill them both. And then he left the house and that was the last she saw him alive."

She sat back in her chair, smugly satisfied to have delivered yet another version of that night, unaware that it had plenty of competition.

"So she didn't know how he found out," I said.

Paulina shook her head. "Didn't say. What difference does it make? You find out your wife's a whore, that's all that matters."

Maybe not to Zina, I thought.

As it had been with Saline, it was a huge relief to get away from Paulina. There was something about their sensibilities, their perspective on reality, that I found dispiriting. I nearly dashed from that garish apartment, leaving repeated thank-yous and gracious refusals of homemade chocolate and exotic cookies behind in my wake, my first full breath taken when I reached the Volvo in the poorly plowed parking lot.

Inside the car, I collected myself. I dug around the half-dozen depleted packs of Marlboro Lights until I found an unsmoked cigarette, and I lit up, running the engine to make heat to battle the cold coming in the big crack in the window required to let out the smoke.

As I sucked on the cigarette, I pondered. I took it as a matter of faith that no one in any criminal case—client, witness, cop, or victim, if still living—ever tells the complete truth. Only bits of it. Our job as legal professionals was to mix and match the stories and interpret, to mine the known facts and build logical composites out of the assorted, partial truths.

Which left a lot of room for subjective judgment, which could be a bad thing, depending on who did the judging.

As to the Buczek case, everyone who survived that night was lying, in one way or another. Some of the stories overlapped, but there was no central narrative and only one agreed-upon fact: Tad went out into the snowstorm sometime during the evening. Everything else was up for grabs.

Lies aren't all bad, however. When there're a lot of them, it means there's something in need of being lied about. Two versions of the same story is a tension point, what Harry would call a "leveragable opportunity." A term that always made me think of Archimedes shifting his fulcrum around until figuring out how to move the earth.

I thought I could finish the cigarette, drive, and ponder at the same time, so I backed out of the space and carefully drove through the crowded parking lot to the street, where I made a right-hand turn to go back to my office in Water Mill. With the regular four lanes of Montauk Highway reduced to one and a half per side, I was feeling especially cautious, frequently looking from side to side and checking in my rearview mirror. Which is how I noticed the black Chrysler 300, not an unusual car in the Hamptons by any means, but more notable by the look of the driver and his passenger.

My negative guardian angels.

My heart gathered revs until it sounded like a tom-tom drum inside my head. I ignored that, as well as the adrenaline ripping through my veins, and concentrated on the reality behind me.

It was broad daylight. I was on Montauk Highway, a busy thorough-fare. I knew they were there and felt somewhat sure they didn't know I knew. So I forced myself to drive in a perfectly normal way, though I wondered what my normal driving looked like.

I drove on the highway until a left turn presented itself, a road that headed north toward Seven Ponds and, beyond that, North Sea. I took it as calmly as I knew how. The Chrysler fell in behind. At least then I was sure, although less secure, since the road was lightly traveled and ran through some thinly populated areas. I kept my speed down despite urgent signals from my more primitive parts, the ones charged with opting for fight or flight. I rejected both and kept on driving.

I took out my phone and called Sam. He didn't answer, of course.

I headed up that way anyway, gradually gaining speed. I continued to redial Sam, on the off chance he'd finally answer. I hit a long straight stretch of road and let my speed creep up over the limit. The Chrysler kept its distance, maintaining a steady five car lengths between us. Soon after, I was on North Sea Road, heading north. This was a much more heavily traveled route, even in this weather. I had to nudge the speed up even more to keep pace with the cars and trucks. The Chrysler tucked in behind me to keep others from getting between us.

I called Sam again and cursed his misanthropic ways when he didn't answer. Then I started to question my strategy. Why not just call in the cavalry, Joe Sullivan and his indomitable beat cops? Those sworn to serve and protect, paid for with my own tax dollars.

Because that would be that. The cops would stop them, hold them, and release them after their lawyer showed up, because all we'd have is my testimony and identification via security cameras, which the worst lawyer in the world would be able to contend well enough to bust them out of jail, and I'd never see them again. Two others would take their place.

I didn't know what Sam and I could achieve on our own that would be better, but I wanted to give it a try.

My phone rang. It was Sam.

"They're behind me!" I yelled. "In a black Chrysler 300. It's them, I'm sure. I'm heading toward Oak Point."

"Do you have the Glock?" he asked.

"Are you kidding? Of course I have the Glock."

"Stay on the line."

I could hear the sound of him running, crunching over snow, telling Eddie in stern terms to go back to the house and stay. Good luck with that, I thought. Then the sound of a car door opening and shutting with a thud, a change in the tone of the background noise.

"You still there?" he asked.

"I am."

"Are they still there?"

"They are. At a respectful distance," I said.

"Do they know you've spotted them?" he asked.

"I don't think so. But how would I know?"

"If they follow you onto Oak Point Road, don't turn in my driveway, go all the way to the end."

Sam lived at the tip of Oak Point, a peninsula that thrust into the Little Peconic Bay. His driveway, which he shared with Amanda, was the last turn before the road went through some marshy wetlands and then through a narrow dune above the pebble beach.

"Okay. Do you have a plan?" I asked.

"Stop at the beach, pull the Glock, and stay behind the front of the car. Bullets don't go through engines."

"Good tip. What'll you be doing?"

"I don't know," he said. "Play it as it lays."

"You've never played golf in your life."

When I reached Oak Point Road, I slowed and turned, like it was the most normal thing on earth to do. My eyes, welded to the rearview mirror, saw the Chrysler turn behind me.

"He's still there," I said to Sam.

"Stick to the plan. Keep your cell on speaker so we can communicate."

Oak Point Road had barely enough room for two passing cars in the best of circumstances. With all the snow, it barely had one, which made me wonder how you dealt with oncoming traffic. I slalomed my way past the little houses on either side of the road, most of which had unplowed driveways, a testament to second-home status. The Chrysler was still back there.

I drove past Sam and Amanda's driveway and around a gentle turn to the end of the road, delineated by a sturdy crossbar. I made a quick turn, took the Glock out of the sack I called a purse, opened the door and, police-style, rested the barrel on the hood of the Volvo.

I saw the Chrysler approach, pass Sam's driveway, then slow at the sight of my car parked perpendicular to the road. They stopped. Then Sam's 1967 Pontiac Grand Prix shot out of his driveway behind the Chrysler, completely blocking it in. The driver of the Chrysler put his car in reverse and tried to do a three-point turn, but immediately got the rear wheels stuck in a snowbank. Now they were broadside to me and barely thirty feet away.

I took a deep breath and, letting it out slowly, shot out the Chrysler's front tire. Then, remembering the cop's advice back at the range, took my time with the second shot, which blew out the back tire as it spun in the snow.

I looked up at the driver just in time to see the blur of a big automatic swinging toward me through an open window. I dropped down behind my car and heard two thuds, accompanied by two pops that echoed in the near distance.

I hoped Sam had something in mind beyond pure improvisation, not thinking I could survive an all-out gunfight. I tried to calm myself and get comfortable with the two-handed grip on the Glock.

I heard one more thud/pop and then a scream of startled rage and pain. I heard Sam yell my name, and I stuck my head around the front of the grille. I saw Sam pulling the driver out of the car with one hand, with a small baseball bat in the other. The automatic was on the ground. Sam kicked it in my direction.

The driver was Yogi, the taller one. Sam had him by the scruff of the neck, and every time the guy tried to twist around, Sam whacked him on the head with the bat. Boo Boo by now was coming around the front of the car, a gun of his own pointed at Sam and Yogi as they slowly backed up.

"Go ahead and shoot your friend!" Sam yelled at Boo Boo. "Then Jackie will shoot you and we'll be done for the day."

"Why don't I shoot you instead?" said Boo Boo.

"No!" yelled Yogi.

"Go ahead and try," I called. "You're still a dead man."

Boo Boo's head turned in my direction, with his gun still pointed at Sam.

"Drop the gun and you can walk away from this," said Sam.

He tapped Yogi on the head again.

"Drop it, for chrissakes!" Yogi screamed.

"And live another day," said Sam.

"More than I can say for you," said Boo Boo, tossing the gun into the snowbank to his right.

"Hands on your head," I said to Boo Boo as I came around the Volvo, my gun still trained on his chest. Sam patted around Yogi's overcoat and down his sides to the ankles and back again. Then handed the idiot off to me. He walked over to Boo Boo and frisked him with one hand, keeping the bat at the ready with the other. Yogi held his right forearm, his hand dangling in an unnatural way. His pale, oily face was clenched tightly.

I stuck my gun barrel into the side of his head.

"Did I mention that these things can just go off on their own?" I asked in a calm, even voice.

He stood quietly, immobile, his eyes fixed on Sam as he brought Boo Boo over to where we were standing.

"Here's the deal," I said, taking the gun away from Yogi's head. "We know who you are and who you work for. We want to know why the interest in the Buczek case. Why's it so important?"

Yogi let out a dry chuckle.

"Not happening," he said.

"What's your connection to Ivor Fleming?" I asked. The two heavies looked at each other. "What is it?" I repeated.

"If you know who we work for, you know we ain't talking," said Boo Boo.

I knew he was right. Whatever level of coercion required was way beyond what Sam or I were willing to do. We really had no leverage.

"Okay, you don't have to tell me. I already know," I said. "I'll just make sure Fleming learns I heard it from you."

Boo Boo smirked.

"Big whoop," he said. "Who cares about that little Chink."

"You care enough to do business with him," said Sam, catching my drift.

"The boys in Brooklyn do business with a lot of people," said Yogi. "You don't know who you're fucking with. They'll do shit to you nobody can imagine."

"You'd think Tad Buczek would know better," I said.

"Tadzik was like this to us," said Yogi, using the friendly diminutive of Tadzio and resting a closed fist on his chest. "Our brother. It was your Guinea that killed him. This cannot stand. You just need to get him a jolt upstate. We'll take it from there."

"What if he didn't do it?" I said. "What're you, working for the DA?" Yogi finally turned his head to look at me. "I know for a fact it wasn't Franco," I said. "Don't you care who actually did it?"

Yogi looked like he was coming to grips with a shifting paradigm, though he likely wouldn't know what that meant.

"Some people might," he said.

"Then let me find out and quit trying to terrify me to death," I said, jabbing him in the side with my gun. "Tad was family. Do you think I give a crap about his killer? You can have him as soon as I'm sure I got the right guy."

Their silence seemed to indicate a new perspective.

"See, fellas," said Sam, "we're actually on the same team."

"We'll be talking to you later," said Yogi.

"Great. Love a good conversation."

I kept the two of them covered while Sam retrieved their guns. Then, using a thick rope out of the trunk of his old Pontiac, Sam pulled the Chrysler out of the snow and cleared a way for me to drive by. Which I did once we had the two of them back in their car, Boo Boo now in the driver's seat.

I parked the Volvo behind Sam's house and joined him in the

Grand Prix, which he backed into the driveway so we could watch the road and wait for the tow truck I called to come haul away our new friends.

"What did you mean by 'Go ahead and try'?" he asked me when I climbed into the preposterous car.

"I didn't think he was good enough to hit you," I said. "But if you don't take risks, how do you get anything done?"

"Nice job with the tires, speaking of which."

"Thank you," I said, feeling a surge of exhilaration, realizing in the relative calm of the car that I was nearly dizzy with it, my bloodstream so saturated with adrenaline I could feel it seeping out of my pores.

I shared this with Sam.

"Winston Churchill said, 'There is nothing more exhilarating than to be shot at without result.'"

"I was motivated," I said.

"Did we learn anything?" he asked.

"Did we ever."

"Really."

That was when I fully grasped why my heart was soaring up in the clouds. Those dumb, vicious thugs who'd hang their own mothers before letting one scrap of useful information pass their lips had graced me with a wonderful gift. The one scrap that completely reshuffled the deck.

"The playing field's getting rearranged," I said, giving voice to my thoughts. "The paradigm is shifting. Can you feel it?"

He put his hand on his stomach. "I thought it was just gas. What I get for eating right before a brawl."

Soon after we waved at Yogi and Boo Boo being ferried away by the tow service, the Chrysler in a flatbed listing badly to port. We sat there and talked for another hour about nothing in particular, which was often the case with Sam. It wasn't until after he backed up next to my

Volvo and checked for internal damage from the three bullets in the fender that he told me that he was proud of me.

"You showed a lot of starch back there," he said, which for Sam amounted to lavish praise. "Kept your head."

Which had the effect of nearly ruining my machismo mood. So I showed him what I was really made of and pretended not to recall the utter indifference my father had toward offering approval of any sort, a tendency he managed to take with him to the grave.

I just gave Sam a thumbs-up and drove away.

19

My laptop had two important messages waiting for me. One from Randall Dodge that he had an external hard drive loaded with my requested material, the other from UB45JK asking me to IM her at the first opportunity.

"Hello there," I wrote UB. "What's up?"

She shot right back. "I got a hit on Zina. Got there before Gyro's whoopee-do Interpol dude."

"Get out of here."

She sent me a URL that took me to a Facebook profile page. Having never used Facebook, I had to sign up. After a bit of information sharing that I loathed giving up, I got in. I searched with UB's URLs. And suddenly, there was Zina—her picture and an unreadable name.

"Sorry, I totally can't read Polish," I wrote to UB.

"It isn't Polish. It's Russian."

I stared at the Cyrillic letters but couldn't tease anything out.

"Does it say Katarzina Malonowski?" I asked.

"Close. She's Katarzyna Malonov'skyy. A Russian. Could be of Polish ancestry, since Malonowski is a common Polish name. Fancy Interpol man didn't know to try the Russian spelling. Heh-heh."

"I've never been on Facebook," I wrote. "I thought people exposed their whole lives."

"She's got everything but her picture blocked. It's usually the other way around."

Not if you wanted someone to know what you looked like, I thought.

"You are brilliant," I wrote to UB.

"I'm a Dystopriot Warrior, second grade. We are fearless and intrepid."

"Now that I'm signed up, I could send her a message?" I asked.

"You could. Her profile wouldn't be here if it wasn't an active account. Let me know how that goes. I've become emotionally involved."

I promised her I would. After we logged off, I sat and stared at Zina. Or was it Zyna? The adrenaline rush of the earlier fight came flooding back. The virtual world proving yet again it could reach out and grab the real world by the throat. Though now that I had what I had, what did I do with it?

I decided to write Randall while I pondered that.

"This is excellent news," I wrote, thanking him for the satellite images.

"I couldn't let you log on, but I could download the stuff you wanted. I put all of it on an external hard drive, which is a physical thing I can just hand over," he wrote back a few minutes later. "If you want more, I can go back and get it. No one's the wiser. You can watch it on your pretty little laptop at home. In your underwear if you want."

He didn't know how likely a prospect that was.

"I'm on my way."

Before I got to Randall's, I stopped at the food store and stocked up for the next storm threatening to bury the East End till the spring thaw, if it ever came again. Like an automaton, I walked the aisles and loaded my cart with all the merchandise our local emergency nags insisted we have on hand—canned goods, bottled water, batteries and candles (the latter of which they said to snuff out before going to bed—I could see their liability lawyer adding in that one). I threw in a few specialty items of my own—coffee, ice cubes, tonic water, and limes to go with the gin. If I was going to survive, I might as well have some reason to live on.

Of course, there was Harry. I felt a little tug at my heart that he hadn't already asked me to come stay with him. On the other hand, that was the kind of thing he used to do that irritated me, and now I was glad he didn't. But there was no reason why I couldn't call him and suggest it, now, was there?

"And where are you?" he asked when he answered the phone. "I think I hear music."

"I'm in the salty snacks aisle. You prefer nuts to chips, is my recollection."

"I do. Especially unsalted, so you might have to search elsewhere. Planning a party?"

"I am. A snowstorm party. At your house, you and me. I'm provisioning as we speak."

"I'm honored. And already well stocked, as you'd imagine. Though more is always better."

Should I tell him I shot out a car's tires and received a return volley today? How about shoving my gun barrel into a guy's head, or making a deal with the mob to stop harassing me in return for handing over Tad's real killer so they could execute him in prison? What are the proper parameters for sharing the workday with your significant other?

"Let's keep an eye on the sky," I said. "I need to get there before all hell breaks loose."

"Or freezes over."

Randall had the hard drive waiting for me in a little box when I got to his shop. He stuck it in a brown paper bag.

"In case the NSA already has a satellite trained on me," he said.

He supplied a handwritten list of instructions on how to launch the application and navigate among the various times, dates, and locations, as well as how to use the arrow keys in place of the joystick to zoom in and out. I thanked him sincerely, and he thanked me back—for what, I'm not sure.

"You might give that back when you're done with it so I can wipe it clean," he said. "And don't download any files. Read everything off the drive."

"I refuse to be paranoid myself," I said. "But I can act paranoid on your behalf. How's that?"

"Good enough."

I'd planned to take another trip over to the Buczek place after I'd gone through Randall's satellite recordings, but I was in the neighborhood (not really) and there was still some light left in the day (not much) and there was that impulse-control thing.

So I felt the Volvo take over the wheel, guiding me up from Southampton Village to the Seven Ponds area, which by now felt like a second home. Randall had offered to lend me his GPS, which I could use to pinpoint the little building we'd uncovered, but I didn't need it. I was an ex–real estate lawyer. Just show us a tax map and we're like homing pigeons.

And I had my own GPS built into my fancy phone. What a world.

I drove past the Metal Madness entrance and parked on the side of the road, leaving enough room for anything smaller than a dump truck to get past me. I was wearing my full winter regalia, although taller boots would have been advisable. I pulled out my phone and brought up the GPS, enlarging the screen until the red dot of my destination was next to me—the blue dot. Then I set out.

With every step through a stand of new-growth trees I seemed to encounter deeper snow, sometimes reaching nearly to the crotch of my flannel-lined jeans. The only relief came from a few stretches where a layer of ice partway down was strong enough to support my weight. This was nice until the layer broke through, nearly dislocating my hip. I would have cursed the weather, but I'd already done that so much I was sure the spirits who controlled those things had heard enough from me and would turn a deaf ear.

After an exhausting slog that felt longer than it probably was, I spotted a small, cedar-sided building. The shingles were dark gray and partially blackened with age, and the uneven lines told of a weak foundation. The roof, however, looked new. I trudged the rest of the way, actually opening the top of my jacket to let out some body heat.

It was maybe fifteen feet square. It had a front door and at least one window. I tried to look through the glass, but years of crud rendered it translucent at best. I went back to the door and tried the doorknob. It turned.

It felt like I'd entered an entirely different building. Inside, the walls were paneled in fresh, rough-cut cedar and the floor in pine, in nearly the same wood tone, partially covered by a brilliant hand-woven Navajo rug. In the middle of the room was a bed, roughly unmade—thick, bulky quilts randomly cast about. On the side tables were empty glasses. On another table, along the wall, was a half-full bottle of bourbon and an ice bucket, a lump of partially melted and refrozen cubes at the bottom.

I used the camera in my phone to snap photos from various angles. I carefully avoided touching anything with my bare hands and shuffled around the room, smearing my footprints. I thought of Randall and how easy it was to act paranoid on my own behalf.

When I went to leave, I stopped for a moment at the door and looked down the hill through the young, gangly trees toward the center of the property. It was lumpy, as it would be from multiple tracks covered by repeated layers of snow. The trail went straight through to the field below, which is how I could see the figure of a person struggling through the depths, heading in my direction. It was too far away to make out much more than the dark, cold-weather clothing and the determined stride. Just before I turned to flee, the figure looked right up at me, paused for a moment, then redoubled its efforts.

I was in much better shape than I deserved to be, given my indifferent relationship with regular exercise. But if I was going to design the most rigorous physical challenge imaginable, it would be trying to sprint through thigh-deep crunchy snow. Though I had the sight of that dark and relentless form churning up the hill to drive me along, and that was enough.

I thought about the decision to check out the odd little building rather than just go home and slip into comfy clothes, gather intoxicants about me, and celebrate a generally successful day. What is wrong with me, I would have yelled if I'd had the wind.

About the time I thought I'd escaped the threat from behind, I began to worry about what was in front. I'd left the Volvo alone and thoroughly exposed on the street. Not just an abandoned vehicle, but a hindrance to the already beleaguered traffic flow. What was I thinking? Oh, that's right. I wasn't thinking.

As I slogged toward the road, the Volvo came into view, where I'd left it, confident in its circumstances. I should have taken precautions before racing to the car, but eagerness took over, and I almost ran through the final stages of irredeemable exhaustion toward the street and hoped-for salvation.

I made it, pushing the electronic key to open the doors, and collapsing into the driver's seat, heaving cubic yards of air into my lungs and letting them out in a song of pathetic whimpers. I started the car and floored it, racing away from that perfidious place, that capital of misfortune and outlandish acts of compulsive unrestraint.

I used the first three hours of the presumed safety of my apartment to sleep rich, dream-free sleep, a type of self-induced narcosis. In my clothes, on the couch, a glass of wine barely touched. When I woke, it was dark outside, and I had no idea what time it was, much less where I was or what year I'd reentered. I didn't panic, however, assuming all would be revealed within the next ten seconds, which it was.

I was pleased to not be in the house I once shared with Pete up in the woods of Bridgehampton. And to not be in my college dorm room or the vermin-infested pension near Sacré-Cœur I thought so romantic, like any other culturally besotted kid living anywhere but home.

I liked being in my apartment next to my office over the Japanese restaurant on Montauk Highway. It might not be the perfect place forever, but for now, it was a hallowed place.

I wanted to lie there forever, but part of me wanted to get up and move around, maybe dig up some coffee. This part, though a minority voice, prevailed, and I did just that, albeit not without major complaint from the aching, lead-limbed majority.

The coffee had hardly filled the pot when the phone rang. It was Mr. Sato telling me I had a guest waiting for me downstairs.

"Crap." I'd forgotten about him again.

"Shall I tell him you are indisposed?"

"No. Give me fifteen minutes."

I stripped everything off and got into the shower, where I mostly let the hot water massage my body and steam up the bathroom. Showers always had the power to either wake me up or put me to sleep, depending on prevailing circumstances. That night it definitely trended toward the soporific, and it was only a supreme act of will that kept me from shlumping to the floor and drowning in artificial rain.

I made little effort this time to manage my wardrobe, or hair, or makeup. I just showed up at the restaurant in sweater and jeans and a face gloriously unmeddled-with. Angstrom didn't seem to notice.

"Sorry for making you wait. Had a hard day," I said, sitting down at the table and receiving my white wine, a standing order.

"You don't seem the worse for wear," he said, obviously out of kindness.

"Wear would be the least of it."

"What happened?"

File cards flipped through my mind, each holding a piece of information I didn't want to share with the press. This was not the proper format for a healthy conversation. But I had to accept that it never would be as long as the other party was a reporter.

"Nothing really. So, what can you tell me about Ivor Fleming?"

He took a little notebook out of a battered briefcase and flipped it open. It was the same type as mine, just a different color. I held mine up and we had a light communion over notebook preferences.

"There are two schools of thought about Ivor," he said. "One says he's still dirty, the other says he decided after the last prosecution to stop pushing his luck. To enjoy his mature years selling scrap metal and sponsoring community activities. It's pretty evenly split, but the latter camp has the better case, since there's no evidence he's involved in any of the naughty stuff he used to be into, which was just about everything. Most criminals like to specialize, but Ivor liked a diversified portfolio. Probably his business background."

"What do you think?"

"Always the contrarian, I think he's still active. Just far more careful."

"Anything connected to the Polish or Russian mob in Brooklyn?"

His face filled with surprise.

"You know more than you're letting on," he said.

I did a little coquettish move and said, "I might," then instantly regretted it. What is wrong with me?

"Why don't you tell me what you know and not waste our time," he said in as much of a noncritical way as you could speak those words.

"I'm sorry," I said. "That was jerky. I know the Poles and Russians are in some sort of alliance—the Russians operating a large global organization and the Poles contracting out as an independent subsidiary. There are benefits to both, on a local level as well as in their international operations. And that's about it."

He looked impressed. "That's a lot. The configuration you note is relatively new. There's been a lot of bloodletting among all the Eastern European gangs as they sorted out territories formed after the Soviet collapse. They all have a presence in New York, working out of Brooklyn, as you'd have to if you were going to engage in world trade."

"How big is all this?" I asked.

He gave a "who knows" gesture. "Billions. How many? Anybody's guess."

"Where do you think Ivor fits?"

He pointed his finger at me, not rudely, but to make sure I would hear what he was saying. "This you don't talk about. It's exclusive. My research, okay?"

"I won't. Unless it will help keep my client out of prison, then I can't promise anything."

He considered that.

"I believe you," he said. "You're not only direct, you're principled."

Yeah, yeah, I wanted to say, but it would have wrecked the spirit of the moment.

"Okay," he said, "I think he's working in something closely tied to his legitimate business. It's an area he knows inside and out. Much easier to stay under the radar when you're on home turf."

"Scrap metal?" I asked.

He shook his head. "A business consultant would tell you Ivor's not in the scrap-metal business, he's in the business of harvesting an inexpensive raw material, processing and packaging it, and then redistributing it as a higher-margin, value-added product. The processing and packaging is minimal, so it's not like he's really manufacturing anything. At the end of the day, it's the moving around of the stuff that he's really good at. So he's not in the metal business, he's in . . ."

"Logistics."

"Exactly."

A single sharp laugh popped out of me, loud enough to cause Angstrom to pull back and the couple at the next table to shift their wary eyes in my direction.

"That's funny?" he asked.

"Not to me. Logistics is serious business. You don't get any more serious."

"Then why are you laughing?"

"I know the god of the logistic sciences. When people ask, who's the Babe Ruth, the Michael Jordan, the Jimi Hendrix of logistics, they'll say, Harry Goodlander. None better. Broke the mold."

"Your boyfriend," he said.

"You shouldn't know his name. That's personal."

"It was in your background file. I didn't compile it, just read it."

"That makes me very unhappy."

"It's probably worse than you think," he said. "Everybody can know almost everything about everybody."

I knew this was true, I just didn't want to think it was true about me. So I shifted the conversation back to the original topic.

"So you believe Ivor has somehow integrated evil enterprise into his official business. Which you redefine as essentially import-export," I said.

"I do," he said. "The world is now nearly one. Matter flows around the globe like the currents of the sea. Legal and illegal all travel in the same streams. Ivor is a tributary in that system, from his various feeder stations to his plant then out again to trucks, railroads, and shipping docks. Who would be in a better position to serve illicit traffic?"

"What is he shipping and handling?" I asked.

He sat back. "Don't know. Working on that. Could be anything or everything. I don't believe it's nothing."

"As a matter of faith," I said.

"That's right. And I'm an atheist."

"Not me. Agnostic all the way. Hedging my bets."

He liked that, and showed it by grinning and making me clink glasses.

"You are utterly charming," he said, his voice pitched down a notch or two. "That's a professional and personal opinion. The more I learn about you, the more impressed I am. I know it's unprofessional of me, but I'm feeling seduced by my subject."

"Metaphorically," I said.

"Of course."

I looked at him a little closer, in the forgiving dim light of the restaurant. His hands looked a little less delicate and his frame more robust. And the face, which stopped me midstride when I first saw it, was getting even better. Something started stirring down below, even though I told it not to.

"Where do you stay when you come out here?" I asked him. "It's not exactly B&B season."

"We have a travel department at the *Times*. They find secure lodging for reporters in Afghanistan and Somalia. The Hamptons off season are only slightly more challenging."

"You're charming yourself. Is that something you learn in the reporter trade? Flatter your victims out of their information?" I asked.

"Sometimes. You do the same thing when you have to. And thanks for what I think was a compliment."

"So what's going on here?" I asked.

He looked theatrically confused. "Nothing. I'm trying to do a story on you and you're resisting me. Which only makes me try harder. And I think we could have something on a personal level if you'd stop pretending we couldn't, though don't wait too long. Once I start writing the story, I have to follow it where it goes."

I'd already downed two white wines on automatic delivery. When the third one came, I sent it back to be replaced by a vodka on the rocks. Angstrom ordered a scotch and soda, responding to the escalation.

"That's okay," I said. "You're not only abstruse, you're principled." I felt the outer surface of his calf, so barely perceptible it could have been his aura, brushing against my leg.

"You know about Harry," I said. "What about you? I don't have a dossier to pore over."

He smiled a warm, self-deprecating kind of smile, something I rarely saw among the men I knew. Sam and Sullivan were too hard-assed to consider such a thing, Randall too devoid of affect, Harry too ironic. I liked the change of pace.

"Not much to tell. Succession of women disenchanted by the long hours, occasional risk to life and limb, and low pay. Did I mention obsessive preoccupation with appalling subject matter? I didn't blame them. Still don't."

"I know the tune to that song," I said.

"I know you do," he said, looking at me with those drill-through-your-skull eyes.

Then I felt more than an involuntary pressure against my leg.

"So you won't tell me where you're staying," I said.

He told me. A motel on the eastern edge of Southampton Village, about ten minutes from my apartment.

"Unless I stayed with you," he said. "In which case I'm only about two minutes away. Or less, depending on how things go."

I held up my vodka.

"Things aren't going there," I said, "but I will finish this drink with you. And I'll pick up the tab as a thank-you for the information."

He clinked my glass and sat back in his chair, but kept the leg thing going. I gently moved mine away.

"I finally have a source willing to share a lot of information on you," he said.

"Oh?"

"Ross Semple, the chief of police."

"You're kidding. He hates me."

"He admires you tremendously. Had nothing but praise and appreciation. The detective, Joe Sullivan, didn't add much, but he confirmed everything the chief told me. They think a lot of you."

I remembered the same conversation with my mother. I told her my father saw me as an annoyance at best, and she said I should hear him brag about me to his friends. And to this day, I think, Yes, I should have heard him, because I still don't believe it.

20

After that last drink Angstrom and I shook hands and he left for his motel, and I went back upstairs. I went directly to the office and brought my laptop over to the sofa to maximize the comfort factor. The paper bag with Randall's hard drive was sitting on my desk, but it seemed way too technically intimidating to tackle at that point. So I started to wander down more familiar paths, beginning with the standard search engines.

It was relatively easy to track Saline to Kings County Technical College, still very much an ag school back when she was there. True to form, she was nearly invisible, with no record of extracurricular activities or sports. What I needed was her official transcript, which should be confidential, and thus inaccessible by traditional means. I tried that route anyway, halfheartedly, then resorted to Randall's not-so-traditional application, which also didn't quite work. However, I was able to get into her personal file, which some enterprising archivist in the college's administrative office had diligently converted to a digital format.

Included was a recommendation letter to the medical schools she was applying to. According to the recommender, any postgraduate program would be greatly enhanced by her presence. A perfect 4.0 grade point average being the least of her credentials, all academic. Apparently, early in her college career she'd migrated from general agriculture into its underpinnings, settling on dual majors in organic chemistry and microbiology.

I considered people who excelled in fields like that to be denizens of an alien planet. For me, English was the only possible major, since at least I knew the language and had already read a few of the crucial texts in high school. Science and math were subjects to flee from, screaming.

There were other awards and commendations, certificates declaring mastery of various arcane specialties. Then came the other stuff, this not so bright and shiny. Several notes from the school's medical office expressed concern for her health. Poor eating habits were cited. I read anorexia between the lines. Other notes recorded conditions described as exhaustion or malaise. I wondered about this love in officialdom for euphemism. Just say it. The girl was probably depressed and riddled with anxiety. Within each notation was Saline's urgent request that no word of this be communicated to her parents. The writer of the notes expressed openly his or her dilemma—respecting Saline's privacy and upholding the school's right to loco parentis—yet believing her interests might be better served by contacting Mom and Dad.

Maybe if they had, what happened a few years later wouldn't have happened, I thought. Or would have happened earlier.

Saline did graduate, and was accepted into New Amsterdam Medical School. And that's where the Kings County trail ended. So I followed her into the city, where I ran smack into a brick wall. As a medical institution, New Amsterdam had things like HIPAA rules requiring much more rigorous security. Randall could probably sneak in, but I didn't want to put him in any more danger than I already had.

So I jumped back into the land of the legal and drove my search engine around Manhattan for a few hours. To sop up the vodka and white wine, I made a ham sandwich on white toast with butter, my favorite breakfast—comfort food courtesy of my mother, whose culinary repertoire was limited, but always delivered with brio. I think this celebration of food that people not derived from the British Isles would find bland at best was what my family practiced in lieu of actually learning to cook.

I clicked around the Web while I ate and tried to keep toast crumbs from falling on the keyboard and jamming up the keys. So without hardly realizing it, I wandered onto a neighborhood newspaper that covered the Upper East Side. It had gone through the familiar transition from print to both print and online and now exclusively online. Right on the home page, a little window declared proudly that the paper's archives, covering all forty years of publication, were now available with a click of the button.

I clicked. At the upper right of the first page was a search box. I typed in "Saline Swaitkowski" and was startled by an immediate hit. I sat up a little in my chair and went to the article.

A much younger, though far more bedraggled and haunted Saline was being escorted by a female police officer toward the open door of a patrol car, with a headline that read POLICE INVESTIGATE PREMATURE DEATH. The copy read "The *Carnegie Hill Chronicle* has learned from the NYPD that Joseph C. Vargo, a second-year medical student at New Amsterdam Medical School, has died from an apparent heart attack in his apartment on Eighty-ninth Street, between Lexington and Third Avenue. His death was reported by his girlfriend, fellow student Saline Swaitkowski, who called 911 when he failed to wake up yesterday morning. No cause of death has been determined, though according to Miss Swaitkowski, Mr. Vargo had complained of chest pains, and recently completed a series of tests. Officials at New Amsterdam expressed their deepest sympathy to Mr. Vargo's family, and have granted Miss Swaitkowski an unconditional leave of absence."

I went back to the *Chronicle*'s search box and typed in "Joseph Vargo." There were two more hits. One described his father traveling up to New York to retrieve his dead son, the other reporting the results of the autopsy.

"The tragedy of Joseph Vargo has been made so by the discovery that headache medication was the cause of his sudden death last Tuesday. Mr. Vargo, a victim of chronic migraine headaches, was also suffering from a rare form of angina that can occur in people in their twenties and thirties. The potent migraine medicine he was taking was specifically prohibited for people with this type of heart condition, especially at the high dosages he'd apparently administered to himself."

The law school I went to, as a matter of policy, denied the existence of human emotion. In the classrooms and discussion groups in student lounges and faculty receptions, it was all about the clinical application of ascendant ideals over the vulgar preoccupations of flesh-and-blood people actually consumed by the situations thrust upon them. It wasn't until I left those hallowed, insular, and arrogant halls that I appreciated the mission my scattered mind had set upon, and woke every morning glad for it.

What I learned was that the laws we examined and memorized, and the principles upon which English Common Law was based, which in turn spawned our American legal system, accounted for the unpredictability and innately selfish nature of our species. They started with the assumption that emotions drive behavior, what John Maynard Keynes called the animal spirits. It was the academics and clinicians who tried to turn legal theory into soulless, rational calculation.

Consequently, most legal practitioners hadn't the faintest clue what to do with a person like Saline. And their professional equivalents in medicine knew even less. So it was no surprise that the institutions, the mighty system itself, spit her out, as if performing tissue rejection on a foreign body.

For that alone, I grieved for the young Saline, yet another brilliant soul with the curse of differentness, and though my sanity was rarely in doubt, I recognized the plight, identified with the sad conclusions.

Burton called me the next morning, waking me out of a deep sleep, where I was dreaming that Tad's gloomy house had turned into crystalline ice, like the ice palace in *Doctor Zhivago,* and Zina was Julie Christie in a pink velour jumpsuit and white fur hat. I was interrogating her again, but she was speaking Polish, or Russian, and though trying to be honest with me, I couldn't understand a word she said.

I grunted into the phone.

"There's a cheerful hello," he said.

"First word of the day. Sorry."

"I'm here in your parking lot. Permission to come upstairs?"

"You're kidding," I grunted.

"I'm not."

There's a dilemma. Keep your boss waiting versus greet your boss looking like a corpse with a bad hangover. My soggy brain arrived at a strategy—focus on the hair and face, and stick with a sweatsuit for expedience. And thus I had him up in the office in about five minutes.

"I don't know how people can work out in the morning," he said as we climbed the stairs. "Though I admire it."

"Personal discipline," I said. "In all things. Coffee?"

I cleared a space for him on the sofa and started a pot of my best.

"So what brings you here?" I called from the kitchenette.

"I come bearing gifts."

"That's so sweet."

When I got back to the office area I saw him pulling a file folder out of a FedEx box.

"Another case?" I asked.

"Your current case. The private chat-room conversations of Tadzio Buczek and Katarzina Malonowski."

"No sir."

"Yes ma'am. The result of a subpoena signed and expedited by the Honorable District Judge Claire Freyberg, to whom we now owe a large favor. Probably have to paint her house or something."

"Seriously?"

He blanched. "Of course not."

"No, I mean you got the transcript."

"We did. Natrafić.czat.net was unhappy about it, but I had a chat with their lawyer, and here we are." He handed it to me. "I've barely looked at the text; it's nearly all in English. Will save us the translation time. Nice coffee."

I apologized for the absence of crumpets and jelly, something you'd have delivered to you at Burton's on a cart. He graciously claimed no interest in such things.

"Since I'm here and all, why not brief me on the case?" he asked.

I'd known Burton long enough to know this wasn't a subtle way of checking up on me, but rather an honest interest in staying informed, mostly to lend advice and possible assistance. As with other fine men, he knew instinctively that the greater the trust he held in you, the harder you'd work to earn it.

So I went through everything that had happened—the sit-down with Ivor Fleming, chasing down Zina's true identity, uncovering Saline's past, and the shootout with Yogi and Boo Boo, along with a discourse on their employers back in Brooklyn. I also showed him the

stills of the two goons from my security video. I left out Roger Angstrom of *The New York Times,* for unknown reasons, but floated the
theory first put forth by Sam that Ivor Fleming had avoided further
prosecution by finding a safer form of illegal activity. He took it all in,
then gently probed for conclusions that I didn't have. To distract him
from more probing, I talked about the side trip into the Don Pritz case,
including the conversations with Dinabandhu Pandey and also Art
Montrose, whose standing with Burton I was eager to repair.

"Interesting," he said. "I wouldn't have known."

"That's why I'm telling you. Good intentions aside, I think Montrose was wrong. He might have used the best strategy to save Franco
from a worse fate, but I don't think Franco was guilty of anything but
gullibility. I think it was all a setup by Eliz Pritz. On her part, the perfect crime."

I ran through the logic of my argument. He then shot it full of holes,
in a polite way.

"I know I can't prove anything," I said, "but I don't have to. The
only relevance to me is the restoration of faith."

"In Franco's innocence."

"The word 'innocent' may not quite apply, but he isn't guilty as
charged. I can't prove that, either, but I believe it to be true, and that's
all that matters."

"They won't all be innocent," he said.

"Most aren't. That's why it's so important to save the ones that are.
It's the point of it all."

He got up to go. I thanked him for the transcripts and for everything else that was good about my life and would have gone on from
there if he hadn't put his finger to my lips, which gave me a chance to
get the brakes on my brain before it drove off the road, which it can do
under certain circumstances. So then he left me feeling even more
blessedly grateful.

Before tackling the file, I took a shower and downed some coffee, feeling like the impending task called for an alert and unimpeded mind. That was the right choice. A less agile intellect would have assumed the transcripts were of an intimate tête-à-tête between two lonely singles and taken longer to realize it was anything but.

Zina: This to acknowledge receipt. Require dates for specific requests per order #3567vsl.

Tad: Received order on 5/11. Will need two more weeks to confirm supply. Are stateside agents coordinating with other feeder units? Understand need to know, but should avoid unnecessary duplication.

Zina: Understood. Will streamline order. G thanks you for continual quality production.

Tad: T thanks him for quality deposits in accounts.

Page after page of the transcripts was more of the same. Routine business transactions, clothed in euphemism and insider code, though the language was far more banal than exotic. I began to jot down patterns, trying to get a sense of what they were writing about. After a while it began to emerge. Tad was a supplier of something, a source. He identified himself as a feeder, and there were other unknown but noncompetitive feeders operating in other territories. Zina was a buyer, though not the end of the trail. People beyond her were defining demand, which flowed through Zina by way of someone named "G." Between Tad and Zina were other links in the chain, identified only as "stateside agents."

As a person who had spent countless hours entirely absorbed in complex narratives of Harry's involving the movement of things like endangered animals, two-ton automated machine tools, two-thousand-

dollar boxes of saffron, and the occasional single envelope containing a promissory note for a half billion dollars, I knew what I was
looking at.

Shipping and handling. Supply-chain management. Import-export.
Logistics. An art and science lovingly undertaken by some people, but
hardly a romance. Tad and Zina had found a convenient and reasonably
safe way to communicate, though precautions were taken. All of which
indicated an illicit enterprise, which answered one open question. Tad
was dirty. And so was his wife.

Almost involuntarily, I reached for the phone and called Harry.

"Are you ready to take me in?" I asked.

"Happy to be a port in the storm."

"It's not supposed to start until tonight, but I need to pick your
brains."

"Slim pickins," he said.

"False modesty is unbecoming."

"I think that was a compliment."

"I'm expecting a fire."

I threw a pair of silk long underwear, wicking socks, and additional
fleece sweaters into a big duffel bag, along with other overnight neces-
sities, like the laptop, the nat.net transcripts, Randall's external hard
drive, and a spare magazine for the Glock tucked in with the cosmetics.
What girl wouldn't?

The sky on the way to Harry's was a sullen dark gray. The temperature had risen in the last twenty-four hours, but the weather com-
mentators ruined that hopeful sign by saying it was the telltale of a
southwesterly storm, usually the worst of all.

I turned up the heat and switched the radio to classical music to
compensate for all that negativity.

Harry had parked his Volvo facing out toward the road, but I pulled straight in, to better hide the bullet holes. There'd be time to go through all that. He met me halfway to the door and took the heavy bag.

"Should have brought a forklift," he said, heaving the bag over his shoulder.

"You have one? Wouldn't surprise me."

As requested, there was a fire in the fireplace. I let Harry help me disgorge the duffel bag, and we settled in the living room in front of the hearth. Then I made him go through Tad and Zina's interactions, hovering over him and interrupting every five minutes with my earnest interpretations. He ignored me, except for an occasional pat on the hip, and read on for almost an hour. Then he relented and looked over at me.

"You're right," he said. "In every particular."

I swatted him. "Come on. Tell me the truth."

"It's a classic distribution channel. Tad is the field agent, charged with acquisition. He funnels what he obtains through intermediaries who either add value to the product or act as go-betweens with some special advantage, like a relationship with port officials, allowing un-scrutinized pass-through. From there the merchandise is received somewhere in Europe—if it's Poland, probably in Gdańsk—and then distributed from there. Tad is in direct contact with one of the last links in the chain, so he's either set this whole thing up himself, or he's bypassed his immediate buyer and gained access to the people closer to the end of the line. Usually an unacceptable thing even in the legiti-mate world, if there is such a thing. Though it sounds like the former. I think he's set something up with this character G and the two of them have worked out the multistep distribution process. Love to know more about it. Looks pretty cool."

"Cool? What are they trading in?" I asked.

"No idea. Drugs, microchips, nuclear arms, French poodles, wicker furniture . . . it's all the same in the language of commerce. Merchandise, product, shipping, handling, containers, customs, manifests, ports of call. Stuff that has to move and the stuff that moves it."

We took a break from analyzing the Tad/Zina interactions to eat lunch and check in on the storm's progress, which seemed to be holding true to earlier predictions, gathering its strength before slamming into the southeast corner of the Middle Atlantic and then heading up our way. The Carolinas were already succumbing to record snowfalls and desperate proclamations that this kind of thing can't happen here. Harry went off to test his generator and check on his business and I went back to poring over the transcripts.

This was always my greatest failing. The inability to maintain concentration through constant, repetitive tasks. A liability only overcome through titanic effort, it almost scuttled my law school career.

Luckily, the tone of the exchange between Tad and Zina began to change three-quarters of the way through the transcripts, revitalizing my powers of concentration.

Zina: G not feeling good about marketplace in Kraków. Too much Russians.

Tad: Do we suspend operations?

Zina: Not option. Buyers want, want, want. Send more, more, more. More three, five's and seven's.

Tad: Plenty of them, sweetheart.

Zina: Not your sweetheart.

Tad: Just an expression. Don't get your panties in a twist.

Zina: Understood. Forget dealing with American gangster.

Over the following volume of transcript, the narrative became clear. Zina's patron, G, was coming under increasing pressure from a competing organization and was feeling more and more desperate. Zina was getting distraught, and much more emotional in her communications, not for herself, but for G, whom I couldn't help but identify as Godek, her father. It just seemed too personal and conflicted a relationship to be otherwise. I congratulated myself when I hit this line of communication.

Tad: The people on the docks have quit shipment. Say things on your end too f**ked up. Need information.

Zina: G and mama have to leave for a while. Must stop operation for now. Old fight with big rivals here in Kraków getting very nasty. Much bad blood. Not so good. Not sure when next communicate. Please check nat.net daily.

It was almost two weeks until the next post. Tad had likely checked in as directed, but it was not what he probably expected to read.

G: Very bad trouble here. Too much money and too little respect.

Tad: Surprised to hear from you. Where is Zina?

G: Gone to safer place. Not safe enough.

Tad: What about the operation?

G: You will find new customer when I am gone.

Tad: Where are you going?

G: Will not survive this.

Tad: Repeat that please.

G: Will not survive this. Mama refuse to go, but must send Katarzina away.

Tad: Where to?

G: To America. Have a new deal to talk about.

Tad: Lay it on me.

G: Sorry?

Tad: Tell me about the deal.

I stopped reading and ran for some cantaloupe and chilled water. Not that I didn't want to read what came next; I wanted it too much. I needed to slow my fervor, put a governor on my nervous system.

Food and drink in hand, I went back to the stack of papers and read on.

G: I want to send Katarzina to you Tadzik. I will pay.

In the steady back-and-forth of the text there was no place to show a pause, but I was sure G had to wait a bit before Tad responded.

Tad: Explain.
G: Bad blood is with me. Will fight it out here in Poland. Won't spill on Brighton Beach. Too much risk things get out of control. Nobody wants that. You come here and take Katarzina back with you. Only way to keep her safe.
Tad: That's a tall order, chief. What do I do with her over here?
G: Katarzina tell me you like money. You keep her safe forever, money will be yours. Pretty soon, I have no use for it anymore.
Tad: Send a deposit through Brighton Beach. Pass along what you're talking about in round numbers. Then I'll decide.
G: Soon, Tadzik. Have much more money than time.

And that was the last line. There was nothing in the bland, simple text to properly honor the force of those words typed in halfway around the world, yet as intimate as it could be, staring up at me off the page, grim and resolute.

21

I leapt up out of the sofa and paced around Harry's living room like a caricature out of a hammy old movie. There was just too much adrenaline in my system and no place to put it. Son of a bitch, I said to myself. Of course.

I went into Harry's office with the last few pages of transcript in my hand and made him read to the end.

"Holy cow," he said.

"I've got to go see Franco." Harry looked out the window. "It hasn't started yet," I said.

"Let me drive you," he said. He must have seen me stiffen a little. He spun around in his chair and looked at me full on. "Here's the thing. It made me happy that you wanted to weather the storm here with me. So this is where my expectations are. Now, if you go, that happy stuff will be replaced by anxious stuff. I won't get in your way, I just want to keep that happy stuff going until we're back here safe and sound."

He didn't have to add, For chrissakes, Jackie, I don't ask for much. Could you just toss me a bone once in a while?

"Nothing would make me happier than having you drive me to the county jail," I said.

I liked his car, which was the same exact model as mine, yet without all that junk, it felt a lot bigger on the inside. And it was interesting to see what the upholstery actually looked like.

On the way up to Riverhead we played verbal tennis. I served him a question about the Buczek case, and he knocked back a possible answer. And vice versa. This was both helpful and fun, which made me especially grateful I had the sense to bring him along.

"When are you going to bring in Joe Sullivan?" he asked. "He doesn't like it when you get too far ahead of him."

I'd tried not to think about that, knowing Harry was right.

"I've got nothing that would even begin to shake the ADA's case against Franco. So Joe would have zero incentive to chase around all this with me, so theoretically, I have no good reason to pull him in."

"He'd still want you to."

"It's no fun for you to be right all the time. Especially when I'm trying to rationalize."

"Just saying."

We kept the radio tuned to stations with reliably steady weather reports. To our relief, the storm had slowed down some, and was spending some extra time clobbering Washington, D.C., which had effectively halted congressional proceedings and thoroughly gummed up the executive branch. I took that as a sign from God.

"Good, nobody can screw up the country for at least a few days," I said.

"Is that a political statement?"

"Theological."

Since the county jail's principal purpose was to hold defendants over for trial, it was a fairly spare yet congenial place in comparison to the big prisons upstate. The guards were county police who'd earned a chance to live out the last days of their careers walking shackled people in and out of their cells and hanging around unadorned office space. So you didn't have to confront that edgy intensity so often found in street cops.

"Hi there, Jackie. Who's the muscle?" the check-in guard said, looking up at Harry.

"He has muscles, but it's the brain that counts," I said.

"Investigator?" the guard asked, handing me the justification for bringing Harry into a client conference. I nodded, and they buzzed us through the door, then through the next door, which was a sliding wall of bars, and then we were escorted to the conference room where Franco was waiting.

Predictably, there was a moment of alarm when he saw Harry come through the door.

"Jesus."

"Franco, meet Harry Goodlander. He's a friend who helps me on cases."

Franco watched his hand disappear into Harry's massive mitt.

"Pleased to meet you," said Harry.

"Sure, me too."

We sat across from Franco and I sat a file on the table. Inside were the nat.net transcripts; still images of Yogi, Boo Boo, Ike, Connie, and Ivor Fleming; and a printout of Zina's Facebook page.

I let a little silence build, taking the time to study Franco, his once olive-toned face now the color of rancid tallow, with deep lines down both cheeks and across his forehead. He'd shaved off his goatee and had his hair trimmed close to the skull, which only put on more years. It was remarkable to me how quickly people could decline in prisons and jails, but I'd seen it often.

"How are you doing?" I asked him.

He shrugged. "I don't know. Who cares."

I didn't bother to say, I do.

I'd also brought my cell-phone photos of the little shack near the road. I took them out of the file and placed them in front of Franco. He just looked down until they were all spread out, then looked up at me, his face a mask of sorrow.

"Where'd these come from?" he asked.

"I took them myself," I said. "If the cops searched for fingerprints, whose would they find?"

He looked down again.

"They know about this place?" he asked.

"No. Whose prints would they find?"

"Mine and Zina's. I told you we were in bed together."

"But you didn't tell me where."

"What difference does it make?" he asked.

"It makes a difference because you didn't tell me. How come?"

With nearly reverential care, he put the photos back into a neat pile and slid them across the table.

"It's personal," he said.

"There's a good answer coming from a man fighting for his life."

"I'm not fighting."

"Obviously."

"It was our place. Like a little haven. I didn't want to have everybody tromping around in there, getting fingerprint dust all over and turning things inside out. Which I guess is going to happen anyway now. Don't know why it should matter. Everything else is down the toilet."

I hated to see it, but his eyes were filling with tears.

"You never told me how you got started with Zina," I said gently. "How did it happen?"

He looked away and rubbed his face with his shirtsleeve.

"Tad was away a lot. He'd drive off in the box van and be gone all day, sometimes overnight. Zina always seemed to know his schedule, never seemed nervous about him showing up all of a sudden. She'd ask me to fix something inside the house. Hang around while I work, ask me if I want something to eat, so we'd sit at the table and talk about stuff. It's all innocent, since you got Saline and Freddy coming in and out all the time. Until one day when Tad's away and Saline needs to go Up Island for a doctor's appointment. So this time, she just asks me to come visit her at the main house. Then things get started like you see in dirty movies. She answers the door in this sexy outfit, kind of a peekaboo thing on top, you get the idea."

He looked over at Harry, as if his presence increased the intrusion into his personal life.

"I get the idea," I said, drawing his attention back to me.

A flicker of defiance crossed Franco's face.

"I'm a man," he said. "I'd been in prison for a few years, then alone on this big property, trying to keep my nose clean, staying out of bars and other places where you meet women. Not knowing what I'd say if I did meet anybody. 'Hi, I'm Franco, ex-con. What was I in for? Oh, just killing my lover's husband. But I also like evenings by the fire and long walks on the beach.' And now here's this total knockout right out of a teenager's wet dream, what the hell am I supposed to do?"

"I don't blame you, Franco," I said. "I really don't." He wiped his face again and sat back in his chair. "I'm sorry to put you through all this, but I have to." He nodded, and I continued. "Did she ever talk about the intimate aspects of her marriage to Tad? I know they had incompatible personalities, but what about the bedroom? Did that ever come up?"

He shook his head slowly, as if saying no and trying to remember at the same time.

"I really don't think we talked about it," he said. "I just assumed it wasn't so great, otherwise what was she doing with me?"

I put the photos back into the file and fought with myself over what to bring out next. I chose Ike and Connie. Franco looked down at the images.

"Ever see these guys at the property?" I asked.

He studied them for a while, then shook his head. "I don't remember them."

I laid out the pictures of Ivor Fleming, then Yogi and Boo Boo. He shook his head again.

"Them either. Tough-looking bastards."

"You sure?" I said.

"I'm sure. Don't get the point."

"Did you ever go with Tad when he left in his box van?"

"No. Freddy usually did. The idea was for me to stick around the place and keep an eye on things. There's your irony."

"But you and Zina went to the little place up the hill. Not the main house."

"With Saline around? Are you kidding? No love lost between those two. Wouldn't trust Saline as far as I could throw her, which wouldn't be very far. Big gal. But she hardly ever left either of the houses, so the little place made sense."

Sometimes I can lose track of facts in a case, especially when they slip in and out of factual status. So it didn't surprise me that one obvious fact suddenly occurred to me.

"That night, you were in bed with Zina, but Tad was on the property."

He grinned, though not at anything funny.

" 'Holy crap' I think were the words at the time," he said. "He was supposed to be gone till after the snow ended. Who would have thought he'd come home that afternoon? Not Zina."

"That's why he was looking for her. He got home and she wasn't there. You're sure Saline didn't know about the little place?"

"Positive. She would've ratted out Zina in a New York minute. As it was, when Tad headed for the woodshed, it gave Zina time to scoot back down the hill to the big house. I waited for her to get there and call me with an all-clear. That's when I left to look for Tad. I didn't want to be caught up there any more than Zina."

"What if I told you Saline has always known about you and Zina," I said.

He stared at me, processing the idea. "I wouldn't believe you."

"She knew all along, even before you two were in the sack. Do you really think you could hide anything from an intelligent woman virtually living in the same house, watching the new wife's every move?"

The air started to seep out of Franco's nearly regained posture.

"I don't get it," he said. "Why didn't she say anything?"

"That's my question for you."

He shook his head, his haggard face filled with wonderment.

"I don't know," he said. "Sometimes I wonder if I know anything."

I often had the same feeling, I thought, though I didn't say it. I didn't want to give Franco another reason to be despondent. I wanted to be the one glimmer of hope in the bleak gloom that pervaded his view of existence. But I had to.

I took out one of Randall's satellite photos and used a marker to draw a straight line across the property. I spun it around so I could show Franco.

"So, here's the house"—I pointed to it—"and here's your little private cabin. What's right in the middle of those two places?"

He studied the photo.

"I don't know," he said. "Lots of stuff."

"That's true. Including the southwest base of Hamburger Hill. The place where you found Tad's body. Over here's the woodshed"—I drew a circle around a fuzzy white shape—"way on the other side of Hamburger Hill, where Tad was supposed to be shoveling the roof. Yet this photo was taken the day after he was killed, after the storm cleared the area, and there's still plenty of snow."

"It snowed a lot after he shoveled it off," said Franco.

"Ah, but we have a close-up."

I pulled out another image.

"It's been enhanced as far as possible," I said, "but enough to tell the tale."

Franco stared especially hard at this one.

"I don't know what that is," he finally said, sliding the paper back across the table.

"It's the woodshed. It's collapsed. Tad got there too late. The damage was already done."

Franco slid down in his chair—any farther and he'd have slid off onto the floor.

"Here's a theory," I said.

"I don't want to hear it."

"Sorry, you have to. Tad calls you on your cell phone. He's home unexpectedly and wondering where Zina is. You think fast and say, 'I don't know, Tad, but I was just about to go shovel the snow off the woodshed. I'm worried it can't take the weight.' You knew Tad would join in, putting him well out of the way for Zina to run back to the main house. Well, trudge would be more like it, since no one was running through those drifts."

He didn't stop me, so I kept going. "Zina has a head start, but you're not far behind. You follow her footsteps, down from the cabin, through a corner of the big pergola, then up the rise toward Hamburger Hill. And what do you find? Dead Tad.

"What's the first thing you think? Zina ran into Tad and there was a confrontation, which somehow led to Tad turning his back and Zina braining him with a chunk of ice. It was unavoidable. There were Zina's footprints, heading straight from the cabin to where Tad lay dead, and then on to the main house. So you dragged his body down the hill and walked over her path to the main house, obscuring all the damning evidence. Then you called me. Since I, and later the cops, were totally new to the scene, we never thought to search for footprints coming down from the opposite direction into the pergola. You did a brilliant job of focusing our attention where you wanted us to."

Franco just sat huddled into himself, rubbing his hands together and mumbling incoherencies.

"Tell me," I said to him, in as deep and determined a voice as I could muster. "Do you think Zina killed Tad?"

He looked up at me.

"I don't know, Jackie, I really don't," he said. "She could've, that's all I know. It went down like you say it did. It's why I moved him. I panicked, like I said, only not for me, like a dope, for her. And it worked, by the way," he added, with some tattered triumph that barely lasted a second. "Till now," he concluded, and sank back into a fetid swamp of frustrated hopes, self-loathing, and images of persecution.

When Harry and I got back to the car I asked him how it felt to sit and listen to a conversation and never say a single word.

"Delightfully refreshing," he said.

"What do you think?"

"Franco's finally telling the truth. Though probably not all of it."

"Interesting you'd say that. That's what I think," I said.

"Because you're so smart."

"So by inference, as smart as you."

"Don't expect me to argue with that one."

When we made it back to his house the sky was still a sooty gray, but so far no snow. By current reports, the storm was on top of Philly and South Jersey and moving more to the east, causing some optimistic forecasters to suggest it might miss the East End altogether. We thought this sounded like a grand idea, but were almost afraid to wish for it too hard in case that brought it on.

Harry revived the fire and went off to stir up some refreshments. As we ate and sipped wine, I tried to get him to talk more about the Buczek case, but he kept turning the subject to other matters. I noticed.

"Am I talking too much about my case?" I asked. "Are we getting worried it will cause us to lose happy stuff?"

"We are. I want to help as much as I can, but since we've been back home, we've been treading over the same ground."

"Obsessively?" I asked.

"That would be a little too strong."

"No, it wouldn't. You're right, what do we want to talk about?"

"Roger Angstrom."

One of the unfair things about having a fair Irish complexion is it's almost impossible to hide an involuntary emotional response. With people like us, you don't even need a lie detector. You just ask the questions and gauge how much of our face turns pink.

"Don't tell me he called you," I said.

"You didn't want him to. I can tell by your face."

"Damn the bastard," I said, taking my cue from his comment. Luckily, anger and shame can look the same. "I thought he was going to leave me alone."

"It's none of my business, but I'm a little surprised you didn't let me know. Just for the fun of it. *The New York Times* and all."

"It's ridiculous. I don't want to talk to the press about what I'm having for dinner, much less an active case."

"He told me it wasn't about any specific case," he said. "It was about you."

"You didn't actually say anything, did you?"

"Sure. I said I thought you were brilliant, passionate, and absolutely committed to your work."

"You're not supposed to say anything," I said, though in a gentle way.

"He told me he knew that already, and wanted more specific examples. I told him that would have to come from you. He started probing into your personal life, and our relationship, and I said the same thing. So at the end of the call he'd learned that you're brilliant, passionate, and absolutely committed to your work. And that's it. Will make a nice headline, but not much of a story."

Relief flowed through me, which I expressed.

"I think it's really cool that the *Times* wants to write about you," said Harry. "You've done some interesting things, had an interesting life. You deserve some recognition."

"As if you're objective," I said.

"Okay, I'm not. But they are."

This caused me to confront the central question, the one I could openly ask: Why was the prospect of showing up in the newspapers so horrifying? Since I needed a good answer for Harry, I was forced to have one for myself. And with that, it came to me. It was about identity—my identity. The fact that I was riddled with conflicting impulses, that I argued with myself constantly and questioned nearly every thought and notion didn't change the fact that I knew who I was. My personhood, and everything that went with it, was never in doubt. I'd never be able to describe such a confusing tangle to anyone else, but I knew inside my head how it all fit together. The idea that anyone outside of that most private realm could think they could render anything close to the truth was absurd. If I went along, I'd only be doing it out of vanity. Just to see my name in type and my face in a little photograph.

I don't know exactly what I said to Harry, but it was along those lines. When I was finished, he told me he loved me and that he'd henceforth dedicate himself to keeping my life forever out of the media's reach. I'd make Thomas Pynchon look like Jerry Springer. Greta Garbo like Lady Gaga.

Again, the right thing said at the right time, which made me feel a surge of affection although tinged with a pinch of guilt, because I'd spoken the truth, but like we'd accused Franco Raffini of doing, not all of it.

It wasn't until the next morning that harbingers of the next big storm, a scattered snowfall on the tundra we now called home, made an appearance. While still in bed, we turned on the radio and heard that a state of emergency had been declared in Baltimore, D.C., and Philadelphia. At that moment, the heart of the storm was over the Atlantic off the coast of New Jersey and, gaining energy from the relatively warm waters, was slated to miss New York City and most of Long Island but would hit the East End and the islands off the coasts of Rhode Island and Massachusetts like a ton of bricks.

We'd had a peaceful, lazy night, and I awoke more refreshed than I had for weeks. While Harry reinvigorated the fire, I constructed breakfast. So then for at least another hour, the world felt like a soothing, tranquil place, as it often does in the calm before a storm.

Still content, but ready to face reality, I got dressed while Harry set up a desk for me in the living room so I'd have room to work on my laptop with a mouse and Randall's hard drive plugged in.

I spent the first hour going through e-mail related to my other clients, answering most of them or responding in some other way, after which I realized I hadn't really let anything slip while absorbed in the

Buczek case. Then I wrote a brief description of the nat.net transcripts
for Burton, along with my subsequent conversation with Franco. After
sending that off, of course, I was hooked again.

I'd been eager to look at what Randall had pulled from the weather
satellite's archives, though I'd felt intimidated by the technical com-
plexities of such an alien program. These fears were entirely unfounded.
Randall had prepared a home screen with all the images, times, and
dates catalogued. All I had to do was click on what I wanted and up it
popped.

I decided to start with the Buczek property a few weeks before the
storm and move slowly forward from there. I had a choice of speeds—
jumping ahead at one-hour, two-hour, or six-hour intervals per mouse
click. Or I could see everything at two-times, three-times, or six-times
in fast-forward. You could also review in normal time, but that would
take weeks. I picked three-times fast-forward and stared.

Tiny cars zipped in and out of the driveway. Ant-sized people scurried around the grounds, coming and going from the main and staff
houses, and in and out of the big storage barn. It almost immediately
became pretty boring, but I forced myself to stay alert anyway—not my
favorite thing.

When night fell, darkness filled the screen, and there was nothing
to see but pinpricks of light, so I went to six-times speed and raced
through the night to daylight, pale as it was, and occasionally too misty
to see much detail. Clouds also presented a challenge, and there were
days when there was nothing to see but gray and white.

I went through a few more twenty-four-hour cycles like this with
nothing to show for it. Then I saw a pair of people walking up the path
to the little building I'd checked out the day before. I froze that image,
noted the time code, then went in reverse to earlier in the day until I
saw a box van leaving the property. I went forward again and watched
the two enter the building, where they stayed until nightfall.

Presumably, they left during the night. The van returned the next morning. I watched a lot more carefully after that, slowing things down to a stately two-times speed. Which is likely how I saw "the thing."

That's what I called it, as an unidentified mass connected to the area at the foot of Hamburger Hill directly opposite from where Franco had found Tad Buczek. It was large enough to appear as an anomaly within the image, though shadows shifting through the day obscured its true shape.

I went back in time again with an eye fixed on that location and saw the thing appear again about a week before. It was a mistier day, reducing the shadow effects. I slowed down to real time and watched as long as I could stand it. Then I got up and poured more coffee. When I got back to the screen, the thing was gone.

I snatched the mouse and used it to jump back to when the thing was in view again. So focused on the thing, I didn't immediately see the white box van moving down the driveway. It drove past the main house, up a slight embankment, and down a path that led around to the back of Hamburger Hill, where it disappeared into the man-made monument. And the thing swung shut behind it. Not a thing, of course.

A door.

22

I ran into Harry's office and announced that we had to go back out again. He spun around in his chair and calmly said, "Really."

I yanked him out of his chair and brought him by the hand to the living room, where I made him watch a replay of the white box van driving into Hamburger Hill.

"Wow," he said.

"This is bigger than wow. We have to go look."

"How bad an idea is that."

Goddammit, I thought, not even twenty-four hours later and we're back at the old dilemma. I swallowed my next thought: Sam Acquillo, older and smaller than you, wouldn't hesitate a second even if conditions were twice as bad—something I'd never, ever said to Harry, to my eternal relief. Not least of all because Harry had also saved my life when the circumstances called for it, deploying his massive size to good effect. More so because the comparison was irrelevant. I would never tie my romantic heart to a person like Sam, no matter how much I trusted and admired him. I wanted my heart tied to people like Harry.

"It's not a bad idea," I said. "It's my idea, and I'm going no matter what. I just thought you'd want to come along because being around me makes you happy."

Even with him sitting down we were nearly at the same eye level, so I could see him soften and the amused warmth I liked so much spread across his face.

"I'm sorry. Let's start that over again. Wow, we have to go look. Who's driving?"

"Dayna Red."

"The Wood Chick."

"The snowplow operator."

I ran back to my computer, looked up the number for Specialty Hardwoods, and called.

"There's another blizzard coming through," I said when she answered. "Shouldn't we be driving in it?"

"Of course we should," she said. "Driving where?"

"Back to the scene of the crime," I said.

"You don't hear that every day," said Dayna.

"How many shovels do you have?"

"One."

"Bring it," I said, and gave her directions to Harry's.

While we waited for her to pick us up, I climbed into long underwear, synthetic wicking socks, flannel jeans, and a fleece top. I checked on Harry, who was doing the same.

"Doesn't it make you pine for palm trees?" he asked, pulling ski pants over his own very long underwear.

"You keep promising global warming. How many snow shovels do you have?"

"Two."

"Perfect. And bring your pickax. We might be chiseling through ice."

To avoid overheating, we waited for Dayna in the driveway. The snow had graduated to the next level—the flakes were still small and light, but there were more of them and the wind had clicked up a notch from calm to breezy. The two Volvos wore a thin skin of white.

"Consider yourselves lucky," I said to them. "It could be worse."

"You're talking to the cars," Harry said.

"You don't?"

Dayna and her truck showed up soon afterward. It was a serious truck with a capacious cab, though I'm sure the sight of Harry gave her pause. I jumped in first, and in a few moments we were in a cozy situation. I introduced the two of them, Dayna threw the wheel-mounted transmission into drive, and we were off.

"You're a good sport to do this," I said to her.

"Who doesn't like to go out and play in the snow?"

The storm's timing was perverse. Anyone who hadn't kept track of recent weather reports had made it to work in the early morning, when only the light stuff was coming down, and now they'd seen the error of their ways. The radio was filled with near-hysterical admonitions for everyone to get home and stay home, for God's sake. All they had to say was this storm was looking to be even more ferocious than the last big one, and people would get the point. Since "home" for ninety percent of commuters was to the west, Montauk Highway was already jammed. Our route was east, then straight north, one blessing.

After zigzagging our way around the prevailing traffic and maneuvering around cars already slid off the road and locked in place, Dayna asked me if I still wanted to do what I wanted to do.

"I'm trying to save that dumb son of a bitch's life," I said, "no matter how hard he makes it for me."

"That's Jackie's job," said Harry. "Saving dumb sons of bitches' lives."

"They don't all deserve it," I said. "I'm not sure Franco does, but that's not the point. Jeez, it's really snowing."

Suddenly it really was, the flakes so densely packed there was almost no air left to look through. The radio had warned of whiteout conditions. Now I knew what they meant. We were forced to drive at impossibly slow speeds just to avoid rear-ending another truck in front of us. Worse, the ground temperature was now out of sync with the wet, fat flakes that froze into sheets on contact, creating a nearly frictionless surface. Even Dayna's four-wheel drive was barely up to keeping us on the road.

Which meant the other drivers were really in trouble. Every few yards another car or truck was rammed into a snow embankment, their drivers and passengers either sitting in mute misery or pointlessly trying to push their way out of trouble. These were the biggest hazards we faced, as a fleeting moment of traction would cause the stuck vehicle to lurch out into the street, often sideways to traffic. More than once Dayna swerved an instant before colliding with an oblivious and briefly ecstatic driver, who'd immediately find himself buried in the opposite bank. I'd close my eyes and brace for impact, then open them again in wonder that we were still intact.

"Wow," I said, "how did you miss that guy?"

"I used the Force. Not the dark side, in case you're wondering."

It was far better when we finally crossed Montauk Highway and worked our way up the back roads, already deep in snow but far less traveled. Better snow for Dayna to deal with. She settled into third gear and literally plowed ahead.

To help me resist the urge to chatter away and mess up her concentration, I switched around different radio stations. This gave us a range of perspectives, from "this is really bad" to "this is insanely bad." Then the governor came on everywhere and confirmed the second opinion.

He announced that he was ordering all roads in Suffolk County closed and warned that drivers of snowbound vehicles could be waiting a long time for rescue, given that municipal plows and emergency crews could barely move around themselves.

Dayna pressed on, unfazed by all the apocalyptic talk, her eyes forward and face set in a slight grin. She was enjoying this, which Harry pointed out.

"Me and Jeffrey sailed around the world when we first got together. There's nothing out there that can match weeks of running downwind through the Roaring Forties. Talk about tricky driving."

"What haven't you done?" I asked.

"Saved a son of a bitch's life."

We started to relax a little before turning a corner and almost smashing into a pair of trucks that had already smashed into each other. The road was blocked. We jumped out to see what was what. No one was hurt, but neither truck (one a van, the other a small pickup) was going anywhere. And consequently, neither were we.

The driver of the pickup rolled down his window when Dayna knocked. He didn't answer when she asked if he was all right. Harry tried in Spanish and he nodded. I don't know where the conversation went from there, but with the help of the other driver—an Asian guy who had his own shovel—and Harry's considerable contribution, we moved the little pickup to the side of the road, clearing a path for Dayna to squeeze through. I gave the Spanish guy my card after telling him through Harry if he caught any trouble for moving his vehicle, I'd fix it. He looked completely reassured, which was touching. His confidence was well placed, but he didn't know that.

We moved more cautiously after that, if that was possible. We passed a few more vehicles that had succumbed to the slightest of inclines, but all were safely pulled over in full surrender.

"Man, it's slippery," said Dayna. "Four-wheel drive is a bare minimum."

"I once drove across a frozen arctic sea in a box on treads, like a cross between a minivan and a tank," said Harry. "That would work. And I've also sailed the Roaring Forties, so I totally dig what you mean about that."

Dayna looked across me at Harry. "Oh yeah? Ever danced naked on peyote in the jungles of Belize to the songs of enraged howler monkeys?"

"No."

"Okay, then talk to me when you do."

It was silent in the truck for a little while, then Harry said, "Ever capture a pair of live *Theraphosa blondi* tarantulas in Venezuela and hand-deliver them to a hemophiliac billionaire living in a nuclear-bomb-proof cave in the Swiss Alps?"

"Don't take the bait," I told Dayna. "He can do this all day."

This was the third time Dayna had been to the Buczek place, so she knew the way. When we reached the top of the drive, we saw it was already well filled with snow. She dropped the plow.

"So what's the plan?" asked Harry.

"We call on Zina and ask her permission to search Hamburger Hill. If she refuses, we leave and spend the trip back apologizing. If she agrees, we go find that door."

"And if it doesn't open?" asked Dayna.

"We improvise."

With that, Dayna pulled into the driveway and we were headed down the hill, the truck's engine revving under the load and snow flowing out from the right-hand side of the plow like a white wave breaking on the shore.

Having run this route a few times, Dayna took us to the house with confidence. I felt myself start to feel some regret at the idea of barging in on Zina, which I easily shook off, pushing Harry with my shoulder and saying, "Let's go."

The three of us went up to the front door and I rang the bell. Saline answered, looking alarmed.

"There's nothing to be concerned about," I said. "We're here to see Zina."

"Nothing of concern?" she said. "We're in the middle of a blizzard."

"Not quite the middle, ma'am," said Harry. "It's going to get a lot worse."

"Please tell her we're here. It's extremely important," I said.

The door closed and we were left to silently wait on the porch. I hated this part, where you stood outside and looked at a closed door, wondering what was happening on the other side. This time, the door opened again.

"Come in," said Saline. "You can wipe your feet on the mat in the foyer. The rest I'll just have to clean up later."

She said that last bit mostly to herself. I felt a little bad, but no way would I take off my boots.

Zina received us in the living room, sprawled as she often was on a love seat, wearing an outfit not all that different from the one in my dream. It seemed like Zina had perfected active loungewear—comfortable clothing made to look like you wore it to do something uncomfortable, like lifting weights or filling out tax forms.

"You always blow in with the storms," she said to me. "Does that mean something?"

"Probably. You might remember my friend Dayna Red, and this is Harry Goodlander."

He reached down and they shook hands.

"Sorry to bother you," he said.

"You might be; Jackie certainly isn't. She's always push, push, push. Come on, isn't that true?"

I told her Harry and Dayna would go sit in the kitchen with Saline so we could speak in private. After they left, I unbuttoned my parka and dropped into the opposing sofa.

"It is true, I push," I said, without apology, "and you've been patient with me. I want to be patient with you, too, but the questions are piling higher than the snow out there."

"I've told you everything I know."

"You've told me nothing that you know," I said.

She frowned and smiled at the same time. I'd seen the look before. It was supposed to express strained credulity but did the opposite.

"What a thing to say."

"Is your father still alive?" I asked. She held my eyes but didn't speak. "After you left Poland, did he survive?" A crimson blush began to form around her neck, spreading upward toward her face.

"Who have you spoken to?"

"Did he?"

Darkness fell across her pale face. "No. They killed him. My mother watched. She's now in the crazy hospital, so they might as well kill her, too. Who are you talking to? What are they going to do to me?"

There was a question I hadn't even thought to ask myself. Not that it mattered. I didn't have an answer.

"I don't know who they are," I said. "I only know your life was threatened and Tad went over to Poland and rescued you. For a price."

She looked behind herself toward the kitchen.

"Saline knows none of this," she said, her voice pitched to a near whisper.

"I wouldn't bet on it," I said, but just as quietly. "You and Tad were only officially man and wife," I said, taking a chance, "not in the real sense, with all that goes with that."

Her nearly regal feline poise began to sag.

"That's very personal," she said.

"Sorry. So's Franco's life, which you don't seem to appreciate."

"That's not true," she said, looking away.

"Then quit lying and tell me what really happened that night."

She looked back at me, her eyes becoming more slanted as they closed nearly to a squint. "You ask a lot to come into my home tracking water everywhere and calling me a liar."

"You let us in because you don't know what I know, and you want to find out. You might not know our legal system, but you figure it's better talking to your late husband's family member than the cops. And you're certainly right about that."

She swung her feet down onto the floor, as if to become better anchored against incoming threats. She held her head in her hands and talked into the Persian rug.

"Tad was supposed to be gone for two days, but the storm was so bad they shut down the highways and he couldn't get to where he was going. There's a little cabin up near the road. It was built for some old Buczek long time ago. Franco fixed it up enough for us to meet there." She looked up again. "But you know this already, don't you?"

I nodded. "Franco told me. And I've been there. I've seen it."

"You can go up there," she pointed toward the ceiling, "and see our bedroom. Two beds. Part of the deal, he has to make everyone believe we are husband and wife. But you're right, in real life just on paper. The only thing that happened up there was a lot of snoring. Unbelievable. No one could sleep through that."

Another flurry of questions flew like startled birds into my brain, but I stayed on track. "Tad called Franco, looking for you."

She nodded. "Franco tells him he was about to go clear off the woodshed, which was the truth. He was worried it would collapse from too much snow. But now, it would be a good way to get Tad away from the house so I could sneak back in, then make up some silly story about taking a walk in the storm. I ran down the hill as fast as I could with all the snow, and when I get to the house, he's not there. That's all I know. I never saw him again."

"You didn't run into him along the way?" I asked, almost casually.

She perked up in her seat. "Who, Tad? No. That would be disaster."

"There was a disaster. He was killed," I said. "Franco found him on the path you took to the main house."

She struggled to understand me, or confuse me further, it was hard to tell.

"Me kill Tad? That's impossible. He catch me out there it would be the other way around for sure."

Not impossible for Franco, I thought, who trod the same path. But I didn't say it.

"When you got back to the house, what did Saline say?" I asked, without conceding to her denials regarding Tad. "Weren't you concerned about her?"

"Saline wasn't there. She was back in her own house, I suppose. No reason to be here." She looked toward the kitchen, fixing Saline's location in the present.

"Where did Tad go when he left for long periods of time? What was he doing?"

"I don't know," she said, too quickly.

"Yes, you do."

"So you're a mind reader? You know what's up here?" She pointed to her head.

"What's under Hamburger Hill?"

She stiffened but held the set of her face. I could only imagine the terrors and stresses of the life she led in Poland and Russia, the types of people with whom she did daily business and the types of pressure they could apply. She would have a natural resistance to revelation, an instinct for half-truths and subterfuge.

"I don't know what you are talking about. It's a hill."

"You're giving us permission to go look for ourselves," I said, taking out my phone. "I've got the Southampton police on speed-dial. They won't have to ask."

She pulled up her feet again and lay down on the couch, putting her clasped hands between her knees, tucking into herself.

"Suit yourself," she said.

So I did.

Back in the kitchen, Dayna, Harry, and Saline were sitting on stools around a counter-height butcher-block table drinking coffee and munching on sausage and peppers, bits of ham, pickles, beets, and olives.

I grabbed an olive and announced to my partners that we had a job ahead of us, should they still choose to participate.

"You can come too, Saline," I said to her.

"I don't understand," she said.

"We're going out to take a look around Hamburger Hill. Anything specific we should focus on?"

She dropped a half-eaten pickle on the plate. She put both hands flat on the table and stared at me.

"You can't just do that," she said. "This is private property."

"Zina gave her permission. Sure you don't want to come?"

"Why do you want to do this?"

"Why shouldn't I? Come on, guys, let's go," I said, and led my gang out the door to Dayna's pickup. I unfolded a still shot from the satellite video I'd stuck in my coat pocket. We looked it over, brushing snowflakes away every few moments, and established our bearings, plotting a route along the path I'd seen taken by the box van.

"Do you think your truck can manage it?" I asked Dayna.

"For sure. It's actually easier in deep snow to get a grip. If we have to plow, I'll plow."

The first part of the trip took us farther down the main driveway toward the staff house. I had my eyes on the still, trying to plot the best place to turn off, so I didn't see what Dayna and Harry saw, I just heard "Uh-oh."

It was another pickup, about the size of Dayna's, also with a plow slightly raised. Freddy was at the wheel. We were in a deep valley of plowed snow, inside a stand of young pine trees, with little room to pass by. Freddy slowed, but didn't stop until his plow came up against ours with a slight bump. Dayna put the shifter into first gear and stood on the brakes. We heard Freddy's engine racing and felt our truck slide backward.

Dayna let out a little yap of surprise. She let off the brakes and pressed the accelerator. We stopped sliding and held our position. Harry rolled down his window and yelled, "Hey, what're you doin'?"

Freddy suddenly backed up, causing us to lurch forward. Dayna braked and we watched him pull back. Harry put his hand on the door handle, but I stopped him.

"Wait," I said, a split second before Freddy sped forward again, wheels spinning, and plow rising. Dayna frantically shoved the plow lever forward and the truck in reverse, though we'd barely gotten under way when Freddy's truck hit. Freddy had ballistics on his side. His head would've only slammed back into the headrest; ours pitched forward, along with the rest of us. Dayna at least had a hold on the steering wheel. Seated in the middle without a seat belt, I was the least secured, and if Harry hadn't thrown his long left arm in front of me, I'd have gone through the windshield.

"You fucker!" Dayna yelled, shoving the gear lever back into first gear and hitting the gas, slamming into Freddy's plow before he could retreat and locking up the two trucks like rams in a mighty contest of engines, gears, and tire treads.

At first it was a stalemate. Harry held on to me and braced himself with his other hand on the dashboard. The engine roared, and we shifted side to side, though stuck in place. With the plows raised, we couldn't see much of the other truck, but could hear the scream of his spinning wheels and see the plume flying from the tires like the tail off the back of a hydroplane.

Dayna called him a few more impolite names and then did something surprising, and a little alarming. She took her foot off the accelerator and put it back on the brake. After pitching backward for an instant, we lurched to the left and then stopped. Dayna had cocked the steering wheel, causing us to crunch into the hardened snowbank. Freddy kept shoving us without letup, but we stayed in place. Dayna then put her truck back into gear, only this time in second. Harry saw what she did and said, "Hah."

Dayna let out a growl and started to accelerate as she eased off the brakes. We moved forward, very slowly at first, but then more quickly. We could hear the rpms from Freddy's engine rise and fall as he tried to regain traction, but his wheels just spun with little effect while our higher gear ratio and lower torque led to the opposite effect.

We heard his engine drop all the way off and felt a thud as he hit his brakes, and then pulled Dayna's trick, turning backward into the snowbank. The instant he hit, Dayna slammed her truck into reverse and pulled back a few feet, using the plow controls to both lower it and change the angle of the blade to the hard right. We could now see Freddy's truck, forty-five degrees off the center line with his rear end buried in the tall bank and his wheels spinning as he tried to regain forward momentum.

With her plow cocked to the right, and back in second gear, Dayna drove into the front left corner of Freddy's truck, catching the side of his plow in a way that allowed her to shove the pickup sideways and farther into the snowbank until it was perpendicular to the driveway and hopelessly jammed in place.

Dayna stopped pushing and stepped on the brakes. Harry jumped out of the truck and grabbed his pickax out of the bed on his way around the rear bumper. I followed him and was around the truck in time to see him swing the flat end of the tool, like Mickey Mantle going for the stands, right into Freddy's passenger-side window. Freddy thought this was a good time to leave his truck and run. Harry anticipated this and, like a giant arboreal ape, clambered over the hard cover protecting Freddy's truck bed, and ran after him.

It took me a bit longer to get to the other side, but again, just in time to see Harry, with his loping stride, quickly overtake Freddy as he slipped and scurried over the slickened driveway. Harry came up to Freddy's side, spread his right hand across the other man's back and pushed. Freddy went splat, arms and legs splayed, spinning on his big belly across the frictionless surface.

Harry slid, too, but stayed on his feet, rotating around so he faced toward the other man, who was trying to wriggle to his feet. He might have made it, but I got there first and jumped on his back. Freddy went back down and I went with him, gripping the hood of his heavy down coat and pulling it backward, which had a decided choking effect.

I let go when Harry got back to us. He grabbed me by the shoulder and helped me scramble off Freddy's back. We watched Freddy struggle to his feet. Harry reached out and grabbed a wad of Freddy's coat at the neck, holding him at arm's length, which in Harry's case was pretty long. Freddy looked at Harry's other hand, which was pulled back in a fist the size of a fruit basket, and dropped his arms in defeat, the ongoing snow speckling his round face and thinning gray hair.

"Please don't," he said.

"You can let him go," I told Harry. He looked over and saw the Glock in my hand. He released his grip on Freddy and stood back.

"You're not going to kill me," said Freddy, somewhat hopefully.

"No, but I might shoot you in the foot. How do you think that would feel?"

Dayna walked up. "Jesus, man," she said. "What kind of a nutcase are you?"

"You can't go up there," Freddy said to me. "It's private."

"It's not up to you."

"Zina doesn't know what she's doing."

"We're going," I said. "With or without you."

"We are," said Harry in his most convincing basso profundo.

I held the gun on Freddy while Dayna and Harry moved his truck, yielding just enough room for her to slip by. When they reached the place where Freddy and I were standing, I said to him, "Here's the deal. If you make us search for the door, and we don't find it within an hour or two, I'll give up and call the police. Then there's nothing I can do for you. If you show me where to go, I'll help you."

"What are you talkin' about? What door?" he said.

I shook out my still of the satellite video and gave it to Harry to show him. He stared at it for a while, then looked up at me through his slitty little pig eyes.

"This ain't legal," he said.

"Get with it, Freddy. It's a new world out there. There's no hiding anything anymore."

He just stood there in sullen refusal. With Harry's help, I got him to sit in the back of Dayna's truck with me as we drove to the spot I'd picked out to make the turn toward Hamburger Hill. Dayna plowed out an entrance, then pushed into the drifts. She made slow but steady progress, though Freddy and I got jostled around a bit.

"Offer's still open," I said as we came up to the hill and started to follow its contours around to the left. He continued to look at me, his florid face pinched in anger, but at the moment I was ready to pick a spot, he pointed at the hill.

"It's there," he said.

I tapped on the rear window. Dayna stopped and looked back at me and I showed her where to go. We drove up to the base of the hill and everyone got out and grabbed a snow shovel and followed Freddy as he tramped up to the very foot of the mound. We watched him burrow by hand into the snow, tossing some aside and digging out a small hole. Then he stopped and, after securing his footing, pulled back, bringing a large piece of the hill with him.

He was holding the corner of a canvas, painted in a classic camouflage pattern, off of which heavy chunks of ice and snow slid to the ground. Harry got next to him and helped shake off the rest. Behind the canvas was a gray metal door in a sturdy frame that jutted out from the brown and green foliage covering the side of the hill. Freddy opened his coat, unclipped a heavily laden key ring from his belt, and held it up.

"Like to see you get through that door without this," he said with evident pride.

"We appreciate it," said Harry, taking the key and using it to open and push in the door. He gripped Freddy as I had by the hood and motioned him to go first. Dayna and I followed them out of the blowing snow and into absolute darkness.

Luckily, this only lasted a moment. Harry had found the switch, which he threw with one hand while still holding Freddy with the other.

"Wow," said Dayna, astonished, and her being a woman not so easily impressed.

23

My first thought was "Welcome to Lucifer's Foreign Auto Repair and Body Shop." The room was huge, with steel joists more than thirty feet overhead, and I-beam posts strategically placed to carry the load. Along the wall to the right was a lineup of exotic cars—Ferraris, Bentleys, ancient Porsches and Maseratis, midcentury Corvettes and Shelby Cobras, MG Midgets and a Lotus Elan. I was nearly blinded by the profusion of shapes and colors, so unlike the cookie-cutter bodies and monotone silvers, whites, and blacks that filled modern parking lots.

It was like a Concours d'Elegance with corrugated walls instead of red velvet providing the backdrop.

In the center of the room, spaced beneath overhead racks with pneumatically driven tools—drills, reciprocating saws, and impact wrenches—were partially disemboweled versions of the same, their engine parts and body molding neatly stored in rolling steel bins. In the aisles between each workstation were block-and-tackle mechanisms hung from tracks mounted to the ceiling for transporting the bins to another set of work tables at the other end of the room.

It was, to coin a phrase, a disassembly line.

To the left was an entirely different matter. The wall was lined floor to ceiling with industrial-strength metal racks filled with all manner of mangled junk. Twisted pieces of car body in a variety of colors, balls of crushed appliances, rusted cables, conduit in every possible diameter, and electric motors of every possible size by the hundreds.

Parked against the same wall was a white box van. Twenty feet to the rear of the van was a tall door held shut by a big hydraulic piston.

"Now we know why nobody boosted Tad's Maserati," I said. "He was doing the boosting."

It made me smile, I couldn't help it. Madman Tad might have been criminal, but was he really mad? Angry, yes, but also one who delighted in angering others, specifically the well-fed and self-important who'd moved into his old neighborhood, who turned his farm country into a riot of architectural excess and pretension. It was as if his life's work was to unsettle theirs with his brutish behavior, terraforming, and crazy art, and finally, stealing their toys, chopping them up and selling the pieces.

"For how long?" I asked Freddy.

"Six, seven years," he said in a low voice, as if hoping the authorities wouldn't hear him.

"Where does everything go from here?" Harry asked.

Freddy shook his head. "No way, José," he said. "I want to make it out of jail alive."

"We'll talk about that. Give me a dollar," I said to him. He was naturally confused, but did as I asked. "Okay," I said, stuffing the bill in my coat pocket, "I'm now your lawyer. Don't say a word to anybody, especially the cops, about any of this without me present. Nobody touch anything," I added to the others as we followed Freddy on a brief tour around the shop.

He described the process, most of which was self-evident, of shipping in the cars, gutting the engine compartments, and stripping out the interiors, then the more difficult job of carving up the bodies without damaging delicate sheet metal.

"Any make it out of here intact?" Harry asked.

"Oh, sure," said Freddy. "You always got your special orders." He took us over to a whiteboard where they'd kept track of the process and degree of required deconstruction. "See here? 'Seven series BMW, 2009, full drive train plus rear axle.' Don't ask me any more about the ordering. Tad handled all that. I just broke down the cars and helped with the loading and unloading."

"And stealing?" I asked.

He leaned toward me. "That, too," he whispered in my ear.

"Very impressive," said Harry, who was standing nearby looking at a large control panel covered in gray metal boxes, switches, round meters, and LED readouts.

"Don't touch any of that," said Freddy with some urgency. "You never know what'll start up around this place."

That piqued another thought. I pointed toward the ceiling. "Like the big sprinkler?" I asked.

That made him uncomfortable.

"Might be," he said. "That was Tad's thing, too."

I was beginning to feel a little time pressure. Joe Sullivan wouldn't expect me to call something like this in immediately, especially if I had a client involved, but he would expect a defensible "as soon as possible."

I took out my phone.

"Anything else you want to tell me?" I asked Freddy.

He shook his head.

I was about to push the speed dial when I thought of something. "What about Franco? What was his part?"

"Didn't have one," he said with a grin. "Dope never knew nuthin'."

"What about Saline?"

He shook his head vehemently. "Absolutely no. No, no, no. She's gonna kill me when she finds out. Probably divorce my ass."

While we waited for Sullivan, Dayna plowed a path from the side door into Hamburger Hill all the way to the road. Harry walked around with his hands in his pockets and amused himself looking at all the nice cars, auto parts, and industrial equipment. I spent the time trying to get Freddy to give up more information, which he stubbornly refused to do.

And so a new attorney-client relationship started out like most of them did: the client surly and tight-lipped, the attorney filled with hope, professional fervor, profound skepticism, and disbelief.

After Sullivan showed up, read Freddy his rights, and bundled him into the back of the marked SUV, we drove down to the main house to talk to Zina and Saline. Rarely had such a startling revelation—that there was a massive exotic-car disassembly operation hidden under an artificial mountain—been met with such passivity, bordering on indifference. Saline said something like "I knew those boys were up to no good," and asked to talk to Freddy. Joe told her she could come by after they'd had a chance to question him, with his new lawyer present, of course.

Zina made some odd promise about returning all the cars to their rightful owners, as if that would be up to her. Sullivan told her there'd be plenty of time to sort that out, and to please stay available until further notice.

On the way to his ancient Bronco, which I planned to ride in to HQ, I said to Sullivan, "So you'll be back for a visit."

"Oh yeah."

Dayna took Harry home after Joe promised he'd get me there before the roads became completely impassable.

"If it's too bad to drive, she can sleep in a cell," Sullivan said. "Be a good lesson for her."

"A lesson on what?" I asked.

When we were alone in Sullivan's truck, he said, "Okay, Counselor, what's your theory?"

"Without incriminating my client?"

"Of course."

As it turned out, I had one, though it took some care to give voice to the concept.

"Remember all the crap the neighbors would give Tad whenever he did anything? It's not surprising he'd hide his studio away from the prying eyes of building inspectors and zoning authorities. So it's logical that Hamburger Hill would be his first creation. I don't know how he got started in the chop-shop business, but I'm willing to bet he got to know Ivor Fleming when he was building out Metal Madness. Those sculptures are immense, involving a lot of metal in all sorts of configurations. Fleming's legitimate business, General Resource Recovery, is really the only place on Long Island where he could get what he needed."

"We've heard from snitches for years that Tad was mixed up in the rackets. Never cars or car parts. More like warehouse robberies, hijacking semis, or transporting untaxed cigarettes. Garden variety mob stuff. Why, I don't know. He had plenty of money. Was never charged with anything, much less convicted, so we'll never know."

But I knew. It was just plain old orneriness. It wasn't the money, it was the sport, the adrenaline rush, the knowledge that you were sticking it to a society you felt never accepted you, even though you'd never given them a chance.

"Tad designed and built the whole operation, what Harry calls the supply chain," I said. "He'd harvest the cars from the East End, and probably other parts of Long Island and maybe Connecticut, bring them here, chop them up, and ship the results to Ivor's facility. Ivor packs up the parts inside containers, completely encased in scrap metal and impervious to inspection. Not that inspections were much of a danger in the port he shipped through in Brooklyn—a favorite export facility for the Russian and Polish mafias."

"Old friends of Tad's."

"Exactly. As were the guys on the receiving end in Europe."

I told him about Tad and Zina's chats on nat.net. I wasn't positive whether the information would help or hinder my defense of Franco Raffini, but it just felt unwise to keep it from Sullivan. I had to have a little faith in my instincts.

"So you think the same people followed her over here and killed Tad?" he said.

"It's a really good possibility. Like Franco once said to me, just because you think something is true doesn't mean it isn't. It's Occam's razor. The most obvious answer is almost always the right one."

"Don't know about that. I'm a Gillette man myself."

"Zina herself could be in real danger. It'll actually be good for her to have the property crawling with cops for a while. From what I've read, the feuds inside these Eastern European crime outfits can make Capone-Moran look like a love fest."

"You're still gonna have to prove it to the ADA," he said. "She's really liking Franco for this thing."

I knew that. But now my hopes, ever eternal, had yet again sprung some new life. I had a path, a way to go. I could fill in my version of Sam's boxes and arrows and connect them all. I just had to do the work.

"And you should watch yourself as well," he said. "I don't think those people hold our cops and lawyers in the same high esteem as our homegrown punks."

"No worries there. I've got reverse guardian angels."

"Whatever the hell that means," said Sullivan. He leaned into the windshield and used the back of his wrist to help the defroster clear off a layer of frost. "Man, this weather sucks. If I wanted to live at the North Pole, I would've moved there."

Ross Semple was at HQ to greet us like an indulgent grandparent on Christmas morning. He was so elated over the chop-shop bust, for a second I thought he was going to wrap me in a bear hug. I sent out a very loud vibe that this was not an impulse worth succumbing to.

We sat around and chitchatted while Freddy was photographed and fingerprinted, then we all retired to the big interrogation room with the one-way mirror and recording equipment. One of the most intimidating places on earth, something that hadn't escaped Freddy's notice. Like Franco before him, he'd already taken on the look of a desperate and doomed man.

By prior agreement, I let Joe Sullivan run the interrogation as long as the questioning followed the path to Ivor Fleming, and with luck, beyond. Freddy's obdurate posture in the chop shop notwithstanding, after an hour of Sullivan's verbal pummeling, combined with offers of lenience in return for cooperation, he'd spilled the whole plate of beans. The eventual prosecution of Ivor Fleming had a new lease on life, and the thought of controlling the bust from Southampton had Ross Semple in soaring delight.

After that, I followed Sullivan into Ross's office, where we called the ADA and set a bail hearing for the next day. I shared with Ross what I'd told Joe on the way over, and he offered up a few suggestions of his own on how to proceed with my investigation. Everyone was full of cordiality and goodwill. It was like we were all part of the same family. None of this cops-and-lawyers stuff. I noted that out loud.

"We love you, Jackie," said Ross, offering me a cigarette, which I refused. "Making you happy is really all we live for."

Right at that moment, it was almost possible to believe that.

As promised, Sullivan got me to Harry's, though it took nearly an hour to travel what normally took about fifteen minutes from the north end of Hampton Bays to the Village of Southampton. Part of this was due to frequent stops along the way to pull motorists out of snowbanks and deliver others to safe havens like the fire station or the diner on Montauk Highway. It's what you get when you hitch a ride with a dyed-in-the-wool cop.

Along the way, I got to hear more about his new life as a nearly divorced person.

"Did you know you could watch a game on TV while simultaneously consuming an adult beverage without having to hear that you are wasting your life and all prospects of financial success?" he asked.

"I didn't."

"It's true. And if you happen to come home late, you haven't necessarily ruined a perfectly good meal, because it's where?"

"In the freezer?"

"Exactly. Amazing, huh?"

Harry seemed very glad to see me, though he always did. Despite the ongoing storm, I was glad Sullivan hung around long enough to have a beer and chat it up with us, giving everyone a chance to enjoy the day's remarkable events. And even more for the chance to extend some social warmth to the big towheaded cop, my affection for whom I'd felt defenseless against since I saw him at Tad's climbing out of that rusty Bronco.

After Sullivan left, the jolly spirit was sustained, and Harry and I found ourselves in the living room sitting in the dark, the outside lit to the hilt by floodlights in the trees and under the eaves, allowing us to watch the snow pile up as a sublime and absorbing act of beneficent nature, not the rampaging fury it actually was.

24

I didn't get back to my office until the middle of the next day, forced by a minor client emergency to retrieve a paper file containing information inaccessible by my sleek silver laptop, as barbaric as that sounds.

My client, a nervous Brazilian with a green card who'd started as a cleaning lady in Southampton and now sat on a fortune in oceanfront real estate in São Paulo, was afraid of computers. The trip to my office wasn't that big a deal since the road crews, still smarting from their perceived slow response to the last storm, had cleared the roads at a frenzied pace. The sky was now a bright blue, the wind but a gentle breeze, and the snow a friendly thing that wrapped the Hamptons in a downy white blanket. Since everyone had been cowed by hysterical news reports into staying inside until April, the roads were relatively clear, and I made the trip in nearly normal time.

It was another pleasant thing to have the parking lot behind my building already plowed, and to see Asian gentlemen from the restaurant busily heaving snow off the sidewalks. I punched in the code at the outside door and made my way up the stairs and into the welcoming embrace of my second-story domain.

I retrieved my robe and slippers from the apartment and brought them over to the office. Still chilled from the drive over, I stayed in my clothes. It took some furious digging to come up with the paper file, which for some reason had found its way inside a catalog offering discount patio furniture, gardening tools, and lawn ornaments. Having neither garden nor lawn, it's no wonder I couldn't find the damn thing.

I called the client and worked on her case for about an hour. Then I spent another hour scanning the information and turning it into electronic files that I could save in multiple locations, whether she liked it or not, and sent it to our home office, rescued from the physical reality to which it was once confined.

After that, I spent the rest of the afternoon doing work for other clients in less urgent, though valid, need until both my short-term to-do list and conscience were completely cleared.

Then I went back to the Buczek case.

I leafed through the case file, which was ten times too big to fit inside a gardening catalog, looking for unexamined material. I've read about breakthrough archaeological finds happening not in the field, but in the basement of a museum by people who merely looked at an artifact with fresh eyes. It was the same with the law. Much of the time, the most important fact or angle on a case is right in front of your nose, and you just haven't seen it yet, or given it the proper interpretation.

Neither of which happened to me as I slogged through the piles of paper, photo images, and Post-it notes. It wasn't until I pulled the still shot from Randall's satellite program out of my back pocket that I realized the path inadequately traveled.

I went over to the laptop and opened the application. I knew the problem: It was the boredom factor. My brain is designed to leapfrog from thing to thing, patternless and impulsive, not just hunker down, wait, and stare. This was a job for other people. But then, I balanced my checkbook every month, a job I hated even more. If I can do that, I can do this, I told myself, turning on some Mississippi Delta blues and pouring a glass of wine so at least something else was going on.

After more of this than I could stand, I took a different tack, more to my liking: I used the fast-forward and scanning functions to jump around—forward and back in time, faster, slower, zooming in and out, in real time and frozen in place. This seemed like a lot more fun, probably encouraged by the white wine and a roach I was thrilled to discover in the top drawer of my desk. Why I was looking there, I don't know.

I was about to move on to something less monotonous when I found myself looking at the week before Tad was killed, and then the week after—the middle few days, of course, obscured by the big storm. Something stopped me, and I went back to review the action again.

Randall had set up the application so I could open different images in separate windows, allowing for side-by-side comparisons. This was the first occasion for me to use that feature, and it took a while to set up, but eventually I had two exact views of the Buczek property captured about a week apart.

It was the giant sprinkler on Hamburger Hill. Before the storm, the three twisted tubes were barely visible. When I zoomed in, the reason was apparent—they were laden with snow, blending with the ground below. A week later, after almost two feet had fallen, they were bare.

And in a different position. They'd moved.

The ringer for the outside door went off and I nearly jumped out of my skin. I whipped my head around to the monitor and saw Saline Lumsden trying to look through the peephole in the door. I went over to the control pad and pushed the intercom.

"Hello, Saline, what's up?"

"Oh, you're there. I was hoping I could talk to you."

"What's the matter?" I asked, disappointed by the intrusion.

She clutched at herself and shivered. "Do we have to talk over this squeaky little speaker?"

"Of course not."

I buzzed open the outside door and went out in the hall to wait for her. She clumped up the stairs in heavy workboots, clutching a large canvas bag to her middle. When she saw me at the top of the stairs, she gave me a wan smile.

"I'm sorry to bother you," she said, "but I have some dreadful news."

"Oh dear," I said, waving her into the office. "Come in, let me clear a spot for you to sit. Can I get you anything? Water?"

A fold-out couch and two overstuffed chairs constituted my conference room. I gave her the couch.

"No," she said weakly, "I don't need anything. It's just nice to sit down. I'm so tired all the time."

She still held the bag with both hands, so firmly I hesitated to suggest she stow it somewhere. Maybe she thought it would disappear into all the junk I had strewn around, a reasonable fear.

"So what's what?" I asked. "You said you had news."

"Freddy's dead," she said, looking up at the ceiling as if to signal his new location.

"Oh my God. What happened?"

She shrugged. "I don't know, people just die. At least I got to say hello to him at the jail. He wasn't happy there."

"Was he sick? Did he take medication?"

She looked like she hadn't considered that before. "You're right. Maybe that's it. He took too much of his headache medicine. That can be very dangerous."

My cell phone rang, causing me for the second time that day to jump up in my chair. I looked at the screen. It was Joe Sullivan. I asked Saline to excuse me, that I'd keep it short.

"I just heard the news," I said to Sullivan.

"What news?"

"Freddy Lumsden. He died, right?"

"He did," said Sullivan. "About five minutes ago. We just gave up on the CPR. How did you know?"

I looked across at Saline, who was searching around her fabric bag.

"I'll tell you later," I said. "Thanks for the information."

"You all right?" he asked.

"Yeah, I'm fine. But keep your cell phone handy," I said, and hung up before he could say more.

"Saline," I said, as evenly as I could despite the ball that was forming in my throat. "What did you do?"

"What I have to do. Who else is going to do it?"

"Do what?"

"Deal with people who have some notions in their heads that one just can't accept."

"Like Freddy? What notions did he have?"

"He was planning to tell them everything. I knew he would. It's his personality, to be the helper, to make everybody happy. It's a good quality, but not in every single situation," she said with exasperation.

"The night Tad died. What happened?" I asked, and held my breath.

"It wasn't Freddy's fault. It was Tad's. See, it's that personality thing again. Tad had to give the orders, had to tell everybody what to do."

"The sprinkler sculpture on Hamburger Hill," I said.

She looked surprised. "Did Freddy tell you that? I knew he would. Damn, why can't he just listen?"

"Before the big storm we had a lot of freezing and thawing. Ice was building up all over the place, including the sprinkler. With all that new snow on the way Tad was afraid the tubes wouldn't bear the load. He turned it on."

"No he didn't," said Saline, "Freddy turned it on. Tad was outside, halfway around the other side of the hill, and wouldn't you know it a big piece of ice went flying off that ridiculous thing and hit him right on the head. Smashed his skull right in."

Part of me desperately wanted to reach for my little digital recorder, but I was afraid to break the spell of the moment.

"The police told me he might have survived the head wound," I said. "That a stab wound actually killed him."

"Survived? What sort of survival do you think he'd have? Do you know what happens in this part of the brain?" She turned her head and pointed to the back of her skull. "It's where you keep your visual cortex. He would have been blind for sure. And who knows what else had been damaged. The left parietal was also involved. Lots of stuff goes on in there."

"You finished him off. You killed him."

"No, it was a coup de grâce. You know what that means? The mercy blow. It was the only merciful thing to do."

"What did you use? A screwdriver, ice pick?"

"No pick, just ice," she said matter-of-factly.

"An icicle."

"They were lying all over the place. I inserted the pointy end here"—she pulled up her hair and put her finger beneath the occipital bone—"and just stomped on it. Simple."

That explained the absence of a murder weapon. It melted.

"And you were going to let Franco take the fall. Doesn't seem too fair," I said.

"That obnoxious gigolo? Who cares? Nice to have him gone. We got that extra bedroom back."

Even in the most loony conversation, there's usually an interior logic of some sort. I strived to find it here.

"Saline," I said gently, "you're not going to get to use that bedroom or anything else in that house. You've committed two murders. You'll never get out of prison."

She smiled a tight little smile.

"Well, you see, that's where this comes in," she said, pulling a fat syringe out of her canvas bag. "It works under pressure. You just hit the button on top."

I grabbed the nearest stack of papers and threw it in her face. There were some heavy items in there, so it made an impact. She cried out and put her left forearm in front of her face. Still brandishing the syringe, she stood up from the couch. By then I was on my way to the control pad for the alarm system. If you pushed two of the numbers at the same time it was the equivalent of a panic button. I didn't get there in time—Saline and her syringe blocked my path. I heaved another stack of papers, which were in ample supply, though she was ready this time and easily swatted them away.

I backed deeper into the office. She followed me, keeping a steady distance between us.

"Saline, don't do this. I'm your best hope," I said to her.

"I don't want your help. I can help myself just fine. Always have."

"We're family."

She guffawed. "Fat lot of good that does. They turn on you in a second."

I backed up against my desk, then spun around and snatched up my laptop. Saline backed off a step or two before I had a chance to heave it at her head. She used the hand with the syringe to bat it away, but the crack of the heavy aluminum casing told a story. She switched the syringe to her left hand and put the injured arm against her chest.

"I think you broke my ulna," she said in her usual flat tone. "That really hurt."

I looked around for something else to throw. Saline made a tentative move toward me.

"All I have to do is touch you with the needle," she said. "There's no point in trying to get away."

"Wanna bet?"

I tossed the security camera monitor at her, followed by Randall's external hard drive. And a few ceramic coffee cups found scattered about the desk. Saline successfully fended off the barrage. She was a really big woman and, by the look of her, not easily dissuaded by flying objects.

She moved closer and I did the only thing left for me to do—risky, but unavoidable. I scooped up my terrycloth robe and moved in close enough to throw it over her head. She slashed at me with the syringe, missing by a whisper, though I was already on my way toward the door, not to hit the panic button this time but to retrieve my coat, dropped carelessly on the floor, weighted down by the Glock in the outside pocket.

She kicked at me, but I leaned out of the way, dove to the floor, shoved my hand into the coat, and felt the familiar composite contours of the automatic. I pulled it out of the pocket, and as soon as Saline had stripped the robe off her head, screamed, "Freeze!"

"I'm not afraid of that," she said, the words bursting from her lips.

"Drop the syringe, or I will shoot you. I really, really will," I said, sighting down the muzzle pointed at the middle of her chest.

She seemed undecided. I wished the Glock had a hammer to pull back, to signal my earnest intent, but all I had was the unwavering barrel. I told her I'd shot people before, and would do it again without hesitation.

"I think you would, now that you mention it," she said. "You're almost like a real Swaitkowski. All pigheadedness and crazy fantasy."

And then she stuck the syringe directly into her chest and pushed the button.

25

To enjoy a funeral can cause a person to feel the worst kind of cognitive dissonance. You're sad, but even when the occasion is the result of a horrible tragedy, you normally get to see people you haven't seen for a while, indulge in ancient religious majesty, and if it's a nice day, get a little fresh air in an interesting place, which the Polish graveyard in Southampton certainly was.

I also got to wear my funeral outfit, a sleek black dress with a single strand of pearls, which more than one mourner has favorably commented on.

Saline's funeral was no different. Father Dent did another masterful job sympathizing with her choice to truncate her troubled life without actually condoning suicide, a mortal sin. With characteristic diplomacy, he also bypassed mention of her role in killing Tad Buczek and her husband, Freddy Lumsden, the latter of whom after all was a Presbyterian and thus already conveniently damned.

Franco Raffini—whom I finally sprang after long days of wrangling with the District Attorney's Office—opted out of the event. I couldn't blame him, considering all the trauma he'd been through and the scant support he'd received from Southampton's Polish community.

The other notable person missing from the affair was Zina Buczek, who'd disappeared a few days after Saline's death, and a day before the ADA had decided to charge her as an accessory to the chop-shop operation. It was later discovered by Sandy Kalandro that she'd managed to extract almost two million dollars from her share of Tad's estate, a process she began the day after Franco found his body. Where the money went, and if she was able to follow, were unanswered questions.

Paulina was there, naturally, and less than entirely friendly. I don't think she would ever fully believe that Saline had wreaked so much havoc, or that she would have killed herself rather than face inevitable ruin.

The rest of the family was cordial enough, Tad's massive criminal enterprise having distracted everyone from the circumstances of his death, which the ADA had decided to rule an accident and save everyone a lot of complicated bother.

Being the only surviving person with full knowledge of the case, I owed a lot of my success in persuading the prosecutors to the unwavering support of Ross Semple. He'd been a homicide detective in the city for years, and still had close contacts in the Carnegie Hill precinct, at this point mostly retired. They told him they'd always suspected Saline, since the deadly overdose of the migraine medicine sumatriptan was delivered by needle, and Mr. Vargo's prescription was for pills alone. These suspicions were bolstered by statements from the couple's friends that their relationship was rocky, with Mr. Vargo apparently beginning to see other women. However, given they were both med students with easy access to pharmaceuticals, it was too hard a case to prove.

I had no problem believing it. My unproveable hypothesis had Saline as a woman for whom men were a constant disappointment. First her young boyfriend in the city, then her husband, whom she saw as an ineffectual sap. Tad himself, for whom she probably felt unrequited love (they'd lived together in that house for a lot of years—you have to wonder how unrequited), was at least a single man until he brought home Zina, which must have been a crushing disappointment. Until Zina took up with Franco, and then a little less so.

Since she'd killed the boyfriend and got away with it, and recovered from a serious emotional breakdown, the act had become no longer inconceivable but even justifiable by her own warped moral code.

Her death was the end of Saline and the question of Tad's murder, but it was just the start of another string of events, the most satisfying of which was a sting operation mounted by a team of Long Island detectives on Ivor Fleming's alchemy business, with Joe Sullivan in the lead. As predicted, containers filled with scrap metal routinely left the plant with engines and transmissions, electronic sensors and controllers, wheel assemblies and sometimes complete cars. It was yet to be seen if the trail could be followed into Brighton Beach, though I seriously doubted it.

And even after all that, I had one piece of unfinished business. Using old phone records, I determined that the call to Donald Pritz was indeed made from his own house, on Franco's cell phone, which he had reported lost two days before. I also tracked down the guy who had been instructed by Eliz to deliver the rotisserie at a very specific time on a very specific date and to leave it unassembled.

I uncovered some other interesting things on the big life policy Donald had taken out right before he died. The insurance carrier, whose interest aligned neatly with mine, obtained testimony from an agent that Eliz had pushed for the coverage and that Donald thought it entirely unnecessary.

With Franco's credibility at least partly restored, and safe from prosecution via double jeopardy, the ADA was willing to listen to his side of the story and reopen the case. Ross was also willing to investigate further, and the upshot of the whole thing was I got to ride in the patrol car when Southampton Town Police drove over to arrest Eliz Pritz for second-degree, premeditated murder.

I wanted to tell her she shouldn't have been so rude the last time I came to call, but by then, the impulse seemed petty.

Roger Angstrom got his story—actually, several stories—on the life and death of Tadzio Buczek, on Eliz Pritz, now dubbed the Black Widow of Remsenburg, and one on me. I cooperated as much as I thought client confidentiality would allow, but told him that would have to be the end of it. I apologized for any behavior that might have misled him into thinking I had any personal interest. In doing so, I reaffirmed my heart-and-soul commitment to Harry Goodlander, who, thank God, never had to know such a thing was ever in doubt.

I was at his house the night Long Island broke the all-time record for both snowfall and continuous cold temperatures. We'd set up a double bed in the living room so we could lie there and sip Champagne, nibble on pâté, and watch what turned out to be the last big blizzard of the year.

"Maybe Armageddon's not so bad," I said.

"Adaptability. Humans are good at it."

"We're also good at selfishness and cruelty."

"Only a few of us. Statistically, you're far more likely to encounter acts of kindness."

"Ever the optimist," I said.

"Glass half full."

"That can be remedied," I said, using the Champagne bottle to top it off.